The Vanishing Groom

HELEN GOLTZ

The Vanishing Groom – The Lady Mortician's Visions, book 7.

PUBLISHED BY: Atlas Productions

First published 2025.

Copyright © Helen Goltz

Cover design, as always, by the wonderful Karri Klawiter, Art by Karri.

PLEASE NOTE: This book is written in British-Australian English.

Dedicated to…

Miss Eliza Emily Donnithorne, an Australian bride jilted on the morning of her wedding in 1856, who may have inspired the character of Miss Havisham in Charles Dickens's novel, *Great Expectations*.

And to those readers who have had their heart broken but dusted themselves off, put their chin up, and still believed in love.

Dear reader, please know that no animals are ever harmed, stolen, injured or die in my books, including Julius's big hound, Rufus. So rest easy and read on. I proudly support the WSPA (World Society for the Protection of Animals) and Animals Australia. I thank them for their continued efforts to make the world kinder to animals.

PLEASE NOTE: This book is written in British-Australian English.

Chapter 1

Brisbane, Australia. Wednesday, 1 July 1891. Eleven degrees at 5am, warming to a high of 21 degrees.

'No one knows I am dead.'

Phoebe Astin woke with a fright. The room was dark, but the smallest gap in the curtain allowed a sliver of moonlight to cast a soft glow.

It was a feminine room; a timber bookcase housed Phoebe's favourite books, the dolls she had outgrown but could not part with, hats, ribbons and sentimental trinkets. It was the space she had occupied since suddenly losing her parents at age nine and being brought to live with her grandparents, along with her brothers, Ambrose, then eleven, and Julius, fourteen.

Phoebe looked around. Had she imagined the voice?

'I am sorry to have woken you, but no one knows I'm dead. I might lie there until I decay, and I cannot bear the thought of that.'

Phoebe sat up and swung her legs out of the bedcovers. 'Of course, do not distress yourself. I can assist,' she whispered so as not to wake the household.

The young lady sighed with relief, her shoulders slumping. 'Thank you. I heard from a former nurse that Miss Phoebe Astin of *The Economic Undertaker* could see the dead and assist them. You helped her some time ago.'

'Nurse Charlotte Faithful?' Phoebe brightened, remembering the no-nonsense lady whose heart had given away with a scare.

'The very same. And I am Miss Alma Thornton of 87 Dornoch Terrace, Highgate Hill. Please call me Alma. You may well be the very last person on earth I ever speak with, Miss Astin.'

'It will be my honour, and please call me Phoebe,' the ethereal young lady with the long blonde wavy hair said, as she rose from the bed and reached for her robe. 'You have passed recently, then?'

'Just this day, but I live alone. I am sorry to wake you, but I had no sense of time on the other side. Now I see it is very early, the moon is still out, and the dawn is only starting to break.'

'I am happy to rise; I assure you I have had plenty of sleep,' Phoebe whispered.

'Will you come and find me – that is – will you find my body? The door to my house is ajar, so you can enter easily.'

'Has someone harmed you and departed, Alma?' Phoebe asked, alarmed. 'If a crime is afoot, I know a very capable detective.' She was only too pleased to have the opportunity to recommend her beau, the tall, dark-haired, rugged Harland Stone.

'No. There is no cause for concern; I leave the door slightly ajar as my fiancé may return and require entry.'

'He does not know you have passed? Were you ill or did you die suddenly?' Phoebe asked, tying back her hair and selecting a dress to wear.

'I have been ill, but we will soon reunite,' Alma said, her distress obvious, so Phoebe did not press her. 'It could wait until dawn breaks, but I am not sure how long I can remain with you. I'm quite new to being dead.'

Phoebe smiled. 'And I am afraid I don't know the rules and regulations that come with being on your side. I shall wake one of my brothers and we shall find you, your body, that is.'

Alma smiled. 'Thank you, Phoebe, how kind you are.' The spirit turned as Phoebe dressed warmly for the crisp winter morning and, when ready, Phoebe suggested they slip out the front door and call on Julius.

'My eldest brother is up with the larks, and will accompany me.'

Phoebe knew every step that creaked, and how far to open the door so it did not groan, and soon, she had slipped out of her grandparents' house without stirring the household. Hurrying along the dimly lit street as pink light broke on the horizon, Miss Alma Thornton walked beside Phoebe, not visible to the early morning workers they met along the way. And despite her companion being ghostly rather than full-bodied if needed, Phoebe felt safe.

It was three streets to Julius's home, steep streets, but it seemed silly to hail a hansom at this hour of the morning when one should seek a constitutional. However, there were a few drivers and their horses out and about at first light.

'Good morning, Miss,' a lamplighter said from his ladder as he began his daily duty of distinguishing the night's lamps.

'Good morning, Sir,' she said with a nod and a smile and hurried on. The faster Phoebe walked, the quicker she warmed up, but it was a little wet underfoot, and she took care not to slip on the morning dew.

'Good morning, Miss,' a polite young scoop boy said, ready on duty to collect the horse droppings as his young friend appeared with the newspapers for the day and also greeted Phoebe.

Phoebe returned their greetings and, to her surprise, a shop owner opening his doors said, 'Hello ladies, I hope your day ahead is pleasant.'

'Thank you, Sir,' Alma said, her eyes wide with surprise, and Phoebe gave a small laugh as they moved further away. 'Goodness, I wonder if he has always seen the spirits.'

Moments later, Phoebe pointed to a large house halfway down the street and said, 'that is my brother's house, and a lamp is on.' She repeated the address of Alma's residence.

'That is correct. Then I shall see you at my home soon, Phoebe, and thank you.' With that, plain but presentable Alma Thornton disappeared.

Widely regarded as the most handsome of men, Julius Astin, the eldest of the Astin siblings, placed a rug over Phoebe's legs before nudging the horse along. She quickly shared it with him.

'It is too early to be out wandering alone,' he said, concerned. 'What manner of people might be lurking?'

'A lovely lamplighter, a paper seller and a scoop boy, greeted me. Plus, a shop owner who could see Alma, greeted us both.' She gave a small laugh. 'That took Alma and I by surprise.'

'How odd,' Julius agreed. 'So she is dead from an illness but has no one to claim her?'

'I did not ask that, nor did she say. Alma just said no one knew she was dead. There may be a parent, grandparent, brother or sister somewhere. She mentioned a fiancé and implied their reunion was imminent.'

Julius gave a small hum of interest, and they sat in silence, comfortable in each other's company and stillness, unlike their brother, Ambrose, who, despite the hour, would talk with abandon. In good time, Julius turned the trap onto Dornoch Terrace, and the pair admired the architecture and surrounds.

'Miss Thornton appears to be a wealthy young woman,' Julius said, as he steered the horse into her driveway and jumped down to open the large gates.

To Phoebe's relief, they opened easily, and she reached for the reins to move the horse along. Julius closed the gates behind them, and catching up, easily hauled himself into the trap to steer again. He stopped past the drive where the morning sun warmed a patch of grass, which would keep the horse happy.

Phoebe accepted Julius's hand to alight, lifting the skirt of her loose dress that eschewed the fashion of the time for the more aesthetical designs. Alma awaited on the porch, lit by the golden hues of the morning and looking more ghostly than she had earlier in Phoebe's moonlit room.

'You came. Thank you, Phoebe, thank you,' she said, smiling and clasping her hands. 'As I mentioned, I left the door unlocked, and yes, I know it is not the best practice for a single woman living alone. Hello, Mr. Astin?'

'Hello Miss Thornton. I am sorry to meet you under such circumstances,' Julius said and removed his hat. He noted the door was ajar an inch. 'It is a sizeable house for a lady alone, Miss Thornton. Is there anyone inside now? I should check before you enter,' he said to Phoebe.

'I assure you there is not,' Alma said. 'Despite what I have heard of his demise, I leave it open for my fiancé in case he comes back. You see, he was lost at sea, and should he be found alive, I don't want him to think I've abandoned our love and locked him out.'

'Of course,' Julius said in a consoling manner, but with a glance and raised eyebrow in Phoebe's direction to relay caution in what appeared to be a most odd situation.

'Shall we find you then, Alma, and notify the police of your passing?' Phoebe said.

'Thank you, yes, Phoebe, that would be most appreciated. My bedroom is on the top level, to the left of the staircase. I will leave you to your work.' With that, the former lady of the manor gave a small bow and disappeared.

'Best we get to it, but let me lead in the event someone has taken up residence in Miss Thornton's house,' Julius said.

Phoebe agreed, following her brother inside. The house was like a tomb – chilly and eerily silent. From the entrance hallway, they could see several smaller rooms to the left that were in darkness, their curtains drawn. There was only one door to the room on the right, implying it was a large room, and a beautiful timber staircase led to the second level.

'I am going to open the curtains and doors and ensure we are alone before we go upstairs,' Julius said, moving into the first of the small rooms to the left. He pulled open the curtains, awakening the room with light. Phoebe could see the room appeared sparse with a scattering of tasteful furniture.

As Julius entered the second small room, Phoebe moved to the larger room. The light coming under the door told her the curtains were already pulled, but on gently opening the door, Phoebe gasped in fright and stepped back in revulsion. 'Julius!'

Her brother raced from the sitting room to her side, and his mouth dropped open. 'What on earth...'

Phoebe's hand covered her mouth as she gagged at the smell and sight. It appeared to be a banquet, a wedding breakfast laid out in what would have been a grand style, along the length of a large timber table, with all the gleaming cutlery and glasses. But no one had removed it. How long had it been there?

The smell of rotten food filled the room, rodent faeces littered the table, and the tiered wedding cake was filled with holes from guests of the animal and insect world feasting at leisure. Phoebe had worked on decayed and water bloated bodies, but the shock of the decaying feast with the cloying smell made her retch with the horror of it.

At the sound of a scurrying rodent, Julius slammed the door closed. 'We can assume the grief from loss or abandonment has caused Miss Thornton to lose her wits.'

Phoebe hurriedly stepped away. She swallowed, and taking a deep breath, said, 'We best find her body then.'

'Why don't you wait with the trap and horse?' Julius suggested, and she shook her head.

'She will not be as decayed as the wedding breakfast; Alma told me she has just passed.'

'Nonetheless, allow me to enter the room first,' Julius said and started up the stairs to the next level. Phoebe followed.

Miss Alma Thornton's bedroom door was open, and they could see she was in no great state of disrepair. Julius nodded for Phoebe to follow.

'Good Lord,' he said, approaching the bed. Miss Thornton lay in repose in her wedding dress.

'She has no wedding band,' Phoebe whispered. 'I suspect Alma died of a broken heart.'

Chapter 2

TWO DAYS LATER...

The Courier –Morning edition

A JILTED AND DECEASED BRIDE

A HOUSE WITH ROMANTIC HISTORY

AN UNDISTURBED WEDDING BREAKFAST

An exclusive report by Lilly Lewis.

A stately, handsome house on Dornoch Terrace, Highgate Hill, has a story attached to it as romantic as the most devout worshipper of the imaginative or lovelorn maiden could desire.

A young woman, Miss Alma Thornton, aged 23, the last of her immediate family line in Australia, was engaged to be married. Elaborate preparations for the celebration were undertaken, as was customary. The wedding-day came, the marriage feast was prepared, the guests assembled, the carriages were in readiness to convey the bride and bridesmaids to the church.

Everything was ready except the most important personage – the bridegroom. He failed to appear, and the wedding had to be postponed.

Romance affords no more pathetic picture than that of poor Miss Thornton waiting anxiously, expectant for the bridegroom who never came. Her lover disappeared most mysteriously and within weeks was believed to be dead on a passage to India.

This unexpected termination to what should have been the happiest day in Miss Thornton's life completely prostrated her. To some extent, it interfered with her reason, which is hardly surprising.

Neighbours tell your reporter that from that day onward, Miss Thornton's habits became decidedly eccentric. She did not leave the house, shutting herself from the world almost completely. Miss Thornton lost all interest in the ordinary matters of life and was as much removed from them as if she had become a member of the most strict religious order.

Hoping her beloved would return, Miss Thornton propped the front door open a couple of inches, but she prevented concerned neighbours and her parish priest from entering. The most singular feature of the entire episode was the fact that the wedding-breakfast was never removed. It remained gradually mouldering away on the dining room table for as many weeks until the day of the despairing lady's death.

Yesterday morning, two unfortunate souls checking on Miss Thornton's welfare entered when she did not answer their call; the door was ajar in the hope the wayward groom might return. Sadly, they discovered the decaying feast and Miss Thornton's body, still in her wedding dress. They hurriedly summoned the constabulary, who notified the next of kin.

Finally, there was nothing left but dust and decay – some would add, a fitting emblem of the lady's blighted life.

Reporter Lilly Lewis knew any articles with female subjects would land in her lap; she was, after all, the only female reporter on staff. But writing the story of the deserted woman found dead of a broken heart in her wedding dress was too gothic for her liking.

Placing the newspaper down, she looked at the reporter beside her—Fergus Griffiths—her partner for several very successful crime stories to date. 'I will be writing Penny Dreadfuls next.'

Fergus grinned as he sat back and ran his hand through his brown, foppish hair. 'My article was awash, and I am not even covering the shipping news anymore!' he said in jest. 'At least your story had drama.'

She grimaced, her blue eyes studying Fergus. 'It is frustrating when we finish a big story and then have to start at the beginning again, digging, waiting, hoping for the next big investigative piece.'

'What I wouldn't give for a court case again, like the trial of Zachariah Beaming that we reported on.'

'Oh, those were happy days,' she said, smiling enthusiastically.

Fergus laughed. 'You make it sound as if it were years ago, not months ago. Nevertheless, Lilly, your story on the deceased bride was well written, and if the neighbours want to speak ill of the dead or be melodramatic, that is to your advantage.'

'Thank you as always, Fergus, but I would have liked a quote from Miss Alma Thornton's aunt who came to claim her and an insight into the cad who deserted Miss Thornton rather than exaggerated statements.' Lilly gave a small shrug. 'At least Mr Cowan seemed please,' she said with a glance to the editor's office where, through a haze of cigar smoke, they could see their editor reading the morning edition.

'We need another great mystery, Lilly. A murder, something to get our teeth into,' Fergus said in a low voice, as fellow reporters arrived and exchanged greetings, ready to begin their day.

The handsome, charming and lecherous Lawrence Hulmes stopped by Lilly's desk. He flirted outrageously with her, enjoying her witty retorts and the laughter from the office men.

'A good yarn today, Lilly. Of course, that would never happen to you,' Lawrence said, admiring the brunette beauty with the large blue eyes, enhanced by today's pale blue dress. 'No man would ever leave such a beauty as you at the altar.'

She heard the sniggering laughs and felt the teasing looks. Five brothers had prepared Lilly for the male bastion that was her office.

'That is very true, Lawrence. And not because I am beautiful,' she said in jest, enjoying the laughs. 'But because I would hunt them down, as would my five brothers. When I am finished with them, they would never walk again, let alone up an aisle. But thank you for your kind words,' she smiled sweetly, and he grinned as his co-workers hooted with laughter.

'If that doesn't put you off, Lawrence, you are a man with a death wish,' Ted from the corner added.

'I do like a challenge, but I am guessing you still have that handsome British boyfriend?'

'Yes, and my brothers like him. He is a fortunate man.'

A loud voice bellowed, 'Lewis and Griffiths, get in here,' and the merriment stopped as Lilly and Fergus grabbed for their pads and headed into the editor's office.

Lilly took a deep breath of fresh air before entering. 'Yes, Mr Cowan?' she said, planting herself on the chair in front of his desk as Fergus took the seat next to her.

'What have you got for me, or are you ready for me to assign you another story?'

'We have the sniff of a story from the detectives, Mr Cowan, and should be able to flesh it out for you tomorrow,' Lilly said confidently.

Mr Cowan glanced at the clock and back at his two enthusiastic and youngest reporters. He made a humphing sound of disbelief.

'Given it's the start of the day, I'll give you the rest of it to get your next yarn lined up.' He hit a pile of papers on his desk. 'There's a few stories here I need followed up, but since you are getting a following and the wife enjoys reading your stories, I'll expect something this time tomorrow, then.'

'Thank you, Mr Cowan,' Fergus said.

'And thank you to Mrs Cowan too,' Lilly said, smiling, and both reporters rose quickly as the wave of his hand signalled the meeting was over.

Outside and closer to their desk, Fergus asked, 'Any truth in that?'

'No, but that's never stopped us before. I have nothing on the boil, but...'

'We have one day to change that,' Fergus said with a grin to his writing partner.

Chapter 3

PHOEBE RAISED HER FACE to the sun, closed her eyes, and smiled. Her pale skin rarely saw the sun, and when she did venture out, often on the arm of her beau, Detective Harland Stone, her straw boater kept her protected. But on this winter morning, she welcomed the warmth.

The small trap jostled along, her brother Julius in the driver's seat. Phoebe relaxed beside him. She might not have done so next to Ambrose, who was prone to speed when he got his hands on the reins – most unbecoming for a funeral vehicle.

'It is a beautiful winter's day,' she said happily, opening her eyes and nudging Julius.

'The best time of the year to be an undertaker,' he agreed, dressed in his dark suit and top hat. The gold band of his wedding ring caught the light. 'If only everyone would be courteous enough to die in the cooler months.'

Ambrose, forced to ride in the rear seat with his back against Julius, turned, stuck his head between his siblings and asked, 'What would we do for the rest of the year then?'

'I'm sure we could find an indoor summer business venture,' Julius mused as they turned the corner into the street of the residence they were seeking. 'Good Lord!' Pulling on the reins, Julius eased their pace.

'Goodness me, what is going on?' Phoebe exclaimed at the sight of a long parade of people snaking down the street and numerous traps and horses blocking the entrance to the property. Nearby, residents watched from their properties, angry at the crowds, noise and disruption to their day.

'We are here, and so is everyone else,' Ambrose said. 'You definitely have the right address?'

'Yes,' Phoebe said. 'This is where we came to discover Alma's body, and now it appears the oddity of her situation has drawn a crowd.'

'It's a well-to-do street,' Ambrose said as they passed the neighbouring manors with equally large porticos for guests and vehicles. The rest of the house block was small by comparison; ideal for those not seeking maintenance or the expense of gardeners. Large iron fences surrounded the properties, and a smattering of police officers positioned themselves in front of the Thornton manor entrance gate and at various points along the street to keep people orderly.

'We may have to go on foot from here,' Ambrose suggested, but Julius shook his head.

'Will you alight and advise the police officers at the gate that we are here as requested by the deceased's next of kin?' Julius said. 'They can clear our way.'

'Shall do,' Ambrose said, leaping from the trap and removing his hat. He took off at a good pace.

'I imagine Lilly's story in *The Courier* created much interest in the broken-hearted Alma,' Phoebe said in a low voice, as if saying the words were shameful to the dead.

'And people are insatiably curious. I expect your friend, Miss Lewis, will be here to follow up,' Julius said as they saw Ambrose returning with two police officers in his trail asking the public to make way.

One officer motioned for Julius to proceed, and as they made their way through, Ambrose thanked the public on behalf of *The Economic Undertaker*.

Phoebe heard the comments as they drove slowly on.

'Why does Miss Thornton need an economic undertaker? Look at the size of her house.'

'No point spending good money on the dead.'

'Amen to that,' Julius whispered to Phoebe, making her hide her smile.

'She must have tight-fisted relatives.'

'Maybe there's no one left who cares how she goes out of the world. The fiancé didn't, that's for sure.'

'They are very good, though. We used The Economic Undertaker when aunt died. You'd never know it was cheaper. They were polished.'

Phoebe saw Julius's subtle smile on hearing that last comment and its quick removal as one woman added, *'They are very good looking, too.'*

'At last,' Julius said, arriving at the gate.

'It was a good chance to promote our business,' Phoebe said to him quietly as Ambrose thanked the police constables and jumped back into the trap for the ride to the front door.

Julius guided the horses through the entranceway. 'Very true, Phoebe. Let's hope people think now that if it was good enough for the wealthy Miss Alma Thornton, it is good enough for them!'

Mrs Frances Neale stood in the large bay window of her niece's property and watched the parade of people outside egging for a better view.

'Disgraceful,' she muttered several times, clasping her hands in front of her tiny frame, which seemed frailer in the dark mourning gown. There was nothing frail about Frances Neale.

She had been in mourning for quite some time – first for her elderly parents, then for her brother, Harold, and now for his daughter, her niece Alma.

'Good and right on time,' she said to the empty room on seeing the vehicle coming up the path with *The Economic Undertaker* livery. It was not the hearse as the burial was not today, but Mrs Neale had requested their presence to discuss matters pertaining to her niece's funeral, and she knew exactly what she wanted.

She watched as the small party alighted from the trap and the young man driving saw to the horses' needs first; Mrs Neale approved. A good sign of character. The rumble of voices told her that her driver, promoted to doorman, was checking their names against the list of approved visitors before allowing them entry. The Astin siblings were shown to the drawing room, where she waited, noting their glances toward the open room that held the wedding breakfast. Mrs Neale's budget ensured several cleaning staff dealt with the room swiftly and all traces of the rotting display were gone.

'Thank you for coming,' Mrs Neale said curtly. 'I did not bring any additional staff with me, so I cannot offer you tea. I am sorry.'

'Of course, Mrs Neale. Julius Astin at your service. Please accept our condolences on behalf of myself, my sister Phoebe, and my brother, Ambrose.'

She nodded to each person during introductions. 'Thank you. Please sit down.' The party moved to the two couches in front of the bay window, with Phoebe sitting beside Frances Neale and the men sitting on the opposite couch. 'You are a very handsome family.'

Ambrose gave her a small smile appropriate for the occasion. 'Our grandparents would agree with you, Mrs Neale.'

Frances Neale chuckled. 'No doubt. My niece Alma was a plain girl with a large inheritance. Her mother and brother passed away on the ship to Australia, and her father, my brother Harold, doted on her. He passed last year, and Alma became a very wealthy young woman.'

'And now she has passed away so young too,' Julius said sympathetically. 'You are no stranger to loss, Mrs Neale.'

'I am not. Thank you for your consideration, Mr Astin,' she agreed, giving Julius an appreciative look. 'My niece was also foolish and easily taken by a pretty face and smooth talk. Alma's father, if alive, would have prevented her abandonment and mistreatment. This would never have happened.' She waved a hand at the crowds outside.

'The heart wants what it wants, Mrs Neale,' Phoebe said softly and drew the sharp gaze of the woman her way.

'It does, young lady. You have read the letters of Emily Dickinson. Very good.' The middle-aged woman sighed. 'Yes, we are all fools for love. I see you are married, young man.'

'Only recently, Mrs Neale, and happily so,' Julius said. 'So, how may we be of assistance to you and the late Miss Thornton?'

'Yes, best we get to the heart of the matter,' she agreed. 'Another practical soul like myself, well done, young man. I have a most unusual request, and if you don't wish to carry it out, I will understand and hire another undertaker.'

'Understood,' Julius said. 'What have you in mind?'

'I wish to have my niece prepared early tomorrow morning for a final viewing to take place from eleven to one o'clock, please.' She paused.

'We can easily manage that,' Julius said. 'Phoebe is our mortician and will present your niece respectfully.'

'An interesting profession, young lady,' Mrs Neale addressed Phoebe, but did not object. 'How long will you need?'

'If there are no visible injuries, two hours will more than suffice, Mrs Neale, most likely less,' Phoebe responded.

'She died of a broken heart. The only visible signs are the discolouring of her skin and the gauntness from her suffering.'

'I am no stranger to working with those afflictions, Mrs Neale,' Phoebe assured her. 'If you have a portrait of Miss Thornton in life, I will style her in the manner that her friends and family recognise.'

'Excellent. There will be a handful of friends at most, but many viewers.'

'In that case,' Julius continued. 'Ambrose and I will both be on hand to manage the mourners. Hopefully, with the assistance of the police, if these crowds continue to gather.'

Mrs Neale and the Astin siblings turned their gaze to the crowds shuffling along outside the window to see the house, as if viewing a painting in a gallery.

'I will request the police maintain their presence,' Mrs Neale agreed. 'I would also like to book Alma's funeral with you as discussed with your senior man yesterday.'

'Our grandfather, Randolph,' Phoebe confirmed.

'I believe you have requested our top package with the plumes for the horses. We've booked it for two o'clock with Father Morris of St. Patrick's church,' Ambrose, the recently promoted Operations Manager, confirmed.

'Thank you, that is correct. Alma is to be removed straight after the viewing and taken for burial, please.' Again, Mrs Neale glanced at the crowds outside with displeasure.

'We will need to leave at exactly one o'clock to make the two o'clock funeral,' Julius advised her, 'even if your viewing is not complete, although we have found a two-hour window is ample time for viewing.'

'I agree,' Mrs Neale said, giving her approval.

'May I ask why the crowds are here?' Ambrose enquired.

'The newspaper carries a story about the heiress bride, jilted at the altar, who refused to leave the house or to change out of her wedding gown.'

'But sadly, she would not be the first to have experienced such dishonour,' Julius said.

'No. But the reporter wrote the story as a melodrama.'

The Astin siblings exchanged subtle looks, knowing their dear friend, Miss Lilly Lewis, was the writer.

Mrs Neale continued. 'The article exposed Alma, writing that, in her state of shock, my niece abandoned the wedding breakfast and refused anyone entry to the house to clear it.'

'I recall the story, Mrs Neale,' Phoebe said sympathetically.

'I would have had the wedding breakfast removed immediately had I known Alma was not in a state to manage its clearing. Some people rise in adversity; others wilt. However,' she conceded, 'the article held an element of truth. Alma would not change out of her wedding dress except to wash. She was heartbroken and humiliated and had I known of her state of mind, I would have had her committed; I don't live nearby,' she explained. 'It is of some consolation that the doctor claimed she weakened quickly and did not linger long.'

Mrs Neale delivered the news factually, as if emotions were not to be shown in public or were a sign of weakness.

Ambrose, having recently had his heart broken by Miss Lilly Lewis, sympathised. He had unintentionally inflicted the same pain on Miss Kate Kirby when his affections for Miss Lewis became known. 'How terribly tragic,' he said.

Mrs Neale nodded and sighed. 'It was true that Alma would leave the door ajar in case he returned, at great risk to her personal safety. I heard if she closed the door due to ill weather, she would leave a note on it advising she was in residence and if there were no answer, to persist and not to abandon her again.'

'Oh, that is heartbreaking,' Phoebe said, her hand going to her heart.

'It is. The treachery of men,' Mrs Neale said, making Julius and Ambrose most uncomfortable.

'Do you know what became of the groom?' Phoebe asked.

'Yes. I heard he died on the continent. After abandoning my niece, he departed our shores and fell ill on the ship and died, buried at sea. No more than what he deserves. Alma refused to believe it as the silly girl held hope he would return. Why she would have him back is beyond me. Of course, the money he stole from her is long gone. I have drifted again, back to the matter at hand...'

'What is your wish that you would like us to carry out, Mrs Neale?' Julius asked.

'I would like every lady present to pay their respects.' She indicated the crowd outside and saw the three Astin family members' eyes widen in surprise. 'Yes, every lady wishing to file past my niece in the time allotted must have the opportunity to do so. Let them see what heartbreak men can cause and thus go forth more wisely.'

There was a stillness in the room before Julius said. 'Every lady? Strangers? Women in the long lines outside?' he clarified.

'Yes, Mr Astin,' Mrs Neale said firmly. 'No men are to enter except for yourself, your brother, and the constabulary. Ladies only. As many as arrive and can file past in the two-hour window are welcome. Can you carry that out for me?'

Julius looked at his brother and sister and then responded, 'As you wish, Mrs Neale. As you wish.'

Chapter 4

WHILE THE BOXER CURRENTLY fighting in the ring had never made it known he worked for the police force, Detective Harland Stone suspected word spread fast; there were always contenders ready to take him on while other men of his size struggled to get a sparring partner.

It was early in the evening, before a large crowd had gathered at the club that he and his friends frequented, and Harland was keen to get a boxing round under his belt and let off some steam, intending to relax for the rest of the evening.

As the lady partners of Harland, undertaker Julius Astin, and private investigator-artist Bennet Martin were meeting this evening for their regular *Vexed Vixens* gathering, the men were free to enjoy a gents' night at the club.

Sitting at a table on a balcony level was the coroner, the ruddy Scot, Dr Tavish McGregor, who accompanied the detective and secured a table for four. They were expecting Bennet and Julius to join them at any moment. After a day with the dead, Tavish enjoyed seeing the living, and Harland appreciated the amiable company.

Harland had weathered three hard rounds; the men were matched physically, and there was money at stake. Neither man liked to be the cause of a lost bet or to lose face. The two men stood ready for the final round.

'You're going to lose your money, Jonesy,' one of the regular drinkers who had a prime seat called to his mate, who stood ready in the ring, doing his best to intimidate Harland Stone. 'What was it you were going to do? Down him in two rounds?'

Patrons laughed as the referee took his place to start the next round.

'Duck and weave,' Harland muttered to himself, a reminder to avoid hits to the face. His inspector did not look fondly upon a detective with a black eye, nor was it role model behaviour to display a worse-for-wear face to his protégé, Detective Gilbert Payne. But most importantly, he did not want to stress Phoebe, his belle, by presenting himself bruised or bloodied.

The bell rang, and the men shuffled, raised their fists and began their ritual dance. A quick blow from his opponent hit hard, but Harland had no regrets; he needed this. He was closing a case, a most despicable one, and he needed to hit out in a controlled manner. The thought of the arrest that took place this afternoon fuelled him with anger and disgust. A man who does not fight fair, who strikes the weaker sex and children, is despicable! With a sharp right, he delivered a good blow, knocking down his opponent.

There was a roar from the gallery, and Harland shook out his hand and quickly wiped the blood running down his face; he had got as good as he had given. From the mat, the fighter struggled to his feet quickly enough. A bell rang; the referee raised Harland's arm, and it was over.

Tonight Harland had won, and Tavish would get his money back and more. He saw the begrudging respect in his contender's eyes as they shook.

'A rematch some time?' the opponent asked, believing the man before him got lucky.

'Next time I am angry. I might not beat you otherwise,' Harland agreed with good sportsmanship, and his opponent huffed before spitting blood on the floor beside him.

Harland exited the ring, cleaned up, and, doing up his shirt, rejoined Tavish as Julius and Bennet entered the club.

'Well done,' Tavish said. 'Where did that last blow come from?'

'I was envisaging the scoundrel I put away today,' Harland said, sitting and drinking half of his glass of beer in thirst.

'Ah,' Tavish nodded. 'A man who takes his frustration out on women and children. It's a shame you could not meet him in the ring.'

'He wouldn't step out,' Harland agreed. 'I am not, nor have I ever been, close to my father—'

'No doubt it is hard to be when you are a school boarder,' Tavish interjected, and Harland nodded.

'But he is a man of principle, and I remember his lessons well. It is the duty of men to protect the fairer sex, children and animals. What kind of man does not uphold those virtues?'

'Too many sadly,' Tavish said, and the two men turned their attention to Julius and Bennet, who had made their way to the bar to purchase a round for the group before joining them.

Harland turned back to find Tavish surveying his countenance, and his friend said, 'You did not sustain too much damage.'

Harland winced and patted his right cheekbone. 'It feels like I did, but it is a day until I see Phoebe next, and it will have faded a little by then.'

'Ah, the ladies,' Tavish sighed. 'My twin brother, Brodie, is sailing to our shores as we speak. When he arrives, I will propose to Isabelle, and he will be my best man.'

Harland's face lit up. 'Tavish, that is great news,' he said, slapping him on the back. 'The lovely Miss Yalden. Does she have an inkling?'

'No, and do not mention it, as your protégé may say something to her cousin, Emily. I intend to surprise Isabelle so that she'll say yes in shock.'

Harland laughed. 'You have been courting Miss Yalden for months; I imagine she is waiting with eager anticipation. And I look forward to meeting this brother of yours. Are you identical?'

'No. I am better looking than Brodie, a sad truth for him.'

'Of course you are,' Harland grinned, and the pair greeted the new arrivals. While Bennet bemoaned the chance of having seen Harland in the ring and the conversation soon turned to his opponent, the detective let his mind wander to Miss Phoebe Astin. He, too, wanted to propose, but when? Soon, definitely soon.

Phoebe arrived last at her friend Emily Yalden's home for the monthly *Vexed Vixen* dinner, delayed by meeting Mrs Frances Neale and navigating the crowds outside the deceased niece's home. Julius had done so capably without spooking the horses or collecting anyone underfoot, ably assisted by Ambrose, who waded ahead, charming those in front to clear the way.

Emily Yalden of the *Miss Emily Yalden School of Deportment* regularly hosted as one of the few ladies with her own home and no partner to hurry out the door for the evening. Rushing in, Phoebe smiled at the sight of her closest friends.

'I believe I made it with two minutes to spare and no formal apology for tardiness required to the hostess,' she said in one long breath.

'Bravo, Phoebe,' Emily said with a smile, closing the door behind her. 'We have all arrived, and I can call the gathering to order.'

'You only just beat me in the door, so do not fret,' Lilly said as the close friends followed Emily to the dining table where a lovely spread for dinner lay before them and Violet waited to greet them.

'Don't tell me that terrible manager of yours made you work late again,' Lilly teased, referring to Phoebe's brother and Violet's husband, Julius. 'He is a taskmaster.'

'I shall speak with him; it is not acceptable,' Violet said playfully, taking a seat next to Lilly.

Phoebe laughed. 'It was a very odd client who kept me late. I shall tell you about it later.'

'Ooh, I am starving,' Lilly said, 'and I won't have to compete with Kate for the last slice of your famous quiche, Emily. How I miss Kate.'

'It does seem rather odd without her here,' Emily agreed, looking at the group, which was back to four ladies around the table – reporter Lilly Lewis, mortician Phoebe Astin, dressmaker Violet Astin and Emily herself. 'Although we were originally four and expanded when Violet joined us, so we are back to our original number.'

'I may have a lady who would make a wonderful addition, if everyone is open to a new *Vexed Vixens'* member and if she is interested in joining,' Phoebe said.

'How could she resist? We are most entertaining,' Lilly said in jest, and clinking glasses in a welcome toast and thanks to Emily for hosting, the ladies began to nibble on the spread before them. 'So who is this potential *Vexed Vixen?*'

'She actually met Kate first, and then me. Oh, she has met Violet and you too, Lilly, at the waterside memorial last month,' Phoebe realised. 'I will declare up front I believe my brother Ambrose to be taken with her.'

'The lovely Miss Prout?' Violet asked.

'Yes, I believe she is perfect for the *Vexed Vixens*. A businesswoman, clever and no doubt, good company.'

'So ask her along, Phoebe, if there are no objections,' Emily said, and the ladies agreed.

'That's settled then,' Phoebe agreed. 'She is the first lady monument maker I have ever met. I am sure Miss Prout will fit in well.'

'Has not Ambrose pursued Miss Prout then?' Lilly asked.

'Oddly no,' Phoebe said. 'According to cousin Lucian, I think Ambrose was a little more upset by the end of his romance with Kate than he admitted; he makes light of everything and so rarely has a serious moment. But his confidence seems to have ebbed a little.'

'Well, it is time he got back on the horse, so to speak,' Emily suggested. 'Not implying that Kate or Miss Prout are horses, of course, heaven forbid.'

The ladies chuckled at the thought.

'Yes, I agree,' Lilly said. 'From Kate's correspondence, she is not without her suitors – some handsome and wealthy land owners she would have us believe, so if you think Miss Prout might be interested in your brother, Phoebe, do encourage it!'

'I shall be sure to do so,' Phoebe promised.

'Excellent. Now that we have that sorted, who will begin with what is vexing them?' Emily asked.

'Please allow me,' Lilly said, taking a sip of her water. 'I had to write a most melodramatic article, so vexing!'

'It was very interesting, though,' Emily interjected.

'The lady who died in her wedding dress?' Violet said, 'terribly sad.'

'But it was all true,' Phoebe supported Lilly while not revealing her role in Miss Alma Thornton's burial yet.

'Yes, although I am sure the neighbours embellished the truth. Her aunt would not speak with me,' Lilly sighed. 'I need an investigative piece. It has been two months since Fergus and I had a good mystery to report on. Oh, I know we've had some good articles about catastrophes and dramas in the city, but I long for a good murder.'

The ladies around the table burst out laughing.

'You may laugh, ladies, which is also vexing,' Lilly said, trying to stay serious, 'but truly, it is frustrating. Not even Phoebe's dead are complaining.'

'A sad state of affairs indeed,' Phoebe sympathised, but could not resist grinning at Lilly's antics. 'Although I am pleased no one is going to the other side burdened, I miss having a visit from the detectives, one in particular.'

'Is Detective Stone still walking you home several times a week?' Emily asked.

'Yes, when he can get away, and he is surprisingly regular. We have been to a few recitals as well.' Phoebe looked at Lilly. 'I shall do my best to find a vexed spirit for you, Lilly.'

'Too kind, Phoebe,' Lilly said with a smile. 'I nominate you, Violet.'

'Oh,' she said, surprised and took a sip of water before beginning. 'Well, I have several vexations, although they will sound most ungrateful.'

'You are among friends,' Emily assured her. 'If you cannot whine unjudged amongst us, where then?'

'If you insist,' Violet said with a nod and a smile. 'We have moved into our new business premises, *Beyond the Veil*, and we are now making mourning and bridal wear, as you know.'

'So exciting,' Phoebe said.

'It is. Nellie – Mrs Shaw – is full of ideas, and Mary is longing to work with white fabric,' Violet said, thinking of her youngest staff member. 'It is even more exciting that there may be ladies in this room who need bridal dresses made soon.' She looked at all three with intent, making them laugh.

'You have my business should the day come,' Emily agreed, and Lilly echoed the sentiment.

'I would have no choice,' Phoebe said with a laugh, 'not that I would consider going anywhere else.'

'Rightfully so,' Violet teased her. 'But my vexation is the tradesmen keep finding things to do after they assure us they are done. Goodness, they stomp around, call out to each other, create a mess and have no concept that silk or ribbons are lying nearby or that silence is golden.'

The ladies tried to hide their laughs but could not.

Violet grinned. 'I know it is to be expected,' she said, 'but they are supposed to be finished. They keep returning to do something messy! I cannot mention it to Julius as I don't wish to complain or stress him, but I am close to getting the broom and sweeping them all out with it.'

'I would like to see that,' Lilly said enthusiastically. 'And is married life wonderful?'

Violet sighed happily. 'So wonderful, and Tom truly admires Julius. It is wonderful for my brother to have a man he looks up to and can confide in. I am very fortunate.'

While the ladies agreed, Phoebe felt a pang of loss she never felt when Julius married Violet, as the ladies were friends. But now, the truth of the matter came home to her; he had a new household, and a new brother-in-law whom he was guiding. Julius had truly left the family.

Violet continued. 'But my home life leads to my second vexation; I have no time—nor interest, if I am being honest—to learn to cook. I am sure Julius rues the day when his grandmother, our grandmother, stops sending over meals to help. He has done his best to look enthusiastic about some of my cooking endeavours, and I feel it is my duty, so I don't wish to shirk my responsibilities.'

'I have already warned Bennet that if he thinks I am proficient in the domestic duties, he best seek another lady to court. It does not seem to have scared him away,' Lilly said, pleased.

'I am quite a good cook,' Phoebe said. 'Grandma taught me, so if Harland and I should one day walk down the aisle, he need only fear the ghosts, not my cooking.'

The ladies laughed, and Phoebe provided a solution. 'Sister, do not improve your cooking efforts and I assure you, Julius will soon suggest a cook. Then it will be his idea, and you can say how considerate and clever he is. He does not eat as much as Ambrose but knows nothing else but grandma's best, so it is only a matter of time.'

'A good plan indeed, thank you, Sister,' Violet agreed with a smile. 'Mrs Dobbs let it slip he is eating more at work, and hinted he had spoken of a cook ever so casually.'

'Stay the course, Violet,' Emily agreed, and Violet nominated her to voice her vexation. 'I hope it is about your students. I enjoy hearing of the escapades of the ladies of the *Miss Emily Yalden School of Deportment.*'

'Indeed, they are the source of all my vexation,' Emily agreed. 'Detective Payne, on the other hand, is my source of great contentment.'

'Ah, that is grand,' Lilly teased.

'I am so pleased, and from what Harland tells me, Detective Payne is very happy and often speaks of you in poetic tones,' Phoebe shared.

'Goodness,' Emily said with a laugh. 'I am delighted to inspire. I may become a sonnet! Only three of my students at the moment, however, are inspiring. Four have hope and one is vulgar.'

The ladies all stopped to look at Emily, who had never spoken so negatively about a student, not even the dastardly debutante who had graced her studio some time ago.

Emily continued. 'One does not need to be beautiful or graceful to be charming and an excellent conversationalist. In fact, I have known some very plain women who captivate a room with their wit or confidence. But Miss Martha Hampstead has vexed and challenged me.'

'And have you won the battle? Has she succumbed to some ladylike practices?' Violet asked.

'I think I may claim victory but only after she disrupted the class for many days, belittling what we do and why we do it, ridiculing and ruining the confidence of my ladies, and finding herself ever so close to being dismissed, and I have never expelled a student.' Now, Emily had the attention of all the ladies.

'How stressful for you, Emily, especially in front of your other students,' Phoebe said, recalling how the debutante's spirit had exhausted her.

'Thank you, yes, Phoebe. I felt as if I were a student being assessed and not the other way around.'

'Do tell, Emily; the suspense is killing me,' Lilly said. 'Tell us about your victory.'

Emily took a breath to steady herself. 'It began as she believed our lessons were for women who wished to be under the thumb or to attract a man. I reminded her I was a successful businesswoman and self-made, and I provided examples of inspirational women who used their best assets, be that beauty, brains, charm, contacts, money, to be trailblazers!'

'Bravo, Emily, I wish I had been there for that,' Lilly said. 'Who were your examples?'

'I spoke of Mary Wollstonecraft in 1792, a wife and mother, who wrote "A Vindication of the Rights of Women". That was almost 100 years ago! I told of Charlotte Bronte, who was under five feet in height but whom the poet Matthew Arnold declared was a woman full of "hunger, rebellion and rage", and represented women in her writing as strong. I spoke of Mary Colton, a suffragette with nine children, who balanced home and independence and continues to campaign for the poor. They used their strengths to change their worlds, whether it was charm, talent, beauty, wealth, connections or compassion.'

'Oh, I love this, Emily,' Phoebe said. 'You are amazing. How did Miss Hampstead respond?'

'For the first time in four days, she was silent. Watching and listening. I finished by showing an illustration of Mrs Lucy Stone.'

'I have not heard of her,' Lilly admitted, as did the other ladies.

'I read about her in a journal. Mrs Stone is a feminist; she kept her own name when she married.'

'Goodness!' Violet exclaimed.

'Indeed. I know some of her quotes by heart, and I said one aloud to my girls, as passionately as I could. Mind you,' Emily added, 'there is a risk in that some girls and their mothers do not agree with women's empowerment. But I do. So I addressed Miss Hampstead in particular when I repeated Mrs Stones's quote: "In education, in marriage, in religion, in everything, disappointment is the lot of women. It shall be the business of my life to deepen that disappointment in every woman's heart until she bows down to it no longer. Make the world better". Then, I asked Miss Hampstead, 'Martha, you have made new contacts here. How will you go forth and make the world better with the help of the ladies you have befriended?'

'What did she say?' Phoebe asked, enthralled.

'She was quite taken aback and said nothing. But she was a very different person the rest of the week. She absorbed her lessons, made closer friendships, and she had a gleam in her eye. I am done. Your turn, Phoebe.'

There was a brief silence, and then Lilly applauded, and the ladies joined in rapturously.

'I am inspired now too, Emily,' Lilly said.

'Then you will find the request I had this afternoon very interesting,' Phoebe said, taking her turn. 'As we speak of the vulnerable and strong, let me tell you of a very odd viewing session for my poor client that is about to take place!'

Chapter 5

THE SOFT MORNING LIGHT pouring in through the window where Miss Alma Thornton lay would suffice nicely for the mortician's work. Phoebe, in an attractive cream dress, with her hair tied back with a matching cream lace ribbon, looked a little like a bride herself, dressing to support the deceased before her.

'I am surprised your brothers would not insist you wear mourning wear given you are in public,' Mrs Neale said, and Phoebe could not tell if it was an observation or criticism.

'My brothers do not have a say in what I wear, Mrs Neale,' Phoebe said with no antagonism. 'I cannot spend my life in mourning; those days will come soon enough.'

'Yes, very true and considered, young lady. Can I leave you now if you have all you require?'

'Thank you, Mrs Neale, I have all I need to begin work,' Phoebe assured Alma's aunt, and watched as the lady hurriedly departed to continue her preparation for the day's viewing and funeral.

Phoebe's brothers were already present downstairs with the constabulary, working out how best to create an orderly area for the viewing and for the vehicles of family and friends to come and go. Many were likely to follow *The Economic Undertaker*'s hearse on its way to the cemetery with Alma on her last journey.

Phoebe laid out her powders and draped a light towel around the neck of Miss Alma Thornton to protect the wedding dress, which her aunt allowed the young woman to be buried in. She studied the frail Miss Thornton, selected a base powder, and with her brushes, began work.

'Phoebe, may I interrupt you?' a female voice asked, and Phoebe looked up, expecting to find one of Mrs Neale's staff members, but no living person was present. Alma stood nearby, gaunt in her wedding dress.

'Alma, hello again!'

'Good morning. I hope I didn't startle you. Thank you sincerely for finding my body as promised, but now, I hope to ask another favour as I heard you were a fighter for justice.'

'Goodness, I am flattered by that description and hope to live up to it,' Phoebe said and added, 'I heard of your distress, Alma, and I am so terribly sorry.'

The young woman bowed her head as if ashamed. 'I misjudged his character.'

'You were good-hearted and had no reason to doubt that he was not honourable.'

'Thank you, Phoebe, too kind.' Alma moved to stand beside the beautiful mortician. 'I am opposed to this viewing today... placing me on display for all to see, as if my humiliation was not enough,' she said, her voice rising with anger.

'I do not see it that way at all, Alma.' Phoebe tried to appease the young lady. 'I think you will make a difference to many.'

'How is that?' she asked, surprised.

'Your aunt wishes for women to pay their respects to you, as you lay beautiful in your wedding gown, and I assure you I will do my best to make you look as beautiful as you did on your wedding day,' Phoebe said, and continued. 'They will look upon you and think if one so lovely can be duped, I best be cautious in love myself.'

'I see,' Alma said, considering Phoebe's words.

'If you save one lady from distress and heartbreak by your example today, what an exemplary service that would be to your sex. Do you not agree?'

The young lady held herself a little taller, her head a little higher. 'Thank you, Phoebe, for restoring my dignity. Thank you.'

'So the favour you seek, how may I be of service to you in your last hours before departing for the next life?' Phoebe asked diplomatically. Ambrose would have said, 'Before you are buried six feet under' and Phoebe did her best not to smile as the thought crossed her mind.

'Well, while you work, may I tell you of my engagement and the duplicity that occurred?'

'Of course, Alma. I am at your service.'

The young lady began her story of love and loyalty, eventually concluding, 'I was told my betrothed, Oliver, had died, and I hoped to see him now so he might explain what happened. Just to gaze upon him again...' her voice faltered and then hardened. 'But he is not here.'

'Oh, might he be...' Phoebe indicated down below if he was being punished.

She shook her head. 'No, he is not here at all. He is in fact not dead.'

Phoebe stopped work and looked up in surprise.

Alma continued. 'Phoebe, he stole from me and left me to die of a broken heart. The rotter!'

'Good gracious, so he is very much alive, and you were told an untruth?'

'Yes, I have been thoroughly duped, and I would like justice. Will you help me?'

Daniel Dutton, long-suffering clerk and friend to private investigator and artist Bennet Martin, entered the office with the mail and greeted his aunt, the housekeeper.

'Good morning, Daniel. The kettle's on, and no sign of Mr Martin yet,' Mrs Clarke said.

'Good morning, Aunt. I won't be popular this morning, but I intend to interrupt his painting,' he said, waving a letter. 'Today's mail includes a potential new case for Bennet. He might want this one.'

'And why is that?' a voice said from the top of the stairwell, where Bennet Martin appeared shrugging on his jacket.

'Are you not painting this morning?' Daniel asked, noticing that his boss had finished grooming himself and had even avoided getting paint in his fair hair.

'I have dabbled enough. I am not feeling inspired. Perhaps seeing Lilly tonight will restore my creative powers tomorrow morning. For now, I am bored.' He came down the stairs and greeted Mrs Clarke.

'Tea and toast then?' she asked.

'Yes, please, Mrs Clarke,' Bennet said and followed Daniel into their joint office in the front room of Bennet's modest townhouse. Upstairs were his bedroom and a large front room that he had converted into his art studio, as it enjoyed the light to the best advantage. On the lower lever, a sign outside advised it was the premises of Private Investigator B. Martin. 'What have you then that will have me excited?'

'Perhaps excited is taking it a little far. But a very wealthy man wishes you to conduct a discreet investigation.'

'How do you know he is wealthy?' Bennet asked, sitting in his chair behind his desk and studying the bespectacled, clean-cut clerk who sat to his left, facing the street window side-on.

'Any man worth his salt in business, who has lived on these shores,' he added so as not to insult his recently arrived British boss, 'knows the name Patrick Edmonstone. He made his money in textiles and has three sons, two daughters. All betrothed successfully, and the youngest only recently made her debut.'

'So what does he want with us then since we've established he can pay his bill,' Bennet said in jest, thanking Mrs Dobbs as she served him generously buttered, cut slices of toast and a cup of tea, prepared to his liking. Daniel received an equally large serving.

'I shall read you his correspondence.' He waved the letter before him and began. 'Dear Mr Martin, I ask for your complete discretion and request your services to investigate a delicate matter. One year ago now, my daughter, Grace, was taken advantage of in a most ungentlemanly manner – a promise made and a large dowry stolen. I have been patient, as the police assured me the case was still under investigation, but my patience is wearing thin. I fear the betrayal may become public, and will face that in due course. However, I am hopeful of redeeming some of her fortune and protecting her as a father should. If you are available and I may engage your services, would you be so kind as to make an appointment... etc., etc.' Daniel said with a wave of his hand.

'He sounds like a good father, unless that is just an act to win my sympathy.'

'Perhaps,' Daniel said. 'You do have a very good reputation thanks to your connections.'

'Yes,' Bennet smiled. 'I was most fortunate to make the acquaintance of the detectives and Miss Lewis and to foster those friendships. I have Julius to thank for that.' He looked at Daniel. 'And what makes you think I will want this case?' He finished a piece of toast and began on another.

'A young woman duped, a wealthy family, a cad on the loose. It sounds like something that a talented journalist would eventually get wind of and report. Imagine if you were working the case at the time,' Daniel said, too smart for his own good, as always.

Bennet chuckled. 'Some days, you earn your keep, young Daniel. Make the appointment, and I shall visit Mr Edmonstone and hear more about this most unfortunate duping of his daughter. Then I shall see if Harland can help with access to the police file.'

'I shall send a message now.'

'Let us save the day!' Bennet said confidently. 'I wonder if Lilly knows about it.'

Chapter 6

AMBROSE ASTIN, MIDDLE CHILD, tall, dark-haired and blue-eyed, was fairly confident that he appealed to the ladies, although his love life had been unsuccessful to date. Truth be told, he was a little jealous of Julius finding a bride and cosy home life. At 25, he was next in line to marry, and keen to find the kind of love that would encourage such a union.

He had been at the Thornton manor for over an hour now and was seeking amusement. Julius was liaising with Mrs Frances Neale, Phoebe was applying her wares to the deceased, and he was waiting around, watching as people gathered around the grounds and formed an orderly line down the street, again.

'Ready,' he said, taking a deep breath, and braved the gauntlet of women from the gates to the door. He hurried up the path, leaving the hearse and horses safely to the side, on the pretence of having a message for Phoebe. Ambrose cut a handsome figure in his dark three-piece suit, with a white shirt, a black tie, and a top hat featuring a black band.

The journey on foot was not an easy one, and fifteen minutes later, puffing, he appeared at the top of the stairs and entered the large well-lit room where Phoebe worked.

'Brother!' she said, surprised at the interruption, her powder brush suspended as she studied Ambrose. 'Julius is downstairs. Is everything all right?'

'No. I am in search of a distraction, and it was a challenge to get here! That looks very nice,' he said, moving closer and admiring Phoebe's work.

'I hope it will be,' Phoebe said. 'It is going to be a long day.'

'A drawn-out event,' Ambrose agreed, 'and I have put myself in great danger several times already, entering the house past the pack of women out there.'

'Pack?' Phoebe grinned as she continued to work, while Ambrose stood in the window, hands clasped behind his back, looking down on the grounds.

'They are fearsome in such numbers,' he shuddered. 'And most forward, may I say?'

'You may. I thought they might be angry at any man present, but clearly you have charmed the crowds.'

'I didn't get a chance to speak,' Ambrose declared. 'I have been propositioned, and pelted with handkerchiefs, and barely knew which lady to return them to as they all claimed it was their piece of fabric and lace, and giggled behind their hands.'

'Outrageous,' Phoebe said and could not resist a giggle of her own.

'One lady, who, mind you, was quite attractive, asked me if I believed in love at first sight?'

'What did you say?' Phoebe asked, keen to hear Ambrose's reply.'

'I said, "Madam, I can walk by you again if you do," and she invited me to do so!'

Phoebe laughed but then restrained herself, remembering she was at the scene of a client's viewing. 'That is very clever.'

'Yes, they all seemed to appreciate it,' Ambrose said drily. 'But they got bolder. I am not sure some comments are fit for your ears.'

Phoebe sighed and gave her brother a small shake of her head. 'You and Julius are always over protective. I am only a few years younger than you and have been privy to people from many walks of life. Tell me the worst.'

Ambrose contemplated this for a moment before exhaling. 'Fine then. One Miss said, "You have nice arms. May I feel them around me?" The hide.'

'Oh, very good,' Phoebe laughed.

'Another offered to cook me dinner if I cook her breakfast,' Ambrose said with mock indignation.

'Goodness, that is forward.'

'I warned you. Then, an older lady asked, "Aside from being cute, do you have any other hobbies?"'

Phoebe laughed again. 'Poor you. Was it fun?'

'Very,' he said and gave her a wink.

The folder handed to Detective Harland Stone that morning at the Roma Street Police Headquarters looked as if it had passed through a few hands. The front featured tea stains, weathered corners, and scribbled notes, and the message from the desk sergeant confirmed Harland's suspicions.

'Jilted brides, fortunes stolen... it's been going on for a while, Detective, three years at least,' the sergeant said with a nod to the file he had removed from the internal mailbox and handed to Harland. 'The inspector said he would like to get to the bottom of it. He's under a bit of pressure from the well-to-dos', he added in a quieter voice, thumbing a finger under his nose. 'Looks like he has tasked you with solving it.'

'Thank you, John, a challenge, then,' Harland said, refraining from sighing. It was not the first case that the

Inspector had wanted off his plate and thought he'd see what the new team could do with it.

Harland strode at a good pace down the hallway as he always did to avoid being engaged in small talk about his latest fight or a crime just solved. Since being partnered with the inexperienced young detective, Gilbert Payne, in exchange for winning the coveted role of detective in the Brisbane branch, the two very different men had gone from being ridiculed to becoming a formidable team that had solved every case that had come across the desk. Those who had once dismissed him were now keen to stop and talk about matters and win him over. Harland was a busy man with a long memory for loyalty.

Entering the office allocated to the youngest detectives – the one furthest away from the street entrance – he announced, 'We have a new case, Gilbert.'

'Sir? That is good news. I found that last case most distressing.'

'As did I,' Harland agreed, placing the file on their meeting table in the middle of the room and moving to his desk to remove his suit jacket and hat. 'There is a special place in hell for those who harm the weakest, I am sure of it.'

'I thought you were an atheist, Sir,' Gilbert joked. 'Father Morris will be happy if you've joined us.'

Harland chucked. 'Don't tell him. I like to believe that justice will be metered out in the afterlife if not in this life.'

'It is what keeps many of us honest. I have just filed the last of our notes on the previous case and will have them stored later.' Gilbert placed the lid on the box and moved to clean their notes from the board. 'Is it a murder, Sir?'

'No, theft and fraud, I suspect, but with vulnerable victims. According to the sergeant, it's been around for a while; the Inspector wants it closed.'

'Oh, another,' Gilbert said, disheartened. 'I always feel like it's a test and one day, we will disappoint.'

'It is a different pressure than that of a fresh case,' Harland agreed. 'But we have exceeded before with the fake young boy and the deathly dolls. We shall take the bit between our teeth and do our best, Gilbert.' He returned to the meeting table.

'Yes, Sir,' Gilbert said with a smile, heartened by the rousing sentiment. He finished cleaning the board and, grabbing his pad and pencil, joined his superior.

From the file, Harland withdrew three separate wads of notes, each clipped at the top. He put them in order. 'Three years ago, two, one... these crimes, if linked, have happened every year for three years.'

'So the crime might be happening again now,' Gilbert said. 'Some planning must go into it if the culprit only undertakes this crime once per year.'

'Yes, assuming it is only one person and the cases are linked, I am sure by now he has refined it.' Harland handed the oldest bundle to Gilbert and started on the most recent case notes. Both men read through them silently. On finishing, Harland looked up. 'I have a jilted bride of a wealthy family defrauded, as her father advanced the groom-to-be a sizeable sum.'

'I have similar, Sir – a wealthy woman abandoned. However, the groom did not get away with it and left penniless.'

Harland handed Gilbert his case file and reached for the remaining report from two years ago.

'Same crime, hmm. Three wealthy women were wooed, fortunes advanced and lost in two out of three cases, and their suitor or suitors seem to have got away with it. How has this gone on for three years without an arrest?' Harland asked incredulously.

'I'm sure this dishonourable act happens more often than we know, Sir, so why were these three cases grouped together?' Gilbert mused.

'Good question,' Harland nodded. 'Is the rogue the same person in each case or part of a crime syndicate? It is unlikely these men are using their real names. Let's compare the victims and villains.' Both men thumbed through the pages to find the name and description of the rogue in question. Yelling in the hallway interrupted them, followed by the sound of thumping feet, then silence as someone was bundled away.

Harland read on, 'Last year's victim was Miss Grace Edmonstone, abandoned by Mr Edwin Ownnet.'

'Edmonstone?' Gilbert said. 'I wonder if that is the shipping family headed by Mr Patrick Edmonstone.'

Harland checked the notes. 'One and the same, Gilbert. Money there then.'

Gilbert nodded and read from his file. 'This victim of two years ago is Miss Caroline Gardner, and Mr Walter Tewnon left her at the altar. Gardner... I wonder if that is the Gardner family who made their money in property.' He waded through more pages. 'Yes, here it is. Her father is Mr Arthur Gardner.'

Harland huffed. 'I think we've found the connection. Three years ago, the victim was Miss Winnifred Nash, betrothed to Mr Isaac Wenton. The abandonment of Miss Nash caused her to lose her will to live. She refused food until she was weak and illness overtook her.'

'Tragic,' Gilbert said. 'That scoundrel!'

'Do you know the Nash name?' Harland looked at his protégé with curiosity.

'Yes, Sir,' Gilbert nodded. 'If Miss Winnifred Nash's father is Mr Jacob Nash, then he made his money in grazing land.'

Harland looked at the name and nodded. 'It is Mr Jacob Nash. How do you know these names, Gilbert? I must say I have not encountered them in my circle, but I recognise the Edmonstone name associated with community donations.'

'Mr Edmonstone is a generous benefactor, I believe. About six months ago, an article ran in *The Courier* announcing that the wealthiest man in Australia had died in Sydney. They then listed the wealthiest people in the country at that time. I recall some of those names, as I was curious about the manner in which they had made their fortunes and intended to study them. I want to look after my mother for life and hoped to emulate them,' Gilbert said sheepishly.

'You are a dutiful son, Gilbert. So we have our link. Three of our city's wealthiest men have become targets, apparently because their daughters are of age to marry. Surely, given the connection, these despicable cads are working together.'

'I wonder if they are working for someone, Sir.'

'It is possible, and one might be hard at work as we speak. Let us endeavour to give these ladies justice, Gilbert. We might be best to start with the most recent case – the Edmonstone family.' He read the family's address, and Gilbert noted it down. 'That street rings a bell,' Harland mused.

Gilbert clicked his fingers. 'Yes, Sir, I know why. One moment, please.' The young detective rose and departed the office, as Harland read through the patchy detective notes in the file. It was clear that the previous detective on the case thought the domestic matter was not worth pursuing.

Returning promptly with a copy of *The Courier*, Gilbert placed it in front of his superior. 'Sir, that is the same street where the crowds are gathering to see the house of the woman who died in her wedding dress. Miss Alma Thornton... it's her viewing today.'

'I overhead a constable bemoaning the sight of a decaying wedding breakfast,' Harland said as he turned the newspaper slightly to read the article. 'This is interesting. Miss Thornton was left at the altar, robbed of her large dowry. Does that sound familiar, Gilbert? I think we have found this year's victim.'

'That name, Sir, the name Thornton... it is another of the city's wealthiest sons. Mr Thornton, when alive, made his money in merchandise. I believe he was an astute merchant.'

'It might be in our best interest to compile a list of the city's wealthiest families with unwed daughters of age or about to debut.'

'I shall take on that challenge, Sir. It is a very wealthy street if both of our victims' families live on it – Miss Edmonstone and Miss Thornton. Should we brave the crowds?'

'It might be a good way to kill two birds with one stone, Gilbert. Let's begin with Miss Thornton, as her family is likely to be present for the viewing. If they are too distraught to talk, we will make our way to the Edmonstone household and see if Mr or Mrs Edmonstone are home.'

Harland rose, grabbed his coat and hat, tucking the file under his arm; Gilbert did the same, pocketing his notebook.

'Miss Lewis's article claimed Miss Thornton never changed out of her wedding dress and always hoped her fiancé would return,' Gilbert said as they walked down the hallway. 'Hence the crowds coming to see a curious sight.'

'One lady lost the will to live; another died from the shock of betrayal. These men are despicable,' Harland said, unable to imagine ever doing such a thing to Phoebe. Exiting the building, he took the few stairs down to the street level where a hansom awaited, sure of a fare if they remained around the police precinct.

'Without character and rich,' Gilbert agreed. 'For what is a man profited, if he shall gain the whole world, and lose his own soul? Matthew 16:26.'

'Indeed, but I don't think the groom is thinking about his soul, more likely his creature comforts,' Harland agreed, well used to Gilbert's facts, psalms, and sayings. Sometimes they even proved to be useful.

Chapter 7

THE WEATHER HAD HELD, which was fortunate given the crowds gathered for the viewing of the jilted bride in her wedding dress.

Phoebe finished preparing Miss Thornton for her viewing and was doing her last inspection, walking around the body to ensure Alma looked her best from every angle. Satisfied, Phoebe gathered the bouquets nearby and placed them in a manner most becoming.

'Oh, that is beautiful,' a voice said, and Phoebe turned to see Alma had returned and clasped her hands with delight.

'Thank you, dear Alma. I hope you are happy with your presentation,' Phoebe said. 'Your wedding dress is beautiful.'

Alma moved closer and touched the dress with affection. 'My dream dress. Ivory white brocaded satin with Brussels lace.' She sighed. 'My cousin Sarah was to be my bridesmaid. Her dress was cream woollen crepon, with sleeves and sashes of blue silk... it was Sarah's colour.'

'It does sound lovely,' Phoebe smiled, stepping back to admire the placement of the last bouquet.

'Except that Oliver did not arrive. For an hour, I waited in terror, fearing he was injured and had been in an accident. And then, a note arrived from him saying he could not go through with it.' She looked away, ashamed. 'Phoebe, how could a man who professes to love me do that? Why not send the note before we have all gathered for the ceremony and spare me the humiliation?'

'He was not worthy of your hand, Alma. Such a distressing time for you,' Phoebe whispered.

'Are you finished, Miss Astin?' a loud voice enquired near the door, startling Phoebe and making Alma vanish instantly. 'Oh, sorry, I thought in your profession you would not frighten easily.'

Phoebe smiled at Mrs Neale and explained, 'I work in such quiet surrounds that the living often startle me.'

Mrs Neale walked around Alma's resting body, a smile quirking at her lips at Phoebe's words before assuming her usual stiff countenance. 'Beautiful, thank you, Miss Astin. You have sent my niece off with some dignity restored.'

'It has been an honour, Mrs Neale. I shall depart now and leave you in the capable hands of my brothers,' Phoebe said, packing up her goods.

'I would prefer you didn't.'

'Oh,' Phoebe said, surprised. 'May I be of further service to you, Mrs Neale?'

'Yes. I have been discussing with your eldest brother that it might be best to have a lady present. He will explain my request to you,' she said, as if saying something twice would be a terrible waste of her time. With that, Mrs Neale thanked Phoebe and departed as quickly as she had arrived.

Phoebe sighed and glanced out the window. She did not relish the thought of watching the long line of ladies parade past Alma. But she would do so for the good of the business. She saw Julius approaching the house on foot, and the detectives were with him! Harland and Detective Payne. What perfect timing.

Leaning forward to see the stables at the side of the house, she saw Ambrose had returned to his post and remained with the hearse, while the police constables manned the gate. The horses had been unhitched for now and housed and watered; it would be several hours until the funeral, but Julius thought it best to get the hearse on the premises early. They had never had a funeral that required so much juggling of time and resources – they were, after all, *The Economic Undertaker*.

With Harland on his way, Phoebe took a moment to tidy herself. Although black fabric covered the looking glass, Phoebe used the window reflection to assure herself that she looked presentable. Sounds of footsteps told her the men were approaching, and moments later, the small party arrived in the viewing room with Mrs Neale.

'Miss Astin,' Harland said, addressing her formally in front of the client, but his eyes relayed his delight at seeing her.

Given the solemnness of the occasion, Phoebe tempered her enthusiasm at the sight of the man who had stolen her heart. 'Detectives, good morning to you both.' She hurriedly continued with gathering her items, given impatience seemed to be Mrs Neale's natural state.

The mature woman introduced her niece. 'This is Alma. I am pleased you are taking this crime more seriously, detectives, although it has been months since someone took advantage of her and we reported it.'

'I am sorry for that, Mrs Neale,' Gilbert said. 'We have just received a case file and believe there might be a link to Miss Thornton. We will give it our full attention.'

'We do not wish to intrude today, Mrs Neale, but might we impose on you tomorrow to discuss your niece's situation?' Harland asked.

'I already spoke with the police at the time the fraud took place. Do you not have those notes?' she asked, most annoyed.

'We prefer to speak with the family and witnesses first hand. We will consult the notes, of course,' Gilbert responded on behalf of them both. He did not mention they were in the street to speak with the Edmonstone family and had not yet been given Miss Alma Thornton's case, but no doubt would if the cases were linked.

Harland appeased her. 'I assure you we have experience in matters of this nature and will not waste your time.'

'It is most inconvenient; I am heading home to Newcastle tomorrow. But if you can be here at nine o'clock and no later, I will see you.'

Harland nodded his thanks and confirmed the time.

"Good. Well, I shall be downstairs if you wish to speak with me. I need to remain on hand to greet the family who will be admitted first. Men only for the family viewing,' she said in a warning voice as if reinforcing after that, no man may enter. 'The viewing will start in thirty minutes.'

'Before you depart, Mrs Neale. Could I confirm your niece's fiancé's name, please?' Harland asked, and Phoebe was in awe at how unconcerned he was about the woman's curtness when she felt each remark so keenly.

'Mr Oliver Newton. I rue the day she met him,' Mrs Neale said and turned and left the room. Harland and Gilbert exchanged glances; here, no doubt, rests their fourth and current victim. Gilbert scribbled down the name.

'I am ready to depart, Julius, but I believe I am now to stay?' Phoebe asked her brother.

'Yes, I will explain in a moment, if you will remain?'

'Of course,' she said. 'But first, may I ask Harland, are you looking into Miss Alma Thornton's abandonment and the theft?'

'We haven't received a briefing about Miss Thornton, but we believe it might be linked to several other cases recently assigned to us,' he said.

'May I have a word then?' Phoebe asked.

Twisting his hat in his hands and studying the beauty of Miss Astin with the light behind her haloing her hair and figure in a cream dress that would serve as a wedding dress, Harland cleared his throat. 'Of course. It seems that someone defrauded several young ladies and left them at the altar. Miss Thornton included.'

Julius gave a shake of his head. 'Was not one disgrace enough?'

'Apparently not, Mr Astin,' Gilbert said. 'We have four now,' he said with a nod to the body lying before them, and all eyes turned to the deceased.

'You did a beautiful job preparing Miss Thornton, Phoebe,' Julius said, delighted with her work.

'Thank you, brother. I have never prepared a lady for the next life in her wedding dress.' Phoebe addressed Harland and Gilbert. 'May I tell you what I have learnt if you have time, detectives? It will only take a minute.'

'Please do,' Harland said. We would welcome any insight.'

'Especially as it is likely, we have little to go on,' Gilbert added. 'Mrs Neale seemed most displeased.'

'I suspect Mrs Neale has a propensity to be annoyed,' Julius said under his breath, making them all smile at his out of character informality on a job.

Harland agreed and glanced behind to make sure they were alone and asked, 'Did Miss Thornton appear to you, Phoebe?'

'Yes. She said she was at the altar when she received a note from her fiancé saying he could not go through with the marriage. Several days earlier, to save time and at his suggestion before they honeymooned, she gave him access to her money.'

Harland gave a small groan. 'Later, Alma was told he had died at sea. But now that she is on the other side, he is not there, and very much alive. Mr Newton is here in the country. That is all I have.'

'Thank you, Phoebe,' Harland said. 'We know we are on the right path, at least.'

'Let us step out of the room so the detectives can view Alma, and I shall speak with you about today's change of plan,' Julius said.

Phoebe agreed and, with a glance at the horde of ladies queuing to see the jilted bride, she quickly placed her hand on Alma's shoulder and wished her a peaceful journey to the next life.

Harland watched her depart, and she looked back momentarily at him. It would get him through the day.

Chapter 8

NEXT DOOR TO THE ever-busy *The Economic Undertaker* business, the newly launched *Beyond the Veil* was enjoying outstanding success since its recent opening, despite the unwelcomed appearance of a tradesman now and then. Two doors led to the same room; the black door opened into the mourning wear store where Mrs Nellie Shaw sat on the left, and the white door opened into the bridal wear store where Miss Mary Pollard sat on the right, both in the same large room. Sitting toward the back in the middle of the room behind a dramatic low and wide colourful flower arrangement was the store manageress, Mrs Violet Astin, who could see all that was going on. In each corner was a fitting room, and a door led to the ladies' lunch room and bathroom facilities.

The window display drew many an onlooker. On the left was a beautiful black lace mourning dress and veil, and a unique black mourning cape designed by Miss Mary Pollard. On the right were Violet's wedding gown and veil on display, also the work of the junior designer. It gave Violet great pleasure to glance upon it throughout the day and think of her lovely wedding day and handsome husband, Julius.

Mary glanced up from pinning a hem on a bridal petticoat, and then, smiling, returned to her work. Nearby, Violet and her senior dressmaker, Mrs Nellie Shaw, exchanged smiles.

'Is the view adequate from your new position, Mary?' Violet asked.

'Yes, Miss, I mean Mrs... Violet,' she stumbled over the names as she had been wont to do since Violet married. 'Not only can I see the comings-and-goings at *The Economic Undertaker*, but also the traffic on foot and vehicles heading into the city centre. There is much going on.'

'Excellent,' Nellie said, 'as we are relying on you to keep us abreast of all activity and warn us should management be coming our way.'

'I will definitely do so, Mrs Shaw,' Mary said, taking the role most seriously. 'How lovely it is to work with white fabric.'

'Yes, but your black capes have been in great demand. Do let us know if you would like to work with black again,' Violet teased.

'I will do anything you wish, Violet, Mrs Shaw,' Mary said, alarmed.

'Of course, I know, dear Mary,' Violet appeased her. 'But you are our most talented bridal dressmaker, and if we are to supply both mourning and bridal, then we best put your skills to good use.'

Mary blushed at the compliment. 'Oh! Mr Astin is approaching. Mr Astin senior.'

Within moments, Randolph Astin, resplendent in his grey suit and cutting a fine mature figure, knocked gently on the black door of the store and entered.

'May I enter?' he asked and, seeing no one currently in the store, did so. 'Hello to you, Miss Pollard, Mrs Shaw and Mrs Astin.' He said the latter to his granddaughter-in-law with a warm smile.

'Good morning, Grandpa,' Violet said, enjoying having gained new relatives by marriage, given she and Tom had been left bereft of family.

'Mr Astin, good morning,' Nellie said, and Mary acknowledged the senior Astin in a whisper, hurrying back to her work as Nellie asked, 'Might you have work for us?'

'Indeed, if time permits, ladies,' he said, waving a piece of paper in their direction. 'You have been busy today. I had to wait until your last customer left to duck in between clients.'

The ladies chuckled. 'Fortunately, we have not moved far enough away to be a deterrent to the customer,' Mrs Shaw agreed. 'It is bridal or mourning wear that we can assist with?'

'Mourning clothes are desired by an elderly widow who cannot travel,' Randolph said. 'Is there a chance you could call on her? She is only in the next suburb, and any time of your choosing is convenient.'

'Of course,' Violet said. 'We shall do so now.'

'Allow me, Violet,' Nellie suggested. 'I will take one of our pre-made dresses, and if she is a standard size, I may be able to quickly tack it while there, so she is at least attired for now. I will take her measurements, and we can cut a few more dresses in the coming days.'

'Thank you, Nellie,' Violet said. 'That would be wonderful.'

'Next time, I will send the enquirer in to speak with you directly. They were in a hurry today and asked me to action it,' Randolph said. 'It is a little tricky to ask what size a lady is,' he said with a smile.

'Oh, you could not, Mr Astin,' Nellie agreed with a laugh. 'We all think we are of a fashionable build.'

Violet and Mary laughed at the thought, and Violet added, 'It is fraught with danger, Grandpa.'

'Good, I feel absolved of responsibility, thank you, Mrs Shaw, dear Violet.' Randolph gave the slip of paper bearing the address to Mrs Shaw. 'Charlie will take you in the trap; I shall let him know you are ready to leave shortly, and he will wait for your return, Mrs Shaw.'

'Too kind, Mr Astin, but that is unnecessary if he is busy. I can walk a block and back,' she said, rising.

'I will not hear of it,' Randolph said, 'and I suspect Charlie is keen to have a break from the stables. He has been assisting Phoebe with some clients; however, Julius believed the fewer men present at Miss Thornton's viewing and funeral, the better.'

'The poor jilted bride,' Mary spoke up. 'I saw the story in the newspaper. I would die.' Realising she had promised not to use that expression as Nellie said there was enough death in their business, she inhaled sharply. 'Sorry, Mrs Shaw.'

'I think on this occasion we can make an exception as the sentiment is most appropriate,' Nellie said, ready to depart with a dress and her sewing kit on hand.

'Here is Mr Astin, Mr Julius Astin,' Mary proclaimed, and Randolph turned sharply, a frown on his face.

'I thought he was to spend the day at Miss Thornton's funeral,' Violet said, concerned.

'As did I,' Randolph said, as Julius glanced through the shop window and entered through the white door.

'Grandpa! Miss Pollard, Mrs Shaw, Violet,' he said, finishing last with his wife and lingering a little longer than professional.

'Are you all right, Julius? What has happened?' Violet asked, rising from her seat.

'Do not tell me they have cancelled our services or the funeral?' Randolph said with a glance to the ornate grandfather clock in the corner showing the time to be just on midday and the funeral he had booked due to start in a few hours.

'Do not worry; all is well,' Julius assured them. 'The client, Mrs Neale, thought it best that a man was not on duty at the door where the ladies were to parade past her niece, and I, for one, was happy to depart, and Phoebe agreed to stand in.'

'A wise decision,' Randolph agreed.

'Ambrose will remain downstairs with the hearse; Mrs Neale is to stand beside her niece. The constable will help load Miss Thornton into the hearse so I am not idle for hours, and I shall send Will to meet Ambrose at the cemetery at two o'clock.'

'So you are free this afternoon, lad?' Randolph asked, using his regular term of endearment, despite Julius being the manager of all before him.

'Yes, Lucian is coming over to measure up the new viewing rooms in the store next door, now that the ladies have moved in here, and mark up where to put the adjoining doors. I will be on hand to assist.'

'Excellent, and I have some paperwork for you.'

Julius's face dropped. 'Oh, good.' The ladies hid their smiles.

'I hope Ambrose will be all right,' Violet said, teasing her husband. 'I am surprised he did not fight you to return.'

'Quite the opposite. He has already had many ladies drop their handkerchiefs for his retrieval and no less than five needing assistance up the two stairs into the house,' Julius said with a roll of his eyes. 'Apparently, all do not heed Mrs Neale's warnings of the treachery of men.'

'Well, I for one know many noble men, and it is unfortunate that your client wishes to cast aspersions on the gentlemen of our city to all attending the viewing,' Mrs Shaw said.

'I agree, Mrs Shaw,' Mary piped up. 'My dad is the best man in the world and would do anything for Mum and me.'

'And I concur,' Violet said loyally. 'The gentlemen in my sphere are honourable and protective, if not sometimes vexing,' she said and laughed at Julius's shocked expression. 'Besides, I have known some deceptive women. I don't think bad behaviour is unique to one sex.'

'Thank you, ladies,' Randolph said with a small bow. 'On that note, I shall let Charlie know you are ready, Mrs Shaw, and take my leave.'

'As will I,' Julius said and placed a brief kiss on his wife's hand as Mary whispered, 'How romantic.'

Chapter 9

Arriving at the viewing of Miss Alma Thornton, reporter Lilly Lewis did not enter the large mansion with the line of women snaking out to the street. She had no desire to be admitted; her story was written and had drawn the displeasure of the victim's aunt, Mrs Neale. Today, she was looking for the detectives.

Fortunately, Lilly's wait was brief, and she saw the two gentlemen making their way down the path, drawing the attention of many of the ladies and a chain of whispers. *'Ooh, aren't they the two detectives that were mentioned in the newspaper... the tall one is so handsome... I wonder if they are single... I read they are a formidable team.'*

As they made their way through the gates, Lilly arrived beside them, and received a welcoming smile from Gilbert and a look of relief from Detective Stone when he realised the young lady in the lemon dress accosting them was, in fact, Miss Lewis.

'Do not tell me you are pleased to see me, Detective Stone,' Lilly teased.

'Miss Lewis, on this occasion, I am pleased it is you and not a young lady seeking to make our acquaintance. Are you here to report on the oddity of the day?' he asked.

'No, Detective Stone. I have already covered this story at the request of my editor. It is too close to my former role—births, marriages and deaths—for my liking. I am here intent on tracking you down.'

'Miss Lewis, you have an amazing nose for a story,' Gilbert said as they made their way down the street, away from the crowds.

'Thank you, Detective Payne. I went to the station and heard you were on your way here. Is there something more sinister afoot, or have you been assigned the fraud case?'

When Harland hesitated, she added, 'I assure you of my discretion and will abide by our usual arrangement, if that is satisfactory?'

'It has served us well,' Harland agreed and updated the ambitious young reporter on the possibility that Alma Thornton was the victim of a devilish ruse. 'And now, we are on our way to see the Edmonstone family,' he finished, indicating a large house at the end of the street.

'I know that name,' Lilly said.

Gilbert added, 'The Edmonstone family's daughter was also abandoned and removed of her fortune. One of several young ladies affected.'

Lilly gasped. 'Several?'

'Possibly four, one a year for the past four years,' Harland answered.

'And you believe they are all linked? But why? I've no doubt women are robbed and abandoned all the time.'

'That was our initial thinking too, Miss Lewis,' Gilbert said, 'but these ladies seem to be selected.'

'How so?' Lilly asked as they neared the Edmonstone household.

Harland responded. 'Gilbert made me aware that every year there is an article printed in your newspaper listing the richest and most successful families of our city. We are yet to source the lists, but the victims' names are familiar to Gilbert, and we believe they are from those lists – daughters making their debuts or unwed young women of wealth.'

'Yes,' Lilly nodded. 'I know of the list. It is done in America, and our business writer thought it would be of interest here. I shall source them for you going back five years.'

'That would be most helpful and time saving, thank you, Miss Lewis,' Gilbert said.

'May I enter with you?' she asked as Harland opened the gate and stood to allow her entry.

'You may, but it is up to the Edmonstone family if you may remain.' They took the steps to the front door. Harland rang the bell, and they waited for entry.

'Of course,' Lilly nodded her agreement but soon found herself dislodged and waiting outside impatiently for the detectives to appear. They joined her quickly enough.

'Did you get an audience then?' she asked, keen for the story.

'As expected, Mr Edmonstone is at his place of business, and Mrs Edmonstone would say very little in his absence. The jilted daughter has since been married off, so to speak, and has moved away,' Harland said. 'We will go to Mr Edmonstone's shipping office at the South Brisbane Dry Dock now. And yes,' he said as Lilly opened her mouth. 'You may join us.'

Lilly grinned. 'Thank you, Detectives.' Once in a hansom cab, she continued with her questions. 'Did Mrs Edmonstone say anything of value?'

Gilbert nodded and flipped open his notes. 'We asked for a description and confirmation of the fiancé's name. He was Edwin Ownnet, tall, dark of hair, blue of eyes, a fair complexion, charming and self-made.'

'Self-made indeed,' Lilly proclaimed. 'The treachery of men... some men,' she quickly added.

'And some women, Miss Lewis. Remember Daisy Dorchester's betrayal?' Harland reminded her.

'That dastardly debutante! Who could forget? Let us hope we put this Mr Ownnet away for good. He can enjoy the luxury of a jail cell. That is, you will put him away, I have no doubt. May I have the names of the four ladies?'

Harland agreed, and Lilly hurried to make her notes while Gilbert shared the names and wrote up his notes from meeting Mrs Edmonstone.

Ambrose looked over at his sister and smiled before returning his attention to driving the hearse to St. Patrick's church and burial grounds.

'I believe this is a first,' he said. 'You and me on our way to a funeral together.'

'It is! We could celebrate, except it would be wildly inappropriate and Julius would be bound to hear of it,' Phoebe said in jest. 'Does he talk often on the job?'

'No, and definitely not if there's a chance someone might see us conversing. He is the epitome of decorum. There have been a few exceptions, like the time a family wanted to get gran into the ground as quickly as possible and head to the pub. It was hard for both of us to hide our mirth.'

Phoebe gave a small smile, wary of the fact that she was in the carriage leading a funeral procession. 'I can imagine. There's Will and Claude ahead, waiting for us.'

Ambrose acknowledged them with a wave, and Will alighted from the trap to enter the cemetery grounds and assist Ambrose with lowering Miss Thornton into her grave. Claude remained in the trap to bring Phoebe back to the office.

'Are you sure you don't wish to stay on?' Ambrose asked as they entered the gates of the small cemetery next to the church.

'Quite sure. I have had my dose of people; that will do me for a month or more.'

Ambrose huffed at such a thought. He liked the energy of having people around him. 'Make sure Claude does not go too fast on the return trip.'

'Now you sound like Julius. Most protective of you, brother,' Phoebe said.

'I do sound like him; you are right. Good Lord, I hope it is not catching.'

Phoebe nudged him and hid her smile as they proceeded to the site of the freshly dug grave. Ambrose glanced behind.

'Good, everyone has kept up,' he said, seeing several carriages with mourners behind at a respectful distance.

Phoebe asked, 'Can you see that woman standing up ahead to the side by herself? She is wearing a lovely pink dress, most unusual for a funeral. Perhaps she is here visiting someone and not here for Miss Thorton's funeral.'

Ambrose glanced at his sister. 'Phoebe, there is currently no one in front of the hearse to the left or the right.'

'Oh, thank you, Brother.'

'You see something I don't,' he whispered. 'Is she still there?'

'We are passing her now, and she is on your left. I shall acknowledge her subtly,' Phoebe said, and gave the woman a small nod of her head and a kind smile. The woman returned the smile and turned to watch Phoebe as the hearse passed.

'Is she walking beside us?' Ambrose asked quietly.

'No.'

'Thank goodness for that,' he said and gave a small shudder. 'What does she want?'

'We are in a cemetery. No doubt she is an unhappy spirit. There's Father Morris up ahead.'

Ambrose moved the hearse and horses towards the small gathering of people that included the priest and grave diggers and slowed. The carriages following them slowed and pulled up, the mourning party alighting. Ambrose assisted Phoebe down from the hearse and sent her on her way.

'Hello Will, come then, let us bury Miss Thornton.'

Phoebe approached the lady in pink and glanced around to ensure no one was nearby. Satisfied, she spoke freely.

'Good afternoon, I am Miss Phoebe Astin.'

'Hello, Miss Astin, I know who you are. Forgive me for being so forward and approaching you. I am Miss Winnifred Nash. I came to pay my respects to Miss Thornton, who has now joined me on the other side.'

'How kind of you, Miss Nash. The gentleman up ahead is waiting to take me back to the office. He does not know I speak with spirits. I am sorry to cut you short, but did you have a message for me?'

'Oh, of course. Miss Astin, I will be quick,' Winnifred Nash said, falling into step with Phoebe. 'I too, was a victim like Alma. My fiancé left me at the altar and stole from me and my family.'

'Oh, Miss Nash, I am so sorry.'

'I lost my will to live.'

'Your heart was broken,' Phoebe said sympathetically.

'Thank you, Miss Astin, for your kind sympathy. I am sure he was the same man who broke Alma's heart. Please stop him, Miss Astin. Please stop him.' And then she was gone.

The cad was the same man, Phoebe mused as she neared the trap and Claude, who had been employed by *The Economic Undertaker* for several years, alighted to assist her. He was quiet and conservative, much like Julius, and the pair often partnered if needed, leaving the more gregarious Ambrose with Will.

'Hello Claude, thank you for waiting for me.' She accepted the tall young man's hand as he helped her into the trap.

'My pleasure, Miss Astin. Let us depart then. I imagine this morning's display exhausted you; it would weary me.'

'It was demanding. So many women were pressing in to see the poor deceased Miss Thornton. People are odd,' she said, settling and straightening her skirt in the space between them.

'They are that, Miss Astin. I can attest to that, first hand,' he said, leaping into the trap; the pair exchanged a smile.

Phoebe looked back and saw Miss Nash had reappeared near Alma Thorton's grave. She stood out in her pink dress amidst the sea of black mourners. The young woman gave Phoebe a small wave before fading from sight.

Chapter 10

THE SOUTH BRISBANE DRY Docks was bustling with large ships in port and many small tugs coming and going. Lilly could see how Fergus had no shortage of stories during his time on the shipping news column, even if he seemed too polished to coerce stories from the likes of most of the men present.

Gilbert asked directions from a harried worker, who pointed to the Edmonstone office at the far end of the dock, and Harland moved to the waterside to protect Miss Lilly Lewis from the edge. Gilbert flanked her.

'You are both very gentlemanly,' she said, smiling at the detectives, 'but I assure you, with five brothers, I am quite robust.'

'Nonetheless, Miss Lewis, we must play our part as gentlemen or we will be a disgrace to our sex,' Harland said with a smile.

'In that case, I accept your chivalry,' she agreed as several deck hands whistled at the passing beauty.

They turned to make their way to several small buildings flanked by the dramatic Kangaroo Point cliffs across the river on the far bank.

'Want to go on a date, Miss? I'll show you a good time,' one man yelled, making the workers nearby laugh.

'I have my hands quite full at the moment with these two gentlemen, thank you, Sir,' she responded, making the men laugh and Harland smile at her brazenness.

'A little respect,' Gilbert muttered. 'Imagine if you were here alone, Miss Lewis. Appalling.'

'Thank you, Detective Payne, but I expect nothing less in such surrounds,' Lilly assured him.

As they neared the end of the dock, several more workers whistled and made random remarks to Lilly. A man on a small ferry called, 'There's a seat here for you, love,' he said, patting his lap to Gilbert's astonishment.

'Thank you, Sir, but I am sure that's not a seat I would pay for,' she retorted and won a cheer from his mates on the dock. 'Thank goodness,' Lilly said as they arrived at the office.

'Tell me, Miss Lewis, is it like that for you ladies every time you are out and about?' Harland asked, seething at the thought of what Phoebe might endure.

'Of course not, Detective. We are in a rough end of town, and the men know I am with you. They might not be so disrespectful if I were on my own, a few whistles maybe. I rarely come across disrespect, I assure you.'

She heard him exhale with relief, and the three entered, without an appointment, to see Mr Patrick Edmonstone. Fortunately, being in the company of two detectives assured her of entry, but Lilly was to make her own case to remain. Minutes later, they were shown through to a large office where a gruff, middle-aged man, well whiskered and well dressed, stood to receive them. He seated the party near the window, where a low table rested in front of four large single chairs.

'Detectives, Miss Lewis,' he said after introductions. 'I am not interested in my daughter's story being splashed all over the newspaper like the jilted bride story, Miss Lewis. We must consider our family reputation, and I assure you, Miss Thornton's situation would never have happened had her father, Harold, still been alive. He was a good man.'

'But that's the thing, Sir,' Lilly said. 'No one spoke on Miss Thornton's behalf except the neighbours. *The Courier* will follow the police investigation and report on it, so it is best the truth comes from you, would you not agree?'

When he opened his mouth to speak, Lilly jumped in as a thought occurred to her. 'Of course, my fellow reporter will cover the story, and you can speak with him if you prefer – Mr Fergus Griffiths. I believe you know him from his time on the shipping news.'

'Fergus?' Mr Edmonstone said, surprised. 'He is a sincere young man.' He regarded her in stony silence for a moment and just when she thought she was to be evicted, Harland spoke up.

'Like yourself, Mr Edmonstone, we are pressed for time. I can assure you of Miss Lewis's integrity. May we ask you some questions about the fraudster who mistreated your daughter?'

Lilly could have hugged him, but of course she wouldn't. After the Kate and Ambrose muddle-up, she did not need to be accused of attracting the attention of any gentlemen except her own beau, Mr Bennet Martin.

Taking his eyes from Lilly, Patrick Edmonstone informed them, 'I've hired a private investigator. I'm briefing him later today.'

'Why now, Sir?' Gilbert asked curiously.

'Today is the anniversary of my daughter Grace's failed wedding day. One year to the day. I said I would give the police a year, and then take matters into my own hands. So I have hired a man by the name of Bennet Martin.'

Lilly's breath hitched. *Excellent!* Leads would come her way, courtesy of Bennet.

'That is your prerogative, of course, Mr Edmonstone,' Harland said. 'However, we've just received this case, and my partner and I believe there are links to similar frauds spanning four to five years. We will investigate it despite the appointment, but we have worked well with Mr Martin in the recent past and his insights would be welcome.'

'All right then. What do you want to know?'

Gilbert got out his pad, ready to take notes, as did Lilly.

'How did the young couple meet?' Harland asked.

'A dance for the debutantes that year. It was a charity event run by the church, and tickets were expensive, ensuring the right suitors were present.'

'Except for this one,' Gilbert suggested, and Patrick Edmonstone nodded. Gilbert continued, 'Sir, how would you describe him physically and his nature?'

'He was a tall man, late twenties, dark hair, blue eyed with a strong British accent. He was not long in our country. As for his nature, I am no longer objective, but I found him to be enjoyable company, a fine sailor and a pleasant prospect for a son-in-law. He came from old money, or so he said.' Mr Edmonstone shook his head. 'I could not believe my good fortune that my daughter could meet a man with a strong interest in the sea and merchandise.'

'Did Miss Edmonstone readily return his affections?' Lilly asked.

'She was in love with him and would have no other, despite her mother's protests that she was too young to be serious and settle for the first man she met at her first dance. If only I had been as astute in this matter as I have been in business.'

'I am sure your daughter's happiness was your priority,' Harland offered. 'Did you have an address for him here or his family in England?'

'Yes, but as you can imagine, they have proven to be false.'

'We shall take them anyway, Sir, if you will?' Harland said, and Mr Edmonstone agreed, rising to retrieve a small black address book and a tan leather folder from his desk, both of which he brought back to the group.

'The addresses,' he said and read them out as Gilbert noted them. 'I also have one of the original documents Edwin Ownnet furnished me with... his birth certificate.' He opened the tan folder and extracted a piece of paper. 'The forged wills remain with the bank. He was born in the West Midlands of England.'

He passed it over, and Harland glanced at it. 'Very authentic.' Mr Edmonstone agreed with a sigh, as Harland handed it to Gilbert.

'Goodness,' Gilbert said, and all eyes turned to him.

'What is it, Detective?' Mr Edmonstone asked, and Gilbert looked at his superior, who nodded his assent to share.

'A common spelling error, Sir,' Gilbert said, pointing to the county written in large letters on the top right-hand corner of the birth certificate. 'Mr Ownnet was born in Warwickshire County, but he has spelt it without the "h" in shire. It happens often.'

Mr Edmonstone reached for the certificate to see it for himself. 'Who would know that if you were not familiar with Great Britain counties? How do you know this young man?'

'My Great Grandfather Cyril Payne was born there, Sir. We have his birth certificate in our family tree book.'

Lilly and the senior detective restrained from smiling, and fortunately Gilbert continued.

'Mr Edmonstone, it may seem an odd question, but I assure you it is important,' Gilbert started, and Lilly noted Detective Stone looked at the younger detective, a little fearful of what he might say next. Gilbert continued, 'Can you recall any habits or hobbies that Mr Ownnet had? It may help us move in his circle.'

Harland gave the young detective an encouraging nod; it was a good question.

'He claimed to have loved horse riding and sailing. I also recall that he loved the theatre. Edwin was keener than Grace to attend a show, and she was always happy for an outing.'

Gilbert and Lilly noted the information.

Mr Edmonstone continued, 'I will persist with the private investigator, but welcome your attention to the matter, detectives. Young lady, I ask for your fairness and discretion.'

'And you shall have it, Mr Edmonstone, and justice too, I am sure,' Lilly assured him, and on departing, she cemented her part in the story. 'Detectives, I shall get the rich lists for the past five years and I shall bring it along with Bennet to your office in the morning, if that is suitable?'

'Miss Lewis, you are nothing if not determined,' Harland said with a smile as they made their way back along the docks. 'Shall we say nine-thirty, then?'

As the funeral had concluded, Miss Alma Thornton was bedded in the earth, and Father Morris had departed, Ambrose and Will from *The Economic Undertaker*, readied the horses and waited to pay the Redford men – grave digging father and son, and see the job finished.

Ambrose's eyes widened with surprise, and he smiled. 'It is a good day, after all!'

Will looked up from patting one of the horses. 'How so? What has happened?'

'I believe that is Miss Billie Prout, and I shall go and say hello. Do keep the horses in the shade, Will. I'll be brief.'

Will smiled. 'Take as long as you like, Ambrose.'

Ambrose handed Will the payment for the men, thanked them for their service, and headed to the far side of the small cemetery, adjusting his coat and hat on the way and wishing he was a little fresher after hours spent at the home of the Thorntons this morning followed by the dusty parade to the cemetery.

She was beautiful; of that, there was no doubt. He observed Billie Prout as she watched the two men finishing the placement of a Prout headstone. It was refreshing to see such a pretty dress in a cemetery when black was the dominant colour.

Miss Prout's white and lilac striped dress with little bouquets of flowers sewn around the hemline, fitted so perfectly, revealed a womanly figure. She had pinned her blonde hair back and perched a matching white boater with a lilac ribbon atop her head.

'Beautiful,' Ambrose said, and he saw her look up and smile. He tipped his hat as he arrived. He wanted to appear confident, in control, a man who was comfortable in the world. It was not how he felt; his heart hammered in his chest from being in her presence. Ambrose had not experienced this with Lilly or Kate.

'Well, if it isn't, Mr Astin. We are both in the office today,' she said with a wave of her hand indicating the cemetery.

Ambrose laughed. 'Indeed. Good afternoon to you, Miss Prout, gentlemen,' he said, addressing the group present. A glance told him the headstone was for an elderly man and of a most conservative design.

'Not one of your modern designs, then, Miss Prout?'

'Sadly no, but we just placed that one, and it is one of my favourites.' Billie indicated a modern headstone to her right with a unique shape and design.

'May I?' Ambrose asked, his motive to have her alone for a few minutes, which he successfully achieved.

'Of course,' she said, accompanying him. 'Were you pelted with fruit at Miss Thornton's viewing today?'

Ambrose grinned. 'No, surprisingly. I rescued four handkerchiefs, helped three ladies to their seats when my handsomeness overwhelmed them and declined several brazen invitations.'

It was Billie's turn to laugh. 'Oh, well done, Mr Astin. I am so glad you emerged unscathed. I must say, I am surprised we have not run into each other more, given our industry.'

'It would be a welcome diversion,' Ambrose said. 'Perhaps I may walk you home from work one evening and we can converse in a setting that is not a cemetery?'

'We are finished here, Miss Prout,' one of her staff called, standing and wiping his hands. 'Could you please check that you are satisfied with the placing?'

'Oh, do pardon me, Mr Astin, work beckons,' she said and hurried off, to Ambrose's frustration, but turned back at the last moment, saying, 'Yes, I would enjoy that. Thank you, Mr Astin.'

Ambrose smiled and tipped his hat. What a good day indeed.

Chapter 11

Julius and his young brother-in-law, Tom, spoke in low tones as they sat in the chairs on the front verandah of Julius's Queenslander-style home. Inside, Violet was finishing dinner preparations and had swept them both from the kitchen.

It was dark early and chilly, but the men enjoyed the bracing winter temperature and the moment of quiet in the day. Julius waved to a neighbour arriving home from their day of toil.

Tom, apprenticed with Lucian in Julius's shared carpentry business, said, 'We finished the door and pulley system for your office today.'

'Excellent. I was on hand when Lucian came by earlier to start the fittings.'

'Ah, you had the jilted bride's funeral today. Was it bad? Violet said ladies were queuing to view her.'

'It was odd indeed, but only the immediate family came to the cemetery. I escaped early,' he said, and Tom chuckled. Julius turned to his brother-in-law.

'Tom, I assure you, I love your sister,' he started, clearing his throat, 'but I believe we should hire a cook to prepare the evening meal for us on our return from work.'

'Oh, thank God,' Tom exclaimed. 'I am starving, Julius. I try to eat big at lunch, but it makes me sleepy in the afternoon. I even smuggled some bread and butter to eat later in my room.'

Julius chuckled. 'That is drastic. I am sorry, Tom, I should have acted sooner. I admit I have eaten more of Mrs Dobbs' treats or had lunch out more often, so I could say in all honesty I did not need seconds at night.'

Both men chuckled, then sobered.

'When our grandma died, we had plenty of meals given to us, so Violet didn't have to cook. She's bad at it. Will you tell her or should I?' Tom said.

Julius took responsibility. 'No. I shall brave it. It is my duty. I will word it so that Violet knows I appreciate her contribution during the day and feel she should relax at night.'

'That will work,' Tom said. 'Until she gets with child, then you will have to say we can't part with the cook now out of loyalty, or come up with something else.'

Julius nodded. 'We'll cross that bridge when we come to it.'

Neither of the men saw Violet hovering near the doorway and returning to the kitchen with a smile on her face.

'Let us face it, then. Lord help us, tonight is Shepherd's Pie,' Julius sighed.

'I hate lumpy potato,' Tom grumbled, recalling Violet's last effort, and Julius held back his laugh as they entered and made their way to the kitchen.

'Dinner is served, darling husband and brother, please be seated,' Violet said, smiling brightly at the pair as she removed her apron and indicated the dining room table where she had put two very large servings of mince and potatoes before each man.

Julius grimaced, then quickly hid his expression and thanked her. After Violet said grace and they had digested several mouthfuls, he began.

'Violet, I have been thinking, with your work responsibilities, it is too much to ask of you to return home every evening and cook. I think we should hire a lady to prepare the evening meal for three, and it will also provide much needed work to a local cook.'

'Oh, that is a good idea, Julius,' Tom said, nodding his agreement. 'You must be exhausted, Sis.'

'Not at all,' she said with a wave of her hand. 'I love that I now have a family to cook for, and I've been sourcing some new recipes.'

There was a momentary silence, and Julius tried again. 'Perhaps you could do some baking on the weekend instead. That would be more enjoyable than having to cook at the end of a long business day. You deserve this. I can ask around for someone who might be available.'

'As can I at work,' Tom said. 'I think it should be someone who lives nearby and can get home quickly of an evening once the meal is prepared.'

'That would be best, Tom,' Julius agreed, conscious of the fact that Violet had not spoken. Both men turned to her.

Violet looked from her husband to her brother and back. 'I enjoy looking after you both, but I assume this is a slight to my cooking.' She sighed, and looked hurt. 'Do you not want me to cook for you anymore?'

Julius took a quick breath and decided honesty was best. 'My darling, you are a terrible cook but a wonderful wife and manageress.'

Violet placed her knife and fork down with a loud clatter, and both men flinched. From the few disagreements they had experienced in their brief courting time, Julius knew Violet was not prone to outbreaks or reactions. She would reflect upon it quietly before expressing her view, even if that took a day. He found that very unsettling and would rather have an outburst. The men waited.

After a few moments, he could not bear her silence, nor the thought that he had hurt her. 'I am sorry, I spoke too harshly.'

'No, I am one for honesty and directness every time. So, as the lady of the house, am I not even able to organise the cook of my choosing?'

'Of course, if you wish to do so,' Julius hurriedly agreed in order to appease her.

'Excellent. I agree with you then.'

Julius thought he had misheard. He looked at Tom, and back at his wife. Violet laughed. 'I overheard you both plotting.'

'I think we have been played,' Tom said.

Violet looked very pleased with herself. 'Do not worry the pair of you. I agree a cook would be wonderful, and if you are not upset at the expense that you must incur as your wife is inadequate in the kitchen, dear husband, I am all for it.'

Julius exhaled with relief and reached for her hand, kissing it. 'I am so relieved that I will forgive you for taking advantage of my poor attempts to trick you on this occasion.'

'It was too much fun. I could not resist. Your grandmother, our grandmother, has already suggested I engage a cook, and she has some church ladies interested in the role for a small salary.'

'Thank goodness,' Tom said, stabbing the potato with his fork. 'Can they start tomorrow?'

Julius grinned, and Violet gave them both a smirk. 'You need not be so enthusiastic.'

'Oh, I think we must,' Julius said, teasing her now. 'I am sure I am the only husband who has lost weight since marrying.'

Violet huffed. 'Nonsense. You have been filling up during the day; I have my sources. Eat up then, since this will be the last meal of mine you shall enjoy.'

Julius and Tom exchanged looks of relief, and the shepherd's pie tasted better for the outcome.

A visit from Mr Bennet Martin to the Lewis household always caused much excitement. Not so much with Lilly's brothers, who bemoaned the attention and best cuts given to Mr Martin, but Mr and Mrs Lewis were both excited. It was living proof that their daughter—who harboured ambitions to work in that unsavoury newsroom—still had a suitor, and not just any suitor. The wealthy and attractive Mr Martin would make any parent give praise to the good Lord.

There had been a softening in Lilly's father's view of her occupation, perhaps because he had determined that Bennet Martin's admiration of his daughter's line of work appeared to be genuine, so he decided it was best not to change anything until a wedding ring was on her finger.

Unlike Bennet's last visit—where he met all the family—all hands on deck were not required this evening. So Lilly's eldest brother, Cyrus, was absent, as was her second eldest brother, James, who had since moved out. Thus, six sat comfortably around the table, and at Bennet's insistence, everyone was to call him by his first name.

'I am sorry to have come with so little notice, but Lilly and I are working on a story and case together and need to confer before we meet with the detectives in the morning,' he explained.

'No notice is needed, Bennet, you are always welcome,' Mrs Lewis assured him, but Lilly knew her mother had raced to the butcher and also cleaned the already clean house again.

'My sister seems to find a way to mention you in her stories whenever you help solve a crime,' Samuel said, nudging Lilly. They were the closest in age and the fondest of each other.

'It is not because I am brilliant, Samuel, I assure you,' Bennet said, getting a laugh, 'but I am favoured by the talented writer beside you.'

Lilly smiled with pleasure. 'You are a good investigator, and people open up to you. It must be that British charm,' she teased him. 'The case we are on at the moment is most intriguing.'

'Surely that is not dinner conversation,' Mrs Lewis said, despairing of her daughter.

'It is the most interesting one I can recall for some time,' Elijah, the eldest brother present, said, as he passed the bowl of peas to Bennet.

'Let us hear about it then, Lilly, and I promise after that, Mum, we'll talk of more refined subjects,' the middle brother, Ethan, concurred.

Mrs Lewis sighed but said with a smile to Bennet. 'With five sons, there has been very little refined conversation over the years, so I guess why start now?'

'Because you are a gracious host, Mrs Lewis, and our case is a sad tale of a jilted bride who died in her wedding dress. Best we do not speak of it then.'

Mr Lewis drew a sharp breath, as if it had not occurred to him that Lilly could be proposed to, but left at the altar. 'How cruel and cowardly,' he said, ensuring Bennet was in no doubt about his feelings on that subject.

'Completely diabolical. What sort of man would do such a thing?' Bennet agreed, but before a response was called for, he turned to Lilly's mother. 'Mrs Lewis, I believe you play the piano and sing in a choir?'

'I do, Bennet, just the church choir, but I enjoy the sound of voices in harmony.'

'As does my mother. Might you and Mr Lewis use two tickets to the grand concert at the Centennial Hall at the end of the month?'

Lilly saw her mother's look of delight, and Bennet continued. 'They were gifted to me, but Lilly and I are bound to be too busy to attend, and I would hate to waste them on someone who could not appreciate the performance.'

'Oh, Bennet, I would love to attend in your stead, thank you. Tickets have been sold out for some time, and I believe His Excellency Sir Henry Norman and Lady Norman will be in attendance.'

'A good excuse for a new dress if ever there was one,' Bennet said and laughed at Mr Lewis' reaction.

'Now Bennet, steady on,' Lilly's father said with a wink. 'Don't go encouraging my wife to shop.'

'I am so excited,' Mrs Lewis said. 'Perhaps I might take my sister. Mr Lewis is not inclined to enjoy a concert.'

'A marvellous idea,' Mr Lewis said with a sigh of relief. 'Since I am off the hook, I think a new dress is definitely in order.'

Samuel regarded Bennet and grinned. 'You will be welcome for dinner any day of the week now.'

'Nonsense, Bennet is always welcome anytime,' Mrs Lewis chided her son, and as she rose to remove the plates to the kitchen, telling Lilly to stay seated, the boys leant forward.

'Tell us about the case, then,' Elijah said.

With a quick nod and a glance at the kitchen, Lilly began.

'It was the oddest viewing of a body I have ever seen...'

Chapter 12

Mr Cowan, having heard Lilly and Fergus's update of their developing story, folded his hands across his chest and pursed his lips. It was one of the rare times he did not have a cigar in his hand, and the pair enjoyed the reprieve from a smoky office.

'Possibly four frauds, you say?'

'Yes, Mr Cowan. One a year with the recent death of Miss Alma Thornton—the jilted bride who died in her wedding dress—being the fourth.'

'And they are from our richest families, these jilted girls?'

'We have the lists published each year, and the four families are among those listed, Mr Cowan,' Fergus said. 'It is the act of one man or a contingent of thieves.'

'And Mr Edmonstone, whose daughter Grace was a victim a year ago, will speak with Fergus as they have established a relationship already from Fergus's shipping news days,' Lilly said.

'That is a bonus,' Alex Cowan said. 'All right then. Make it interesting. Make the men villains, the girls pining away, the fathers set on revenge. Do the detectives have any leads?'

'We are meeting them straight after this meeting, Mr Cowan, and we will get exclusive access to anything they have,' Lilly danced around the question.

'Right, off with you, then. Keep the stories coming, one a day for the late edition.'

'Thank you, Mr Cowan, we'll keep the readers across it as it unfolds,' Lilly promised, gathering the skirt of her mint green dress and racing out the door, Fergus in quick pursuit. Returning to their desks, they grinned at each other.

'Oh, I do love the rush of a new investigative piece,' Lilly said.

'So do I. I shall leave you to head to the police station and I shall head to our library and find anything that was filed on the frauds over the past few years, plus the debut notices, and the obituaries for the ladies on your list. If we're lucky, the reporter might still be on our staff.'

'Great idea, Fergus. I shall be back within a few hours and we will confer,' Lilly agreed, and grabbing the lists of the wealthiest as promised to the detectives, she departed in her usual rush.

Phoebe was so relieved to be back in her own room at *The Economic Undertaker* this morning that she stood for a few moments, just enjoying the peaceful surrounds. The light filtered in from the top windows, warming the couch and rug and providing the room with a delightful gold hue. She adjusted the cushion on her couch, did the same with the blinds and watered Florence the fern.

'It is lovely in here,' a male voice said, and Phoebe recognised it right away.

'It is Uncle Reggie, particularly of a winter's morning. I expect Rufus will be bounding down here any minute to stake his claim to the rug in the sun.'

'That is a fetching winter gown,' he said, and Phoebe brushed her hand down the red dress.

'Thank you, Uncle. It is called woollen velvet, and while I know the fashion is to bead and embroider, I like an unadorned dress, particularly if I am to meet with clients.'

'It is most becoming. Please promise me you will never ask to be buried in your wedding dress. What a morose thought!'

'If I die on my wedding day, I may wish to get more wear out of it,' Phoebe teased. 'Otherwise, it is a promise. Is all well with you, Uncle?' She regarded him as Reggie walked, hands behind his back, posture straight in his riding outfit. He was a most handsome man who would never age past his fortieth year.

'I am the picture of health,' he joked.

The sound of bounding down the stairs made Phoebe turn with disappointment at being interrupted so early by the living when she needed a little time to ease into the morning. But her disappointment quickly changed to a smile as Rufus the hound entered. Julius must have arrived.

'Did you miss me yesterday?' she said as he bound up to her for a pat, looked suspiciously at Reggie, and then turned three times in a circle, dropped onto the rug and stretched out in the warm morning sun.

Reggie laughed. 'It appears he missed your morning routine.'

'That is exactly how I feel, Rufus. It is nice to be back in my environment.'

A small sound—the clearing of a lady's throat—made Phoebe turn again to find Miss Alma Thornton in her wedding dress and Miss Winnifred Nash in the pink dress she wore at the cemetery yesterday on first meeting Phoebe.

'Forgive us for interrupting you, Miss Astin,' Miss Nash said. 'I promise we won't delay you. Oh, you have company.'

'Oh, please do not rush away, Alma, Miss Nash. I am happy to be interrupted. Allow me to introduce my uncle, Mr Reginald Astin.'

The small party acknowledged each other.

'Now that we have met, ladies, you have another friend on our side,' Reggie said.

'A happy thought,' Alma said with a smile.

'I am happy that I am back here with select company rather than the hundreds of people that encroached upon us both yesterday. I thought you were most brave, Alma,' Phoebe said.

'An inspiration,' Winifred Nash agreed.

Alma thanked them both and continued, 'Phoebe, he is about to do it again; we are sure of it. It is the same man, and he will woo another lady and break her heart and ruin her. Is there anything you can do?'

'Yes,' Phoebe said confidently. 'I have spoken with the detectives, and I assure you the case is in expert hands. They are our finest.'

The ladies exchanged looks of hope.

'That is a relief,' Winnifred said. 'Despite using different names, my fiancé is definitely the same man Alma was engaged to, who called himself Oliver.'

'Do you know the name of the lady who is being wooed now?' Phoebe asked.

Both ladies shook their heads. 'I do not recognise her,' Alma said, and Winnifred agreed.

'I shall pass that on, and it will make the investigation easier, no doubt,' Phoebe said.

'May we visit occasionally to see if you know more?' Alma asked.

'Please do. I will get an update as often as I can, and let us hope we have justice.' And as someone else thundered down the staircase to visit, the ladies and Uncle Reggie hurriedly bid her good-day and vanished.

Phoebe turned. 'Ambrose!'

'Good morning, Sister. Good morning, Rufus.' The large hound wagged his tail but did not rise from his comfortable position. 'One would think he had had a busy night. You left early this morning.'

'I caught the omnibus with Grandpa, but I understand the attraction of sleeping in with this snappy weather. Where is Julius? Why are you not out on a job?'

'We are about to head out for a collection. I wish to ask you a question, if I may?' He looked uncomfortable, which Phoebe thought was most unusual of Ambrose.

'Of course. What is bothering you?' she asked, sitting on the rug to stroke Rufus.

Standing with his hands behind him, Ambrose posed the question, 'If a lady was open to being met and walked home, how would one go about organising that?'

'I see,' Phoebe said, hiding a smile. 'Well, I would not want the gentleman just showing up at my place of work without notice. Nor would I want to be left wondering.'

'I would have thought the mystery enhanced the wait?' Ambrose said, surprised.

'No, not for most ladies. It means we have to wear our best dresses and fuss with our attire every day just in case he arrives. I would prefer to receive a note nominating a suitable day.'

'Yes, that is a fine idea.' Ambrose nodded and smiled. 'Thank you, Phoebe. Is that the arrangement you have with Harland?'

'No. We have two standing days a week, and if he is not here by the time I depart, I know he cannot make it. Although that has not happened yet.'

'Ah, young love,' Ambrose teased.

'Would this be Miss Prout that you are thinking of walking home? We are going to ask if she would like to join the *Vexed Vixens*,' Phoebe informed him, and Ambrose groaned.

'So if it does not work out with Miss Prout, all the *Vexed Vixens* will be angry with me again!'

Phoebe chuckled. 'No. It differs from our relationship with Kate. But mind you, I do hope it works out.'

'As do I, Sister, as do I,' Ambrose said with a mischievous smile and, hearing Julius bellow for him, he rolled his eyes and yelled, 'On my way'.

'Goodness, so noisy,' Phoebe winced. 'Would you and Julius have time to drop a note to Harland at the Roma Street Police Headquarters for me, please? I have had a recent visitor with a clue that he might find useful.'

'We shall make time. Write your note then.'

Phoebe grinned and, accepting his hand up, hurried to her desk, writing a few lines and sealing the note. 'Thank you, Ambrose,' she said, handing it over.

He waved it at her and departed up the stairs to begin his day; both the younger Astins happy with how life was unfolding.

Bennet Martin shook the men's hands and refrained just in time from kissing the cheek of the reporter, Miss Lilly Lewis. He took her offered hand to shake and kissed it instead.

'What good fortune we all have the same case to work and report on,' he said and laughed at Harland's expression. 'Oh, I know, Harland, you prefer to work cases with your partner, Detective Payne, but here we are, nonetheless.'

Gilbert grinned and appeared to be happy for the partnering, and Harland gave a slight shake of his head and a small smile.

'I do not mind the opportunity to share out notes, as long as we are not reading about the case in the paper before we solve it or hear of facts being withheld by private investigators,' he said wryly.

'Never, Detective,' Lilly feigned shock and nudged Bennet, who agreed. 'And, as promised, I have the richest citizens lists from the last five years.'

Gilbert accepted them gratefully, and hurriedly scanned the list for the victims' surnames. He rose and clipped them onto the board.

'Let us begin then,' Harland suggested.

''Sir, these lists of our wealthiest citizens include the four families that someone has taken advantage of – Edmonstone, Gardner, Nash and Thornton.'

'So, did each family have a daughter making their debut that year?' Bennet asked.

Gilbert shook his head. 'No, Mr Martin.' He pointed to the board listing the four known victims and said, 'Your client, Miss Grace Edmonstone and Miss Caroline Gardner, were the only two girls of debutante age. The other two ladies were older when they were to be married.'

'Fergus is in our archives as we speak, looking for debut notices, the original fraud stories and the obituaries,' Lilly said.

'Excellent, may we see those?' Harland asked.

'Of course, Detective Stone,' Lilly agreed. 'Now, Mr Edmonstone said that Grace met her fiancé at a debut ball arranged by the church, where those in attendance had deep pockets.'

'And he had dark hair, blue eyes, and was from British shores, not long in the country,' Harland added, and all eyes turned to Bennet.

'I assure you I am not wearing a wig and moonlighting as anyone's fiancé nor gaining from it,' he said with a huff of laughter.

'We will hold you to that, Bennet,' Harland said. 'We now need to determine how the Misses Alma, Caroline, and Winnifred met their fiancés.'

Gilbert pointed at the board. 'From what Alma's aunt, Mrs Neale, told us, Alma's fiancé had fair hair, blue eyes, a slight limp from a riding accident and was a salesman. Sir, we need descriptions of Miss Winnifred and Miss Caroline's fiancés.'

A knock at the door had them all turning, and the Sergeant entered. 'Forgive the interruption, gentlemen, oh, and Ma'am. The younger Mr Astin just dropped this in and no, before you ask, he has departed en route to a private collection.'

'Thank you, John,' Harland said, taking the note and closing the door before opening it, assuming it was related to the case.

'Does Phoebe have some knowledge?' Lilly asked impatiently.

'Yes,' Harland said, placing the note on the desk. 'She has had a visit from our two deceased jilted brides, Miss Alma Thornton and Miss Winnifred Nash.'

The small party looked surprised; Alma was only buried yesterday, and Winnifred Nash was put to rest over three years ago.

'They believe the men are the same, according to Phoebe's note,' Harland said.

All eyes turned to the blackboard. 'I fear they might be wrong on this occasion,' Bennet said. 'We only have two descriptions thus far, and there are notable differences in accents and inflictions, such as the limp.'

'Perhaps we should reserve our speculating until we speak with all the families,' Gilbert suggested.

Harland agreed. 'In the interim, Miss Lewis, you are welcome to report that in light of the recent death of Miss Alma Thornton, we are investigating several similar cases. No names yet, please, other than Miss Thornton.'

'Noted, Detective. I will write of it covering a span of years, and the ladies from our city's wealthiest families seem to be preyed upon.'

He nodded. 'There is a risk of our offender or offenders leaving town, but so be it. If they are in the process of wooing someone, that might save one lady.'

'I am going to begin my investigation with Miss Grace Edmonstone's background, as her father is the client,' Bennet said. 'Her friends might recall Edwin Ownnet and how they met at the dance; any such details could help find him or them.'

'I would not discount Phoebe's clue. She has never been wrong to date,' Harland said.

'But she is at the mercy of the spirits and what they choose to tell her,' Bennet pointed out.

'We shall see,' Harland said and bid the reporter and private investigator good-day.

Departing, Bennet offered Lilly a ride back to the newspaper.

'Detective Stone was very loyal to Phoebe,' Lilly said.

'As I am to you,' he hurriedly added. 'It is a privilege to share in the good and bad times with you.'

'That's a pretty speech. We shall see when you are tested.'

Bennet's lips quirked in surprise. 'What would that test look like?'

'Who is to say? If I knew what dramas might befall me, then they might be avoided,' she said in jest. 'So, not a hint of regret that you lost the affection of my dear friend, Phoebe?' Lilly asked without a show of jealousy.

'Not at all. We are quite unsuited. But if I lost you...'

'Then lucky you know where I live,' Lilly teased, and Bennet was sure he had made the right decision. Those spirits appearing were just too frightening for his likening.

Chapter 13

Julius noticed Ambrose was looking happy on their way to collect a body from a private residence and return it to *The Economic Undertaker* for Phoebe to prepare for a viewing. More and more people were choosing not to conduct a private viewing at home and entrust their loved one to *The Economic Undertaker*, who then carried out the burial true to the package purchased.

On offer were three funeral packages. The cheapest named "Essential Funeral" was often purchased by the state for those with no one to claim the body, or by families who did not like their relatives. Julius named the very affordable middle package "Traditional Funeral" to make it appealing; he named the top package, which included plumes on the horses, "Custom", although plumes were becoming less fashionable.

Julius avoided gold or silver references, as he believed it guilted families into paying more, as his grandparents did for his own parents. The middle option made people feel like they hadn't bought the cheapest package. Julius set aside an amount from every "Custom" funeral purchased to cover families struggling to pay their bill. Every funeral included a coffin made at cousin Lucian's carpentry business.

'It is a fine winter's day,' Ambrose said, smiling pleasantly, as if there was no better place to be than riding in a hearse this day.

'What has you so cheery this morning then?' Julius asked. 'My company perhaps, or the thought of another burial?'

Ambrose huffed. 'Both are surely spirit lifting. But no, I had the pleasure of encountering Miss Prout in the cemetery yesterday. She was approving her headstone placement, and I am going to walk her home in a matter of days.'

'Is that so?' Julius said and smiled, before remembering he was driving the hearse, and clearing his throat, affected a sober look again. 'That is great news.'

'That is what I thought. Now, do your best to not draw attention to your handsome face; I want her to be enamoured only with me.'

'If you let me know when Miss Prout visits, I'll be sure to put a shroud over my head,' Julius retorted, and Ambrose barked out a very inappropriate laugh.

As they drove along in silence for a short while, Julius had time to consider Ambrose's comment and take umbrage. 'You know,' he said, 'it was only Miss Lewis who had a fleeting interest in me, which was not encouraged. You could have won her with your charm. Bennet did.'

'Bennet has a lot more to offer than me.'

'He does not,' Julius refuted that immediately. 'That's a ridiculous notion. And Miss Kirby, Kate, didn't care one iota for me. She would have married you in a heartbeat.'

Ambrose gave an indifferent shrug. 'But had you shown even the slightest interest in her...'

'You are being irrational,' Julius snapped, surprising his brother. 'I am not responsible for your single status.'

'I did not say you were,' Ambrose snapped back. 'But you cannot deny that you turn heads, and as you are happily married now, I am glad you are out of the picture.'

'You make it sound as if I sabotaged your relationships. Perhaps if you were more considerate of Kate, you both would not have suffered.' He stopped talking and drew a breath, calming himself. Julius was seldom drawn to anger these days, having worked very hard at managing his temper.

'If I had had a chance with Lilly, I would not have entertained a relationship with Kate. But as Lilly only had eyes for you, even when I was dancing with her... I simply ask that you do not charm Miss Prout.'

'I am a married man,' Julius said in a low voice that betrayed his annoyance. 'And if you remember, I met Miss Prout first and introduced her to you. Please stop talking; we are nearing the house.'

A thousand thoughts were swirling through Julius's mind. He had prided himself on protecting his brother and sister and providing for them. He would never sabotage their chance at love, but had he done so for Ambrose? No, he never encouraged Miss Lewis and had no interest in Kate – he could say that in good faith. Had Ambrose been interested in Violet? Again, he dismissed that thought.

The men approached the house, evident from the black wreath on the front door. A chill had passed between them, and Julius felt most indignant. Hurt. If a woman had the potential to come between him and his brother, he would pick his family every time. But then again, Uncle Reggie had not; he abandoned Randolph, his brother. Would Ambrose have abandoned him if Julius had loved Miss Lewis?

Was the relationship one way? Did Ambrose see him as a hinderance or a domineering brother? Should he have not offered him a role in the business but have set him up in something else more to his liking? He could not process this now; there was work to do.

As they neared, Julius gave a small groan. He could not bear to see a poor family struggling to bury their dead. The situation resonated deeply, mirroring the substantial debt his grandparents had accumulated while raising three unexpected grandchildren after burying their son- and daughter-in-law.

'Down on their luck, this lot,' Ambrose said quietly, 'and the neighbours too, by the looks of it.'

The homes were modest, most likely rental properties, with well-kept yards, but in need of basic repairs. The timber boarding was peeling, the fences had seen better days, except, oddly, for the fence of the property they were to visit. Julius wondered what rent the inhabitants were paying for this lifestyle.

'Name?' Julius asked, and Ambrose reached for the note in his pocket from his grandfather.

'Mrs Ingliss. Mother of three. We buried two of her five children several years back. This is her husband now.'

Julius puffed his cheeks out and exhaled at her misfortune. Pleased to see a large camphor laurel tree to the left of the home, he steered the horses and hearse into the shade. It was winter, but the horses had driven some distance, and the cool rest would revive them before the return trip. Alighting, the men straightened their jackets and made their way to number thirty-nine.

A boy and a girl dressed in dyed black clothes came out of the house and stood on the stairs, watching the men approach.

The eldest, the girl, appeared to be around seven or eight years old and stepped forward.

'Are you here for Dad, then?'

An older boy stood up from behind the fence, a hammer and nails in his hand. 'Tell Mum they're here, Sis,' he said.

'Okay, Jack,' she said and ran inside.

The eldest boy addressed the Astin brothers. 'I'm fixing the fence.'

'It's good to keep busy, Jack,' Julius agreed, and the boy nodded.

'So you are the man of the house now?' Ambrose asked.

'I'm fifteen and old enough.'

'You are,' Julius agreed, diffusing the anger that sprung up in the boy. He remembered the feeling. Then he noticed the other boy studying him with great intent. 'Hello, young man, my brother and I are here to care for your dad. Thank you for letting us.'

'Mum said you are good and we can pay it off,' the boy said, having most likely overhead the adult conversation between his mother and another.

Mrs Ingliss came to the door. 'Oh, good morning to you. Of course we can pay it off,' she assured Julius and Ambrose, as if she feared they would turn and leave. 'Will you come in?'

Just inside the doorway stood another woman, who was introduced as Mrs. Ingliss's mother.

'Can I offer you a cup of tea, gentlemen?' she asked.

'Thank you, Ma'am, but we will abstain while on duty,' Ambrose said, and she smiled at the reference as if the men were serving officers, which they were to the dead.

Julius addressed Mrs Ingliss. 'May we speak in private without the children overhearing?'

'I shall take them to say goodbye to their father before he departs,' the grandmother said and bustled everyone out of the room.

'Do not be concerned with what my boy was saying; I assure you we can pay,' Mrs Ingliss said again, running her hands down her dress in a nervous gesture. Her brown hair, pulled severely back into a bun, combined with her thin frame, gave her a worn appearance.

'Mrs Ingliss, please do not be concerned about that,' Julius said. 'I promise you that your husband is in good hands and will receive our very best attention and a dignified funeral. I would actually like to advise you that there is no cost for the funeral, and no need to pay it back.'

Her face, as well as Ambrose's, lit up with surprise, and then a frown appeared upon her countenance. She waved her hands in front of her. 'Oh, no, Mr Astin, definitely not. We cannot accept charity. I am perfectly capable of paying. I work as a cleaner while my mother minds the children, and my mother sells her baking. My eldest son will soon start working. We have funds coming in.'

'It is not charity, Mrs Ingliss, we assure you,' Ambrose promised, supporting Julius. 'You see, when we have a client who can afford a good funeral but they are not wishing to spend the money on their dearly departed, we include a little extra on their bill. Call it a tax.'

'And we beg of you to keep our secret,' Julius said with a subtle look around, as if looking for eavesdroppers. 'We will deny all knowledge, of course, if you should expose us.'

Mrs Ingliss gave a small smile. 'Your secret is safe with me. You have my word.'

'Thank you,' Julius said. 'As a result, we gift select clients a free burial and coffin.'

'You are not the first and won't be the last, we assure you,' Ambrose said. 'It is a discreet offer; no one need know.'

'And do not be concerned,' Julius continued as she was about to protest again. 'We will maintain the same quality, and our staff will still receive their earnings. It is just that the money comes from the fund and not from yourself. Please accept.'

'With our compliments,' Ambrose added.

Mrs Ingliss drew a deep breath, and for a moment her bottom lip trembled. She gathered herself. 'Gentlemen, for my children, I will most gratefully accept. Bless you both.' She closed her eyes, exhaled, and the weight of the world seemed to fall from her shoulders.

Two days later, Mrs Ingliss was also gifted several mourning wear dresses that fit with the smallest of alterations, with the compliments of *Beyond the Veil*.

Chapter 14

Detective Harland Stone pre-empted the dismissal of himself and Gilbert should they arrive at the doorstep of Mr Gardner or Mr Nash unannounced. Thus, getting on the front foot, he sent a note requesting an audience with themselves and their wives. Both agreed to the time requested, both specifying that for privacy it was to be held at their residences, not at their businesses.

'I can't imagine this life, Sir, and even if I were ever to afford it, I cannot see the purpose of living so grandly,' Gilbert said under his breath as they arrived at the premises of Arthur and Gertrude Gardner. The sprawling mansion with the manicured garden was a far cry from the modest home that Gilbert grew up in.

Harland, however, came from wealth, but spent his childhood in the narrow hallways and draughty bedrooms of a boarding school where the teaching staff believed childhood adversity created strong, resilient men.

'I thought you were going to remind me it wouldn't get me into heaven,' Harland teased his young protégé, and Gilbert chuckled.

'Well, the bible did not say a rich man couldn't enter heaven, just that it would be hard for them to do so. The message being, it is best to share.'

'Indeed,' Harland agreed.

The Gardners were as haughty as their home. Brief introductions were undertaken, and the detectives were reminded of the family's frustration.

'Two years,' Arthur Gardner said. 'We have waited, hoped and desired justice, to no avail. Why the interest now, detectives?'

'We believe we have a pattern, Mr Gardner,' Harland said as the gruff and intimidating man made a sound of disbelief. Harland imagined the power Gardner had over his employees, but the senior detective was not one to cower to bullies.

Nevertheless, Harland knew Gilbert would observe his handling of this situation, as he had done with his superior, so he continued in a calm and professional manner. 'Your daughter may be one of four ladies targeted by the same group

of men. What that formula is, we are yet to determine –
perhaps they are brothers or swindlers in arms. Could you
describe your daughter's fiancé, please?'

'Despicable,' Arthur Gardner said, and his wife gave him a
reproachful look and answered on his behalf.

'Detectives, we appreciate your attention to this matter and
hope you will have more luck resolving it than the former
investigator. Our daughter's fiancé, Mr Walter Tewnon,
appeared to be a respectable, modest, but ambitious young
man. He was quiet of nature, like our daughter, Caroline, and
I would go so far as to say shy.'

'I agree. He was studying bookkeeping, and as my business
is in property, I thought his skills would be very useful for a
future son-in-law. I saw him working in the business in due
course, as did Caroline,' Arthur Gardner said.

'What did he physically look like, please, Mrs Gardner?'
Gilbert asked, ready to jot down the answer.

'He was a tall man with dark hair and blue eyes. He had a
tendency to stoop, but I think that was a matter of confidence,'
she said. 'His parents were abroad, so we never met them.'

'Then, he decided to join them with Caroline's dowry,
leaving our daughter at the altar,' Arthur Gardner said through
thin lips.

'Sir, how did he gain access to Miss Gardner's money before
marriage?' Harland asked, curious.

'They were to travel abroad straight after their wedding, and as Walter presented documents to show he was the beneficiary of several wills, I advanced him the money. I have seen many documents in my time, and they were very authentic. All that remained was the formal ceremony.' Arthur Gardner shook his head. 'I hold myself responsible for a terrible error in judgement.'

'It is hard to conceive of such dishonesty amongst one who seemed so truthful, modest, and in love,' his wife added supportively.

His hobbies also interested the detectives. Here was another fiancé with a strong interest in the theatre, and Gilbert noted the details.

After the interview, the detectives made their way on foot to the home of Mr and Mrs Nash, only several streets away from the Gardner household and an equally lavish abode. Mrs Nash was still in mourning wear for her late daughter – three years had passed. Mr Nash looked weary.

'We made our money on the land,' he said, not embarrassed to talk about wealth. 'My wife and I wish we had never come to the city. If we had just stayed on our grazing property...'

'Winnifred would never have met him,' Mrs Nash finished her husband's sentence, not that it needed to be said.

'He got nothing from us, though. I am not the most trusting of men,' Mr Nash said. 'A country trait, my father would call it. We country folk are slow to trust, but once you are in our circle, we are loyal for life.'

'So, what happened, Mr Nash?' Harland asked, sipping the offered cup of tea in a large drawing room with floor to ceiling windows and a view of parkland before them.

'Isaac Wenton claimed to be independently wealthy, and when he asked to court Winnifred, he showed me documents attesting to his right to legacies from his father and grandparents' wills. I was pleased that he was a man who could keep my daughter in comfort and security.' His voice hitched slightly, and he accepted a glass of water from his wife.

'I am sorry for the distress we are causing by asking you to relive this, Mr Nash,' Gilbert said, 'but we would like justice, as I'm sure you would.'

Mr Nash nodded and continued once he had regained himself. 'It's been three years, Detective, but until my last breath, I will not tire of wanting justice.'

'Winnifred was a good girl,' Mrs Nash said. 'She loved Isaac, but she loved her father more.'

'That is true,' Mr Nash agreed. 'She came to me worried and said he had been pressing her for access to her dowry in advance. He wanted to get his house prepared and finished, so when they were married, it would be to her standard and they could move in without delay.'

'She, of course, told him that was unnecessary,' Mrs Nash added. 'Winnifred hoped to be involved in any repairs and decorations to her future home. Thank goodness my husband was suspicious of this request, and of the delays in the proceeds from his legacies arriving.'

'Without informing Winnifred, we had her fiancé investigated,' Mr Nash continued from his wife. 'There was no house. He lived in a boarding flat. In fact, my solicitor could find no evidence of any wills or legacies coming his way. The paperwork was a very professional forged document. I believe Wenton caught wind of what we were doing, and he abandoned our daughter the day before the wedding.'

'She felt mortified and heartbroken. Winnie stopped eating, sleeping...' Mrs Nash rose hurriedly and with a handkerchief pressed to her mouth, left the room.

'May we have the address of that boarding house, and could you describe this man, Sir?' Harland asked. 'His hobbies also interest us.'

'I still have it,' he said, rising and going to his desk to retrieve a small black book. Jacob Nash scribbled the address and passed it to Harland. 'I will never forget him, and I would love to see him in jail for life,' he said vehemently. 'He was tall, fair of hair, similar to my wife and daughter, and had an engaging Irish accent. I don't even know if that was real.'

'And his interests?' Harland prompted him.

'Ah, yes. He loved puzzles,' Mr Nash said. 'I confess I found that unmanly, but he loved a good play with words and a quiz to solve.'

The two detectives exchanged looks, and rising, they thanked Mr Nash and departed.

As they walked out of the grounds, and toward the street to take the omnibus, Harland mused, 'Two blond men, two dark haired-men, one with a limp, one who stooped, one with a British accent, one with an Irish accent.'

'Two different men perhaps, Sir?' Gilbert suggested. 'Or four men.'

'Or one man. A capable actor could manage those accents and disguises, and as far as we know, there is only one crime per year. It would be challenging to maintain them, but you are right, Gilbert. Some men are capable of great deception. So where is this man or these men now?'

'I shall begin a list of where they resided, Sir, and we could speak to the landlords.'

'Good. Tomorrow's challenge then, Gilbert,' Harland agreed. 'Perhaps we should visit some amateur theatre companies and see if any thespians with the same names are on, or were on, their books.'

'Yes, Sir, I'll add that to our board.'

'While you seek addresses and update the board, I shall talk to the original detective on the case, although I am not expecting to uncover much.'

'Nor I, Sir. He dismissed me when I first requested his time. I think he felt the jilted bride cases were below him.'

'Not even one case was beneath him, let alone four. This is not just a breach of contract to a young lady, but forgery and theft on a grand scale.'

'I don't think he wants us to solve it, Sir. There is an air of resentment among some of our colleagues.'

'It is understandable. I would not like to be shown wanting in my duties, either. Regardless, let us hope we can solve it, Gilbert.'

Randolph Astin smiled at his grandsons as the Astin brothers returned to the reception area, having delivered Mr Ingliss to Phoebe for preparation. There was to be a small family viewing in the morning, followed by the funeral.

'Within days, the pulley system will deliver bodies from this level to Phoebe, directly via the viewing rooms Lucian is completing,' Julius said, pleased.

'That will make our day so much easier,' Randolph agreed, as delighted as Julius with the concept.

'Oh, the Ingliss funeral and coffin are to come out of the Beneficiary Fund, Grandpa,' Julius said casually.

'You are a good man, Julius. God bless you.'

'You would have done exactly the same. Mrs Ingliss has had her share of loss. She is feeding three children on a cleaning wage. It will always be a struggle for her. I wish we could do more.'

'It's been a while since we've given away a funeral, so the fund is healthy,' Randolph agreed.

'It's good of Mrs Neale to contribute to it with her plumes and trimming for poor Miss Alma Thornton,' Ambrose said cheekily.

'And she will never know,' Julius said, looking smug. 'It was the least she could do given our time spent at that long-winded funeral.'

'Well, I have a note to write and send before this afternoon's collections from the hospital morgue. I shall be in Phoebe's room,' Ambrose said and took to the stairs.

Randolph watched him depart before looking to Julius for an explanation. 'A note? I did not know Ambrose could write,' he said in jest, and Julius chuckled.

'He saw Miss Prout in the cemetery yesterday and offered to escort her home one evening. I suspect this is his invitation to her.'

Randolph smiled. 'Wonderful. I will breathe easy when all of you are suitably married. You have led by example and made an excellent match.'

'Yes, I was fortunate,' Julius agreed with a smile that Violet often brought to his countenance. 'Can you ask Will to step up this afternoon, if he is free, and accompany Ambrose on those collections?'

Randolph studied him. 'Of course. Is everything all right, lad? Can I attend to something for you? That is part of my duties.'

'No, thank you, Grandpa; there is nothing pressing. I will organise our weekly advertisement in *The Courier* and check on the other businesses.'

Mrs Dobbs stuck her head around the kitchen door. 'I've boiled the kettle; can I interest you both in a cup of tea and some apple tea cake?'

'Thank you, Mrs Dobbs. I shall summon Phoebe and Ambrose while there is no one in the house,' Randolph said, and moved towards the staircase down to Phoebe's room.

'I need to... I'll be back, but thank you, Mrs Dobbs,' Julius said and, with his hand on the front doorknob, he hesitated. 'Grandpa, can I ask... actually, never mind.'

'What is it, Julius? Speak your mind,' his grandfather insisted.

Julius glanced toward the kitchen and lowered his voice. 'You haven't given me a response for Uncle Reggie. Do not be concerned; he hasn't pressed me. In fact, I haven't seen him for a week,' Julius assured him. 'It's just that I thought you might have wanted to pass on a message by now.'

It had taken some time, but once Julius admitted to his grandfather that he could see spirits, Uncle Reggie shared why he remained on the earth in spirit form – in order to apologise to his brother Randolph for his actions and absence, and he wanted Julius to relay the message. Loving the same woman had not boded well for the brothers; Randolph had won Maria's hand, and Reggie had removed himself from their life.

Randolph drew himself a little taller and exhaled, turning to face Julius. 'I forgive him a hundred times over, as I hope he forgives me for my role in his disappointment. It is just... well, I can't understand why the love of Maria would have kept him away for so long. That it was stronger than his love of the family.'

'His brotherly love,' Julius clarified, as the sentiments were close to his heart at this moment.

'Yes, in essence, brotherly love. I have tried to place myself in his position, but I could not imagine forsaking him. Perhaps I am too sentimental.'

'Perhaps I am too,' Julius said. 'I feel like Ambrose and Phoebe have outgrown the need for me now. Ambrose needs to make his own way, and Phoebe has Harland.' He cleared his throat. 'Too sentimental,' he said again and smiled. With a nod to his grandfather, he hurriedly departed out the front door, striding the opposite way from the *Beyond the Veil* store, city bound.

Randolph stared after him for a moment, thinking of Julius's last words, before calling downstairs to his two youngest grandchildren and rejoining Mrs Dobbs in the kitchen. As Phoebe and Ambrose entered the kitchen moments later, he asked, 'What happened between you and Julius this morning, Ambrose?'

'Nothing,' Ambrose said, accepting a large slice of cake. 'He donated the funeral and...' he paused as if remembering something, but hastily added, 'Nothing untoward.'

'That sounds like something,' Phoebe said, pouring milk into everyone's cups as Mrs Dobbs poured the tea.

'A silly discussion between brothers. Did he say something?' Ambrose asked, eyeing his grandfather warily.

'Not a word, but he asked for Will to take his place this afternoon on your shift.'

'Did he?' Ambrose looked most indignant. 'I see.' And he said nothing more but bore his grandfather's worried looks.

Chapter 15

As Harland was about to depart to speak to the former detective on the fraud cases, the desk sergeant, John, arrived with a small parcel for the detective.

'This was left on our counter, Detective, and none of us saw the deliverer. I am wary of anything not delivered conventionally.'

'As am I, thank you, Sergeant.' He returned to the meeting desk to open it as reporter Lilly Lewis and private investigator Bennet Martin arrived, apologising to the Sergeant for not waiting for his return. Bennet's suit spoke of wealth, Miss Lewis looked charming in a lemon dress with grey trim, and the pair bustled in bursting with news.

'What is this then?' Bennet asked.

'Just delivered,' Gilbert said.

Harland opened the note; his expression relayed his surprise. 'Good Lord!' He read the note aloud.

'So sorry to meet under such sad circumstances, detectives. In her grief at Alma's funeral, Mrs Neale did not think to introduce us. But I had to say farewell to my beloved.'

'Is it from him, Sir? The cad?' Gilbert asked, rising to join the others at the meeting room table.

'It is signed, *"The Vanishing Groom".'* The gathered party was surprised into silence as Harland opened the small box to find a piece of wedding cake. On the top was a toppled bride and no groom.

'This is a game to him,' Harland hissed. 'How has he got away with it for so long?'

'Because no one took it seriously, perhaps, or the family did not want to bring additional exposure to themselves,' Gilbert suggested.

'Now, he thinks he can play us for fools,' Bennet said, including himself in the investigation.

'Do you recall seeing a likely suspect at the funeral, detectives?' Lilly asked.

Harland closed his eyes as he thought back to the male faces amongst the gathering at the cemetery. Gilbert did not speak, as he had learnt to wait for his mentor to gather his thoughts.

Opening his eyes, he looked at Gilbert. 'There were only a few men around the gravesite, and our villain would not have come unless in disguise; Mrs Neale would have recognised him. He must have kept his distance.'

Gilbert agreed. 'There were two, as I recall – a tall man with glasses, reddish hair, and slightly effeminate, and an older gentleman, quite portly.'

'Exactly as I recall it, Gilbert. The younger man present did not resemble Miss Thornton's fiancé in the slightest,' Harland said, reading the description from the board. 'Blond hair, blue eyes, a limp. Well, if he wants to make a game of this, then we will have to be constantly wary.'

Harland packed up the cake and note. Turning to Bennet and Lilly, he said, 'Your visit was timely, but please do not report on the delivery, Miss Lewis, not yet.'

'I shall abstain,' she agreed.

'Do you have information?' Harland asked.

'Yes,' they said in unison and looked at each and smiled.

'So do we,' Gilbert said, returning to the board as Harland now closed his office door and positioned himself on the edge of his desk.

'You caught me just in time; I was heading upstairs. Ladies first,' Harland invited Lilly to start.

'The original news clippings from a year ago through to four years ago cover the bones of the incident and are quite spartan. I suspect pressure was applied to keep the families' shame to a minimum, especially for the sake of the abandoned young ladies. However, there was one interesting little piece.'

The three gentlemen looked at her with anticipation.

'The bank teller mentioned in two of the stories, two years apart, was the same man. Now that might seem trivial, but one would think given his bank handed over the money to a thief, even if they did have the blessing of the family initially, one would forewarn about that a second time.'

'A very salient point, Miss Lewis, well done,' Harland said, stroking his chin for a moment while he thought about this. 'Would you have the teller's name? We will pay him a visit.' He nodded to Gilbert to record it on the board.

'I do. Mr Bailey Sutton.'

'That is hard to top,' Bennet said when it came to his turn. 'I had my briefing with Grace Edmonstone's father. I believe you spoke with him earlier.'

'We did,' Harland confirmed.

'Mr Edmonstone said Grace's fiancé was expecting the proceeds from a legacy and had showed him the paperwork attesting to the money coming his way. As a result, Mr Edmonstone advanced him a considerable sum.'

The detectives exchanged looks. 'He did not tell us that. Perhaps he was ashamed to do so,' Gilbert said.

'Yes,' Harland agreed. 'Mr Arthur Gardner admitted to doing the same. He released funds for his daughter Caroline and her vanishing groom based on the forged will. Mr Nash, however, outsmarted the fraudster and did not lose a pound, but paid the price with the loss of his daughter.'

Lilly shook her head in dismay. 'Do you think it looks like it is one man using the same technique each time?'

'Possibly, but early days yet,' Harland said. 'That is excellent, Bennet, thank you, as it confirms we are dealing with the same modus operandi, at least.'

When Gilbert finished writing this information on the board, Harland summarised. 'So, we have four fiancés. All are tall. Thus far, the fiancés of Miss Alma and Miss Winnifred are similar in appearance – blond haired, blue eyed.'

'And both ladies loved to such a degree that the betrayal took their lives,' Bennet said.

Gilbert added, 'But that appears to be where the similarities end. Miss Alma's fiancé, Oliver, was confident, a salesman and had a limp from a riding accent, no accent. Miss Winnifred's fiancé was Irish with a strong accent and a loved of puzzles.'

Harland nodded and continued. 'The other two men are dark-haired, with blue eyes and different nationalities.'

Again, Gilbert elaborated as requested by his superior. 'Miss Caroline Gardner's fiancé, Walter, was a bookkeeper and a little stooped and lacking in confidence. Miss Grace Edmonstone's fiancé, Edwin, was a keen sailor, came from money, and had a notable British accent.'

'I wonder whether the bank teller is an acquaintance or a relative of theirs,' Bennet mused. 'As he is connected to my client, and organised Mr Edmonstone's advance, I shall investigate that angle.'

'That would save us time, thank you, Bennet,' Harland agreed. 'I would appreciate it if you included Mr Gardner, the other father the teller served, in your query.'

'Of course.'

Miss Lewis, for your story, if you wish to report that we are investigating the link between the four cases and have created profiles for each of the men involved. You may like to add that young ladies should be wary and it is possible a fifth woman is currently being wooed. So if engaged to be married, do not agree to advance your beloved any monies until after the wedding.'

'Thank you, Detective. I will not mention the clerk as that is a loose end, but may I say that several hobbies and interests of the suspects are also under consideration?'

'Yes, that might help. If a member of a small hobby group has suddenly departed and the party knew him to be engaged to be married, it might result in help from the public,' Harland said.

'I would like to profile each lady,' Lilly said. 'I know the families would prefer discretion, but it is a crime, it has occurred, and it is a matter of public record.'

'I cannot stop you from doing so, Miss Lewis,' Harland said. 'I agree that the moment the families involved the police, a criminal case was established. It won't harm our investigation to have the information in your newspaper and might provide us with witnesses.'

'Excellent, thank you, Detective,' Lilly said.

With that, the group disbanded; Lilly returned to the office to write her copy, Bennet to attend the bank and investigate the teller, and Harland left Gilbert to continue seeking the addresses of the fiancés and theatre clubs to visit. He sought the former detective on the case.

Straight after lunch, Phoebe, with the help of Charlie from the stables, prepared her next clients, Mr and Mrs Yates, who had a mid-afternoon viewing scheduled. The aged couple had died within three hours of each other and were to be buried first thing in the morning with the respectable 'Traditional' package from *The Economic Undertaker*.

Phoebe preferred to prepare the bodies as close to the viewing time as possible to ensure they appeared at their very best. Today, with Charlie's help, they could work on the departed couple together. The young stable lad, who aspired to do what Phoebe did, trained with her whenever possible; Phoebe believed him to be most capable.

It was a serene picture; the lady mortician wore a pale blue dress with cream lace trimming, the afternoon winter light softly lit the room as it streamed in through the window and made her hair appear golden. Working nearby, a thin young man with a tinge of red in his hair that the sunlight accentuated, looked respectable in the clean clothes he had changed into for the job ahead.

'That is true love, isn't it?' Charlie said quietly. The pair spoke occasionally as they worked side by side. 'To live together all those years and die on the same day.'

'Yes, a lovely way to leave the world. Their daughter said earlier that they were rarely apart,' Phoebe said. She smiled. 'I believe the number three was important to them. They had three children, thirteen grandchildren, were married on the third day of the third month. Now, they died within three hours of each other. Their viewing is at 3pm.'

Charlie smiled at the thought as he worked from a supplied portrait to get the hairline just right for Mr Yates. Phoebe subtly studied him as she prepared Mrs Yates.

'Charlie, you are a young man with many working years ahead of you. Are you sure you would not prefer to learn carpentry or the business side of being a funeral director? Julius will see to your training in those endeavours, if you prefer.'

'I assure you, Miss Astin, this is what I want to do. It is intriguing work, and we make a difference to families at the end of a life.' He stopped and snapped to look at her. 'Do you not think my work is up to standard, Miss?' he asked, dismayed.

'On the contrary. I think you are very capable, Charlie, and I would be dismayed to lose you,' she assured him. 'You know I am sure if I were away you could step in for me now, and your lessons are almost complete.'

'Do you think so, Miss Astin?' he asked, delighted, smiling as he continued his work. 'I hope that one day there is enough business to engage us both in this role.'

'From what Julius says, it might be sooner than we think. With the new viewing rooms upstairs almost ready, and people growing reluctant to conduct mourning in their homes, I believe we will soon be rushed off our feet with the dead wishing to look their best.'

Phoebe saw Charlie look past her shoulder, and she turned, anticipating someone present. Miss Alma Thornton stood there in her wedding dress, along with Miss Winnifred Nash in her pink frock that she departed the world in. Phoebe pursed her lips to make the silence sign and gave a barely perceptible shake of her head.

'Our apologies, Miss Astin. We will remain quiet until you are alone,' Alma said, and Phoebe gave her a grateful smile.

She turned back to Charlie, who was still looking in the area where the young ladies were standing. Did he too, possess some talent for seeing the dead?

'What is it?' she asked curiously. 'Do you see something?'

He flushed a little and returned to his work. 'It is silly.'

'Then I won't make you share,' she said, 'but you are welcome to do so.'

She saw Charlie swallow before he took a leap of faith and spoke. 'Sometimes I feel the energy of the departed. It might be nothing, and I could be imagining it, but I sense two people in the room.'

'Two!' Phoebe said, shocked at his accurateness. She schooled her reaction. 'Can you see them or just sense them?'

'No. I just feel the shift in the air, as though they are present beyond you there. Perhaps it is Mr and Mrs Yates,' he said, looking at the bodies before him. 'You need not worry. I am not a ghoul hunter or intending to hold a séance in your room. I do not believe in interrupting the dead on their final journey or in the afterlife, Miss Astin.'

'I am not worried at all. I feel the same energy shift,' she admitted.

'You do?' Charlie asked, and his face lit up with relief.

'I always have since childhood.'

'As have I! My mother does not like me to speak of it, but she and my grandmother had the same skill.'

'As did mine,' Phoebe agreed with a smile. 'We shall keep each other's secrets then and welcome the two souls that have joined us.' She did not admit it was not Mr and Mrs Yates... small steps.

On finishing their work, Phoebe declared that the elderly Yates couple looked lovely for their viewing and for the afterlife. She rang the bell on her desk and heard her grandfather's footsteps down the hall to the back door, as he called Claude to come and assist Charlie to bring the bodies to the viewing room. The families would arrive in a couple of hours.

Once the bodies were removed and Phoebe was alone, she turned to the ladies in spirit, addressing them informally as agreed last visit.

'Thank you, Alma and Winnifred, for your patience.'

'We have a lot of time on our hands now, Phoebe,' Alma teased, 'more time than you.'

Phoebe grinned. 'Well, that is a good thing, then. Are you here for an update? I haven't received one as yet, but I know the detectives were visiting the families today, including your parents, Winnifred.'

'My poor Ma and Pa,' she sighed, 'but no, we are here with our own update, Phoebe. We know where Isaac is now.'

'Or, in my case, Oliver,' Alma said.

'You do?' Phoebe asked, surprised.

'Yes,' Alma continued. 'They are one and the same, despite the different names. We are sure of it now. He is residing at a gentlemen's boarding house, and he is wooing another lady.'

'Isaac is going by the name of Joseph Facey. I saw a letter on the table in his room,' Winnifred said, her hand going to her heart as if it still beat.

'I am sorry this pains you,' Phoebe said. 'The heart takes time to heal, and sometimes it won't forget.'

'So true, Phoebe. It should not hurt me after what he did. I should be angry and hardened, but I am not,' Winnifred said, accepting Alma's hand. 'It pains us both.'

Alma agreed. 'Even though it's tainted, one cannot turn off love. I, too, am hurt by his actions and his indifference.'

'Of course. Then we must stop him,' Phoebe declared assuredly. 'I shall note the name he is using and the address for the detectives. I wish to see him first, this cad.'

'It is only a small boarding house, and there is an omnibus stop right opposite, most handy for its residences,' Alma said. 'If you wish to see him, you might watch the house from there.'

'If you get the chance, will you give him a message for me?' Winnifred asked, and Phoebe looked surprised.

'I will. What would you like me to pass on?'

'Just three words. Please tell him, "Winnie says, Adeline".'

Alma gasped and said, 'Yes, please do.'

Phoebe repeated the message. 'May I ask what it means?'

'Of course. It is his mother's name,' Winnifred said. 'He told me his mother was back in Ireland and her name was Maeve. But Adeline is deceased and on our side, and is very ashamed of him.'

'Be careful, Phoebe,' Alma said. 'Do not put yourself in danger for us.'

'Please do not, nor go out of your way to deliver the message. It is only if you find the opportunity,' Winnifred said and requested Phoebe's assurance.

'I will be careful, I promise.' But she was keen to see this rogue "charmer" for herself, and if she could tell the detectives where he resided, that would be a great consolation to the living and the dearly departed.

Chapter 16

Arriving at the carpentry business he co-owned with his cousin Lucian, Julius paused to admire the variety of projects underway. In the back area, he could see the carriages being built. In another large designated area, coffins were being constructed from several timbers but predominantly the cheaper pine, with a few underway in cedar and English oak for those customers wanting the top option. Near the coffins, furniture in different stages of progress was being assembled under the watchful eye of Lucian's supervisor. Julius raised a hand to his brother-in-law, Tom, who he could see working on a carriage in the far corner of the business.

Lucian grinned on seeing him and downed tools to join his cousin. 'You don't look dressed for labour,' he teased, and Julius chuckled.

'No, I'm not sure you could sell what I was capable of making. I'm sorry to interrupt.'

'You own half the business, you need no appointment. Is everything okay?' Lucian asked, nudging Julius towards his office, where it was quieter.

'I won't stay; I just wanted to ask you a quick question if you have time,' Julius said, studying his blond cousin, whose features were akin to Phoebe and the fairer side of the family tree.

'I need a break. Stay and have a cup of tea with me. I wish to discuss a matter with you, too.'

Julius followed Lucian into his office, where they sat and spoke of light-hearted matters until Lucian's secretary returned with two cups of tea and a plate of biscuits.

Alone, Lucian said, 'You first. What is on your mind?'

'Ambrose.'

'Ah, Ambrose,' Lucian smiled. They were the closest of cousins and best friends, and Lucian was the only person who knew Ambrose as Julius did. 'What has he done now?'

'Nothing yet,' Julius said with a grin. 'Although I am hopeful about the union with Miss Prout.'

'As am I. I think since I began seeing Elizabeth, he is keen to partner so we may go out the four of us.'

'How is Miss Jensen?' Julius asked, helping himself to a biscuit since he had missed the chance to have Mrs Dobbs's Apple Tea Cake.

'She is all things lovely. And Mrs Astin?'

'The same, thank you for asking,' Julius smiled. 'Lucian, I don't expect you to break a confidence, but has Ambrose ever wanted to work in his own business? Has he ever spoken to you of wanting to work here, for example?'

To Julius's surprise, Lucian laughed. 'No. Trust me, Ambrose is not handy. Your brother-in-law, Tom, however, is skilled. He can pick up a piece of wood and make something from it. He can fix anything he puts his mind to, and his work is excellent. I love my dear cousin Ambrose, but he would not know what to do with a hammer.'

'As I thought. Has he ever expressed a desire to run a business?'

'No, quite the opposite. He has said many a time he likes the freedom of working in a family business, and while he appreciated the recent promotion, I would not say he is ambitious.'

'Hmm, as I thought too.'

'What's going on?' Lucian asked, reaching for a second biscuit.

'I am probably overthinking it—'

'You?' Lucian interrupted him, surprised, and then grinned.

'Odd I know,' Julius gave him a smirk.

'Forgive me, please continue,' Lucian said, giving Julius his full attention. It was rare that Julius sought counsel not of a business nature.

'Well, Ambrose implied he always has to compete with me, and I am ashamed to say I have no recollection of that. So I thought maybe I should provide him with some other opportunities.' He sighed.

'Julius, you are the best of brothers and cousins,' Lucian said sincerely, and held up his hand to stop Julius's protest. 'You are the handsomest among us; you are the most successful; you have looked after all of us. You are the best of us. But it is not competing, it is measuring ourselves. Not to overtake you, but to be as good. You have role models, do you not?'

Julius could not have been more uncomfortable, and he looked away. 'I am sure none of that is true, but I thank you, Cousin. And yes, I hope to be as calm and collected as Grandpa in adversity. I'm working on that.'

Lucian chuckled. 'Aren't we all? He is like a duck, smooth on the surface, paddling fast under the water.'

'It might be time to step back,' Julius said. 'Perhaps Ambrose and I see too much of each other.'

'As you are close and get on, I don't see why you should step back. Don't worry too much about Ambrose,' Lucian dismissed Julius's concerns. 'He often speaks without measuring his words and would be upset to think he has hurt you.'

'He hasn't hurt me,' Julius quickly deflected, not one for emotional vulnerability.

'No?' Lucian said, studying him. 'Regardless, Ambrose likes to have something to look forward to, and mentioned you were helping him to buy a house. He's excited about that. Miss Prout might just be the woman who harnesses him.'

'I hope so. On your assurances, I won't give Ambrose's mood too much more thought. You wanted to speak with me?'

'Yes. We have so much work, I think we need another apprentice.'

'Lucian, you are an astute businessman! Congratulations,' Julius said sincerely. 'Did you want to get a more senior worker so they could assist straight away?'

'Thank you, Cousin, but no. A woodwork apprentice will work hard and do the smaller jobs to free up my seniors. I don't wish to advertise or do interviews. Do you know anyone? Your last pick, Tom, was excellent.'

'That was good fortune, not selection. But I might know someone. There is a 15-year-old boy who has just lost his father. He was repairing the fence when we arrived to collect his father's body for a viewing. His name is Jack Ingliss, and he likes to be busy.'

'That is good that they have a roof over their head,' Lucian said.

'It was a rental.'

'And he is fixing the fence? Good, he is a boy with a work ethic. If he is interested, I shall meet him.'

'Thank you, Cousin,' Julius said, rising. 'I will invite his mother and Jack to meet with us.' With a grin, he added, 'Are you sure you could not apprentice Ambrose?'

Lucian laughed. 'For the right fee, anything is possible.'

Late-afternoon, Phoebe advised she needed to run an errand, and offered to take the mail to be posted.

'Thank you, my dear. The day had been busy in-house, and I would like to catch up,' her grandfather said, happily delegating the job.

After posting the mail, which included condolence cards with accounts to be paid, and payments to creditors, Phoebe alighted at the omnibus stop on Montague Road, South Brisbane. The stop allowed her to see the corner of Hope Street, and the boarding house where Alma and Winnifred's former beau was in residence. She knew the chances of seeing him were slim, but if he was not working, Phoebe expected he might come and go at his leisure.

She determined to give it no more than an hour to observe the entry and exits while she enjoyed a small sweet bun purchased from the bakery. They were her favourites. It was not long before the door of the boarding house opened and a lady bustled out, swept the step and went back in. It opened again moments later, and tensing, Phoebe relaxed when she saw an older, well-dressed gentleman depart.

Three omnibuses had come and gone now, her treat finished, and she had thanked the driver each time, advising she was waiting on someone before riding. A man of trade arrived on foot and entered the two-storey house. It reminded Phoebe that Lucian's business was not far away, and they would finish for the day soon. She decided it was best to get the next omnibus, or she might not get a seat on board.

Having given up that afternoon on seeing the gentleman who falsely professed his love, Phoebe felt most disappointed, and then the door opened again. A tall, fair-haired man exited, calling out to the landlady and laughing. Charming her no doubt, Phoebe thought, watching him as he hurried across the road to wait for the omnibus where she currently sat. Her heart raced; trepidation, curiosity, even a little fear of what this man could do to a lady.

On seeing Phoebe, he slowed his pace to a respectable walk, straightened his jacket, and smiled at her. He was handsome. Not like Harland with his manly looks, or Julius with his Byronic appearance. More like Ambrose, with his devil-may-care, boyish appearance.

Phoebe's breath hitched. This was him, she was sure of it – tall, fair-haired, and as he approached, she noted his eyes were blue.

'Good afternoon, Miss. May I be of service?' he said with a smile and a small bow. So confident, Phoebe thought. Normally, she would be charmed by his manners, but not this time. Not with the broken hearts he discarded like handkerchiefs.

She replied, most out of character, most coolly. 'Unless you are an omnibus, Sir, I cannot see how.'

He burst out laughing, also an endearing sight, and seated himself beside her on the bench. 'I cannot claim to be one. Mr Joseph Facey, at your service even if I can't be, Miss...?'

Phoebe's eyes widened before she schooled her features; the hide of him. She had the right man – Joseph Facey. Clearing her throat, she nodded, acknowledging his introduction.

'I believe the omnibus is coming, Miss...?' he tried again.

'Miss Jones,' she said, using an alias as she did not want him seeking her. 'I believe I have a message for you, Mr Facey.'

'Is that so?' he grinned, expecting her to be playful and banter with him.

Phoebe stood as the omnibus approached, and he rose to his feet as well. 'It is from Winnifred.'

For a moment, his smile remained, but his brow furrowed as he placed the name. 'Winnifred?'

'Yes, dear Miss Nash.'

A look of anger, then fear, quickly replaced his smile. 'The only Winnifred I know is a deceased young lady, I am sorry to say,' he said haughtily.

'That is her. She asked that I say, "Adeline," and you will know what that means.'

He stumbled backward and then righted himself. 'Who are you? Get away from me.' His handsomeness was gone, replaced by a scowl and fear.

Mr Joseph Facey turned and hurried away, glancing back at her, as Phoebe stepped into the omnibus, accepting the hand of a gentleman to do so. When she looked up at him, she recognised the man right away.

'Julius!'

'What just happened? Was he being too forward? I will get off right now and give him chase.' His face was stormy as he looked behind Phoebe at the man retreating.

'No, no,' she assured him. 'Let us sit and I will tell you all, but you won't like it.' She took his arm to steady herself as the horses started forward and the pair sat.

Julius gave a small groan. 'Tell me you are not meeting him in private.'

Phoebe hit his arm. 'Of course not. How could you think that of me?'

'I am not thinking straight. Were you in danger?' he asked, lowering his voice as passengers glanced their way with interest.

To anyone nearby, they made a handsome couple, but some passengers recognised the recently married business owner, Mr Julius Astin.

'No, I was not in danger as I timed my announcement well.'

'Announcement? Best you tell me then,' he said.

'I will, but don't be over-protective.'

'It is my right as your brother, and I will be,' Julius assured her.

'Then I shan't tell you.' Phoebe turned to watch the passing view and, when there was a short silence, she looked back at her brother with a raised eyebrow, expecting his submission.

Julius gave a small roll of his eyes and sighed. 'I will do my best not to over-react. I don't know what is going on with you and Ambrose of late, but you are both most contrary.'

'Are we? I am sorry, Brother, but I think you will find we have always been that way,' she teased, coaxing a smile from him. 'Can we go straight to the police station since you are here?'

'Really? All right. But start talking, you have me worried.'

Phoebe smiled, lowered her voice, and leaned in closer. 'Thanks to the two ladies, I have found the fraudster.'

Chapter 17

THE DAY'S LESSONS PLEASED Miss Emily Yalden, proprietor of the *Miss Emily Yalden School of Deportment.* Her current batch of ladies were showing great promise with their walking, sitting, dancing and conversation. Even the vulgar Miss Martha Hampstead had fallen into line since Emily's presentation and had become an obliging student.

As the lesson for the day was almost over and they had made good progress, Emily decided to reward the eight ladies present. She had an ulterior motive: to warn the girls of the romance predator who seemed to be in their midst.

'Shall we finish the day with some light conversation practice amongst us?' she suggested, and they all agreed most heartily, taking a seat in the conversation circle Emily had established earlier.

'Miss, may I ask if it is not too forward,' Amy began and Emily nodded, 'the beautiful flowers that arrive each week, do you have a beau?'

The other ladies smiled and leaned forward, keen for an answer.

'Amy, I am pleased you asked that question.'

'You are?' The full-figured, fair-haired miss from an affluent family asked. 'I was sure you would scold me.'

'It is a timely question,' Emily said. 'I am sure you have read the articles in the newspaper about Miss Alma Thornton, written by my good friend, Miss Lilly Lewis.'

'The jilted bride?' Martha asked.

'No, Miss. My father does not approve of my reading the newspaper. He believes it will expose me to radical ideas and make me an unfit wife,' Tess said, and Martha scoffed.

Emily did not comment on Tess's father's views; she did not agree, but her students were her bread and butter and, unfortunately, his opinion was not uncommon.

'I always read the newspaper,' Catherine said timidly. 'I hope it won't make me unfit to be a wife.'

Martha snorted again at the idea, and on this occasion, Emily did not chide her. She would have snorted herself had it not been unladylike. Instead, she continued calmly, 'As Martha said, Miss Thornton was a jilted bride, left at the altar, her dowry and fortune stolen by her fiancé. I would like you all to be wary of men who promise the world and rush you to the altar or request pre-marital access to your income. Reveal your concerns to your father or guardian if you feel something is not right.'

'But you trust your beau, Miss?' Amy asked again about Emily's personal situation.

'Indeed, I do. He is a member of the Roma Street Police Force,' she said discreetly.

'Oh, how exciting,' Martha said and nudged the friend she had made, Betty.

'Does he tell you about the cases he is working on, Miss Yalden?' Betty asked.

'No, he is very discreet and very much a gentleman,' Emily said and saw the disappointing look on Martha's face. 'But we do not want you and your beau to come to his attention. So be wary, young ladies, please.'

'Will you marry him, Miss?' Amy asked.

'And now, we have bordered into the area of inappropriate questions,' Emily said and restrained from sighing.

'My beau wants to write to my guardian and wed as soon as possible,' Martha said, surprising Emily and several of the ladies that she had a beau when, initially, Martha had been so against convention.

'How romantic,' Amy said. 'Is your guardian likely to give permission?'

Martha made a scoffing sound and then, remembering that was not what a young lady did, gave an impish grin to Emily and said, 'My guardian will gladly be rid of me. He is my uncle, and is appointed to manage my fortune until I come of age or marry. Given he believes I am too headstrong, he would prefer I marry so a man can guide me. But I am in no hurry to marry Benson.' She laughed at the thought, as several of the young ladies offered condolences that Martha did not have a father or mother to guide her.

Martha shrugged. 'I have spent half of my life in boarding school and, sadly, I cannot remember my parents very well. I was five when they died. So now that I have finished school, my uncle is determined I become a lady. Here I am!' she smiled at Emily as if challenging her, and Emily returned her smile.

'Given I admire your strength of character, Martha, I will not, on this occasion, pull you up for scoffing, shrugging and speaking far too openly about your situation,' Emily said, pleased with the information. Before she could ask more about Benson, the man who held Martha's affection, the subject changed, but she successfully conveyed her message to the ladies: be cautious with your heart and wealth.

The Astin siblings entered the Roma Street Police Headquarters. Phoebe was pleased to have Julius by her side. On the rare occasions that she had to frequent the station on her own, she felt like a species of bug being studied by all and sundry.

'Good day to you, Mr and Miss Astin. The detectives are in; I believe you are both trustworthy and can find your way there,' Sergeant John said in jest and waved a hand in the direction. The fact that he had several constables and half a dozen members of the public milling around for his attention allowed them to slip through quickly.

Offering their thanks, the handsome pair made their way to the end of the hallway, to the very last room allocated to the newest police team.

Phoebe saw Harland before he saw her. He stood, arms folded, staring at the board as Detective Gilbert Payne appeared to be writing salient points from his notes. Her heart stopped for a moment as she admired his presence.

Julius tapped on the door, and both men looked around. Phoebe saw the look of delight in Harland's eyes before concern quickly replaced it.

'Julius, Phoebe, is everything all right?' he asked, moving to the door and ushering them in, closing the office door behind them.

'Hello detectives,' Phoebe said, and Julius shook both men's hands. 'We have news that I hope will be of use.'

'Anything would be of great assistance, Miss Astin,' Gilbert assured her, and pulled two seats out at the meeting table for them to be seated before returning to his position by the board. Harland hovered in between.

'We would have come to you,' Harland said, and Julius assured him it was no bother.

'We were out and about,' Phoebe added. She dropped her voice as she often did when speaking of the dearly departed, and Julius kept up his ruse that he did not see the spirits. Both looked behind to ensure the door was closed before she spoke.

'Detectives, I believe I have found your offender.'

'You have!' Gilbert exclaimed, his face relaying his shock and then delight.

'This morning, Alma and Winnifred appeared to me convinced they share the same fiancé. They tracked him down,' Phoebe said and explained what had taken place.

'You took a great risk,' Harland said.

'As I have also said,' Julius gave his sister a stern look, and she shook her head slightly at both men.

'I was never in any danger sitting at the omnibus stop, and I did not pass on the message until the omnibus was in sight.'

'But what if he struck you?' Gilbert said. 'Oh, forgive me, Miss Astin. It is not for me to question your movements.'

'But I thank you for your concern, Detective Payne,' Phoebe said to the kindly detective. 'The man's name, or rather the name he is using now, is Mr Joseph Facey.'

Gilbert wrote the name on the board and paused at Phoebe's description of fair-haired and blue eyes.

'That is interesting,' Gilbert said, looking at his notes on the board. 'So you are saying the ladies who believe it is the same man are Miss Alma Thornton and Miss Winnifred Nash?'

'Yes, Detective Payne,' Phoebe confirmed.

'He matches the description of both ladies' fiancé, but not of the other two ladies,' Harland said, reading the board. 'Did Mr Facey have an accent or a limp, by any chance?'

'No,' Phoebe shook her head. 'But he spoke well and was educated, you might say.'

'Whether or not it is the same person,' Julius said, a little annoyed by the detectives ambivalence at being given a name and address of the potential rogue, 'the manner in which he ran off at the mention of the name "Adeline" and "Winnifred" would cast suspicion upon him, surely?'

'My word,' Gilbert agreed.

'We need to pay a visit to Mr Joseph Facey,' Harland agreed. 'If Phoebe's words startled him, he will be wary, so some surveillance may be in order first.'

'Why so?' Julius asked curiously.

'To see if he is currently wooing anyone else,' Harland said. 'It would be good to catch him in the act. In the interim, I would like to see his room and determine if he has any forged paperwork on hand. I shall have a constable on the beat keep an eye on the house tonight.'

Phoebe and Julius rose to depart.

'Tomorrow evening?' Harland asked, and Phoebe nodded and smiled, blushing slightly. 'Thank you, Phoebe.'

'I hope it is of value.' The siblings farewelled the detectives and, once outside, waited at the omnibus rank to return to *The Economic Undertaker*.

'I felt as if they were dismissive,' Julius said. 'Given there are four victims already, I assumed they would hurry to the boarding house.'

'As did I,' Phoebe agreed. 'They do not believe Alma and Winnifred, perhaps. I guess it is a lot to ask that they believe in the spirits they cannot see.'

'Time will tell, but I have no doubt,' Julius assured her.

'Nor I, and I have done all I can,' Phoebe sighed.

'You have, as always, given of your most vulnerable self, Phoebe. You are braver than I. I hope this Mr Facey does not seek you out.'

Phoebe turned to her brother. 'Thank you, Julius,' she said, smiling at him. 'That is very kind of you to say, but I assure you,

you need not worry on my behalf. You have your own family now. Time moves on, does it not?'

She did not know how her words cut Julius, who no longer knew what role he was to play in his brother and sister's life, but both seemed to make it clear he was no longer required in his normal capacity.

Chapter 18

JOSEPH FACEY PACED FROM one end of his room in the boarding house to the other, drawing the curtains but leaving a small gap to glance out, which he did on every turn past the window. He ran a hand over his face and exhaled.

Who was that girl? Winnifred died years ago, three years ago, to be exact. She's dead.

'Maybe I should see her grave, to be sure,' he muttered. 'Adeline, my darling mother.' He looked around as if expecting her ghost to appear and then he moved the curtain to glance outside again. All seemed normal on the street.

'I knew it was time to stop. Now look what's happened. The dead are coming back for me. I should have stopped; I didn't want to do one more; he made me!' he said, as if justifying his actions to anyone listening. To his mother.

Joseph had a plan – to change his life, to live in luxury for the rest of his days and to attract a wife of the class to match his fortune. No one would know about his desperate upbringing. How his father's fists were quick to fly when not holding a bottle. How his mother scrubbed people's homes to put food in his mouth.

He deserved better, and so did she, but it was too late for Adeline. It was not too late for Joseph Facey. One more job and he would assume his new alias – a well-educated, polished British gent, newly arrived on Australian shores. A man of old wealth seeking a home and wife. He would be good to his staff, especially the cleaners. He would look after them, and word would spread that he was kind and worthy of respect.

Of course, he would have a man who would take care of his investments and his funds would continue to grow. He would have a son and daughter, horses, a stable, a garden to wander in and a room to drink his port and smoke cigars. The image obsessed him; it always had, as he stayed out of the way in the rich houses where his mother cleaned.

Alma's dowry was sizeable, but he didn't get to claim the house. If they had married, he would have gained it, but that meant approaching her aunt for the funds, so he took the easier option – the dowry that Alma controlled and he claimed that before the marriage ceremony.

He felt reassured by the large sums in the bank – advances from Caroline and Grace's fathers based on the forged wills and the promise of funds coming; it was a tidy sum. A drop in the ocean for those wealthy men; all they lost was their pride.

Winnifred's father was smarter, and Joseph admonished himself for pushing Winnifred to marry and for presenting legacies from his father and grandfather. He had overplayed his hand, and Jacob Nash had become suspicious. Not a cent from the six months invested with that plain girl.

'Martha is the last,' he said aloud for his mother's sake, should she be looking down on him from heaven. Martha had no parents to contend with, a wonderfully large inheritance and an uncle keen to get rid of his charge.

One more, and he would begin his new life. He glanced outside and saw a constable passing and looking up at the building. Joseph ducked back behind the curtain.

Are they onto me? He needed a plan. A disguise. Joseph Facey had just the thing. His brother.

Detective Gilbert Payne and Miss Emily Yalden followed a well-established mid-week routine. Both liked their routines.

Gilbert arrived at Emily's place of abode in Bowen Hills right at 7pm, dressed in his best suit, shoes polished, hair neatly parted, flowers in hand, to escort her to dinner. Miss Emily Yalden looked sophisticated and modestly dressed in a blue gown with tasteful jewellery.

As always, Gilbert said she looked beautiful, and he was a lucky man and bound to be the envy of every man at the restaurant. This, of course, made Emily blush slightly and, most appropriately, as a lady must always accept a compliment graciously, as she taught her girls. She would admire the flowers before departing and then accept his arm, looping her hand through his, and if the restaurant was nearby and the weather fine, they would walk. Otherwise, Gilbert would retain his hansom and they would continue to the restaurant.

On their first half dozen dates, they tried a variety of places, but being creatures of habit and comfort, settled on three that they favoured, and alternated between them.

Emily insisted on paying her turn, which Gilbert would not allow, and so it was a regular topic of discussion, but the restaurants chosen were modest and of good value. Often, Mrs Payne insisted on treating the young couple, and the pair enjoyed a night out on Gilbert's mother, who heartily supported the union. Of course, Emily sent a note of thanks the next day and shared one small item of interest from the evening – their dishes, the atmosphere, the guests present.

Having ordered their favourite dishes at the Criterion Restaurant that evening, Emily lowered her voice and leaned closer.

'I had the opportunity to warn my girls today about suitors who are in a rush to secure their hand in marriage and their dowries as a result,' she said.

'Very wise of you, Emily. Especially as your ladies are most often from wealthy families.'

'Thank you, Gilbert. It was a difficult discussion to broach when I spend my days telling them not to ask inappropriate or personal questions. But as I have several heiresses in my class, they are vulnerable.'

'Do you know if they have suitors?' Gilbert asked.

'Several do, but they also have astute parents. Martha is a ward of her uncle, but she is as sharp as a knife and has a tongue to match. I believe her suitor, Benson, won't get anything over on her.'

'Benson? Do you know his surname by any chance or anything more about him?'

'Only that he is very keen to marry, which might be a concern, given her wealth. I will see what I can find out. The girls are usually very keen to talk about themselves.'

'Emily, may I say at this point—' Gilbert stopped, to Emily's frustration, as their main course arrived. Both agreed to forgo an entrée in order to enjoy a dessert.

When the waiter departed, Gilbert continued. 'As I was about to say, I have had little time to work on my poetry or thoughts of late, so I may not say this as eloquently as I hoped. I know I have only known you for a short period, and I am keenly aware you are in a more comfortable position than myself—'

'Please forgive the interruption, but that is of no consequence,' Emily assured him. She was the owner of a townhome, the funds bequeathed by a generous aunt, while Gilbert had no property to speak of.

Gilbert smiled his thanks. 'Nonetheless, I wish you to know that my intentions are sincere, and if you had nothing but your good heart to recommend you, it would be the most wonderful gift.'

Tears welled in Emily's eyes, and she blinked them away and gave a small laugh. 'I consider that most poetic.'

Gilbert gave a small smile and a nod of his head in acknowledgement. 'But regardless of your position or mine, I will work very hard to provide for you. There will be times when work demands my attention, but your happiness will always be my priority. I hope that soon, when it is appropriate, you will consider my proposal and not believe it to be rushed.'

Gilbert seemed to hold his breath after his announcement, even though it wasn't a proposal at that moment, but now would be the time for Emily to say if she were not of the same persuasion. He couldn't express the yearning inside him in words. His pulse hammered; the fear of losing her would create not only melancholic poetry but also an enormous, irreparable hole in his heart.

'I have only ever lost my heart to one man, Gilbert,' Emily confessed, and for a moment his face fell as if she was going to speak of a past love, but then Emily added, 'and that is you. When you are ready to begin our life together, I will be very proud to walk beside you.'

All thoughts of the case were forgotten, and the pair were never more in love than they were at that moment. Unlike the false love the disguised Oliver expressed to Alma, or Edwin to Grace, or Walter to Caroline or Isaac to Winnifred. Nothing like that at all. Gilbert was the happiest of men, as a poem would soon convey.

Chapter 19

LEAVING GILBERT TO HIS date, and planning to meet Dr. Tavish McGregor at the boxing club for drinks after work, Detective Harland Stone sent word of his delay and went to Mr Joseph Facey's boarding residence.

He had full faith in Phoebe, but were the spirits always right? Who is to say they were? In the past, some clues had been most ambiguous. He recalled Mrs Tochborn with her child's nursery rhyme, which Gilbert understood the significance of in that instance. Then there were the nurses who warned of their colleagues' deathly doll threats, but not of the perpetrator, leaving them chasing their tales. So he could not help but be sceptical.

'Oh, he is a lovely young man,' the landlady said after Harland made his request at the front door to see one of her tenants. 'If you will wait here in the sitting room, I shall let Mr Facey know a detective is here to see him. I do hope it is not bad news?'

'Not at all, Ma'am. I am hoping he can help me with an investigation... regarding an acquaintance of his.'

Or four aliases rather, Harland thought.

'That's a relief,' she said, hand to heart, and took to the stairs, turning left at the top of the second level and rapping on the door. Harland could not hear what was said, but the landlady returned moments later.

'He is just dressing after bathing,' she said, looking slightly flushed. 'He will be with you in ten minutes if you can wait, Detective?'

'Of course, thank you,' Harland said and, having asked the constable outside to watch the back entrance, Harland kept watch, glancing between the staircase and exterior window, in case Joseph Facey should shimmy past it.

Right on ten minutes later, a voice called from the stairwell. 'Detective, are you there? Will you come up?'

Harland appeared from beside the door. 'Mr Facey, thank you,' and took to the steps hurriedly, reaching the top and entering the man's room as invited.

But this man had a limp. Dark hair, blue eyes. Not the man Phoebe described. Had he told the landlady he was dressing after bathing to don a disguise? Was he the dark-haired cad, Edwin or Walter, who abandoned Grace and Caroline, respectively?

He also had a visible scar on his face, which no one had mentioned in their descriptions, and an iron frame protruding down below his trouser leg around his shoe.

'Would you like to sit?' the man Joseph Facey indicated a chair and took the one opposite, stretching his leg straight in front of him.

Could this be the man Phoebe spoke with, or was he a very competent performer?

'Thank you for your time, Mr Facey. You might have seen the articles in the paper about the four women who have been left at the altar and duped of their fortunes,' Harland said, not waiting for an answer. 'Members of the public have come forward and identified gentlemen they believe could be likely suspects.'

His eyes widened, and he laughed. 'Me? Oh, Detective, I am flattered. Would I be living here like this if I had amassed four inheritances? Trust me, I would be long gone.'

Harland needed to process what the man before him was saying. He was so physically different; could Phoebe have been confused? A thought occurred to him... did she see a spirit, not the living?

He returned to his questioning. 'May I ask how you hurt your leg?'

'I was born with a childhood illness, Detective; it stunted my growth. As one leg is slightly shorter than the other due to a spine injury, the iron frame balances me.'

'And the scar?'

The young man sighed. 'You recall your school years, don't you, Detective? Fellow students always pick on a boy with an ailment, and my school years were particularly hard. The weak are hunted, but you look like you might have been a hunter.'

Harland ignored the comment; it held an element of truth. 'Are you a working man, Mr Facey?'

'I will be soon, Detective. I have just moved here from down south and am living on my savings until I find work. I am a barber by trade... a profession that allows me to stand. My leg aches should I sit for too long.'

Thank you for your time, Mr Facey.' Harland rose. It was either a brilliant performance or this man was physically similar to the fiancés, but Phoebe did not see him close enough to discern that with the scar and iron frame, it could not be him.

Once outside, Harland was not quite prepared to call it a wild goose chase yet and summoned the constable when out of sight of the building. He instructed the young man to let him know if he saw a man of Mr Facey's description leave the building and note, in particular, if he walked without a limp.

'Try to be stealthy, Constable Rogers,' he told the police officer, who seemed excited about the challenge. 'I know that is difficult when you are wearing a uniform, but if you can observe without being seen, look for the scar on his face and the iron frame on his leg. He will come from the second floor.'

'Yes, Sir, I shall report to you in the morning before I finish my shift.'

Thanking the constable, Harland made his way to meet Tavish. On the way, he reviewed all aspects of the case, occasionally forgetting to acknowledge a greeting in passing until the last minute, or not heeding a nearby horse and carriage until a startled cry drew his attention.

He thought about the suitors. Two of them were very good at forging and presenting the promise of fortunes from pending wills. Was it only two men involved then, taking turns at dating a lady? The man he met today had an interesting small collection of books on his shelf, including the recently released *The Picture of Dorian Grey* by Oscar Wilde, and *The Strange Case of Dr Jekyll and Mr Hyde* by Robert Louis Stephenson. Both books are about deception and men changing character. Was it significant?

He saw no evidence of stamps or papers for forging; the desk in the corner and the tables were bare, but that does not mean the papers didn't exist. He wanted to believe Phoebe.

And then he thought of himself as the hunter. Would he have made Joseph Facey's life at school miserable, or would he have protected him? Guiltily, he felt he might not have even noticed the misery of the weaker students.

What he didn't see after his departure was the blonde-haired Joseph Facey, with whom Phoebe had spoken, emerge from the dressing room and congratulate his dark-haired brother, Benjamin, on a sterling performance.

Dr Tavish McGregor clinked his glass against Harland's in a toast, and when the current fight and its subsequent noise died down, he looked at the detective.

'Old Scottish toast,' he said and recited, 'Here's to the men of all classes, who through lasses and glasses, will make themselves asses!'

Harland laughed. 'And through fighting,' he said as a roar went up and a man went down. 'A fine piece of philosophy that.'

'It's longer and written by a reverend, believe it or not,' Tavish admitted.

'I believe it. Like us, a reverend has witnessed men at all stages of life and depravity.'

'A bleak view you have there. Go on, get the case off your chest and then you can relax awhile after,' Tavish invited him to speak. Harland gave an overview, not mentioning Phoebe's visions, and then sat back, spent.

'The bodies tell us nothing that will help your investigation. Both girls died from pining away; it's a disgrace to do that to a lady,' Tavish said with a shake of his head.

Harland agreed. 'If he had not humiliated them, they might have recovered eventually. But we'll never get him for their deaths, only for fraud and theft. That's the great pity of it.'

'Are you fighting tonight?' Tavish asked, with a glance at the rink where the next contenders lined up, full of bravado.

'No. I am still smarting from the last bout,' Harland said, gently rubbing his cheekbone. 'How long until your twin arrives?'

'A matter of weeks,' Tavish said with a grin.

'Two of you, Lord help us,' Harland smiled and let the case rest for a few hours while in the good company of another. But the persistent worry of how he might tell Phoebe the spirits were wrong constantly interrupted his evening.

Chapter 20

The usual morning meeting at *The Economic Undertaker* was a hurried affair. Enjoying their first cup of tea for the day courtesy of Mrs Dobbs and her constantly warm teapot, Randolph Astin ran through the day's requirements.

'As we have no viewings today, Lucian and his men will finish the viewing rooms and pulley system, and then the rooms will be available for bookings and for our use from tomorrow.'

'That will be brilliant, Grandpa,' Phoebe said enthusiastically. 'Every time a body is carried up and down those stairs, I fear everyone will tumble.'

'It will be great to meet the growing demand for viewings,' Julius said, pleased. 'Not to mention no more strain carrying the stretchers.'

'It is a wonderful solution,' Mrs Dobbs agreed.

'And no sleeping in there, thank you, Ambrose,' Randolph added, and the small party laughed at Ambrose's shocked expression.

'I take umbrage at that, Grandpa. I doubt it will be more comfortable than the coffin display, and I can't rest just anywhere.'

As usual, Julius sighed and shook his head at his brother's antics, causing Phoebe to giggle as Randolph grinned and hurried on.

'I have two bookings this morning to discuss funeral packages,' he said and gave Mrs Dobbs the times, who noted them in order to have tea prepared. 'There is a load of fabric to collect from the drapers for the ladies' next door. I have Claude and Charlie doing that in the trap this morning.'

'Oh, good, Violet is waiting on some white lace for a wedding dress,' Phoebe said.

'And why are you excited about that? Is it your dress? Is there something we should know?' Ambrose teased her, leaning forward with expectation.

'No, but when that day comes, I shall definitely ask Miss Pollard to make my dress. The bride-to-be ordered Brussels lace for her dress, and I am keen to see it.'

'Oh, how lovely and extravagant,' Mrs Dobbs said.

'Then why is she using *Beyond the Veil* and not a more exclusive dressmaker?' Ambrose asked.

'We are an exclusive dressmaker,' Julius reminded him. 'Violet's wedding dress in the window is an original gown created by Miss Pollard, and Violet tells me we have had quite a few orders for it. Even an order for it to be made in black fabric as a mourning wear design. I am not sure how I feel about that.'

'Goodness me,' Mrs Dobbs said, blessing herself as she often did at *The Economic Undertaker* kitchen table in matters of life and death.

'How striking,' Randolph agreed, and hurried on. 'Ambrose, there is a funeral at 1pm. The body is to be collected at 12noon from the family's home, and they will follow the hearse on foot to the nearby Toowong Cemetery. Reverend Cummins is officiating. Before that, however, could you go via the police morgue and collect a body for Phoebe?'

'Oh, for the drawing, excellent,' she said, and explained, 'Detective Ashdown needs a sketch done of an unidentified lady.'

'The poor woman,' Mrs Dobbs said, blessing herself again.

'Indeed, let's hope we can assist,' Randolph said. 'Phoebe, if you can have your sketch finished by tomorrow morning or late today, the detective would be grateful.'

'I shall do it as soon as I receive the body, Grandpa. I have no other bodies in-house.'

'Thank you, dear. And Julius, I believe you are seeing your bookkeeper this morning and paying the accounts. This afternoon, you and Lucian are meeting with Mrs Ingliss and her son, Jack, at the carpentry store at two o'clock about an apprenticeship. Right then, that is a busy enough day,' Randolph concluded.

'Wait. Stop. Are you not accompanying me again today, Brother?' Ambrose asked, surprised.

'No. I am sure you and Will can manage. I have appointments,' Julius said.

Ambrose's face fell.

'Harland mentioned he would drop in if they had an update on Mr Joseph Facey,' Phoebe said. 'He was going to put the man under observation last night.' She quickly filled in her family. 'Will you be in-house later in the morning, Julius?'

'I cannot say, but I don't need to be on hand when he speaks with you.' Julius rose. 'Thank you, Grandpa, and thank you for the tea, Mrs Dobbs. I shall get to my appointment with the bookkeeper then.'

With that, Julius exited the room, his siblings looking after him. Mrs Dobbs rose and cleared the table.

'That was odd,' Phoebe said in a low voice. 'Is Julius all right, Grandpa?'

Ambrose added, 'Except for his honeymoon and the time Charlie stabbed him, we have never missed two days of working together. What has gotten into him?'

'Perhaps he has listened to the pair of you when you said you did not need him around as much these days,' Randolph said, a note of sadness in his voice.

'I did not say that—' Ambrose exclaimed.

'When did I imply I did not need him?' Phoebe spoke over her brother.

'Maybe not in words. Best you both get to it,' Randolph said, rising. 'Julius has appointments to ensure the family business remains viable. Let us support that.'

He saw his youngest grandchildren exchange looks and was pleased. Some self-reflection might be to their benefit, and some consideration of Julius, whom it was easy to take for granted as he had always been there for the family, would do them good.

The young constable on the night shift arrived in the office of Detective Harland Stone early before finishing his shift and going home to his bed.

'Ah, Constable Rogers, thank you for calling in.' Harland welcomed the young police officer to take a seat in front of his desk and went to sit opposite. He introduced Detective Payne as the young detective entered the office bearing two cups of tea.

'Good morning,' Gilbert said, placing one cup of tea on Harland's desk and returning to his own with the other and taking a seat. 'I believe you were watching Joseph Facey last evening.'

'Yes, and I can report that no one of his description left the building.'

Harland exhaled, disappointed. 'I had hoped he might have departed without a limp so we could prove he was not the man he claimed to be last evening.'

'Did you take note of any other occupants leaving the building, Constable?' Gilbert asked.

'Yes, Sir.' The constable retrieved his small notebook and leafed through the pages until he reached last night's notes. 'Around nine o'clock, an elderly man went into the building. A lady arrived at 10.45 pm and left at 11.30pm. I believe she was a lady of the night,' he said and cleared his throat before continuing. 'And another tall, blond man left just before midnight and did not return.'

Harland's eyes widened. 'What did he look like, Constable? As much detail as you can remember.'

'I noted it, Sir. He was easily six feet in height, with fair hair, and walked confidently with no limp. He had a brown duffle bag over one shoulder that seemed full, and was hurrying, Sir, as if late for a liaison. The man was wearing a hat, but the wind removed it, and he dropped his bag to hurry after it. That is how I saw he had fair hair. He was clean shaven but had side-burns.' The constable showed the length with his fingers.

'And he did not return?'

'Not before I departed at seven o'clock this morning, Sir.'

'Excellent work, Constable. Thank you for your diligence,' Harland said. 'I will commend you to your superior this very day.'

'Thank you, Sir,' the constable grinned. 'It was my pleasure.'

'You have a detective in you, young man,' Harland said. 'To your bed now, and Detective Payne and I shall visit the premises again and see what we can find out this morning.'

The young constable departed, and Harland looked toward Gilbert, who had risen and was standing before the board, frowning.

'That must have been the man Phoebe spoke with, but he was definitely not the man who spoke with me, unless he was in costume.' Harland sighed. 'He had dark hair, a scar and an iron frame on his leg... and I have been taken for a fool.'

Gilbert replied loyally. 'He is a con man of the highest order, Sir, and fooled some of our city's best businessmen. Besides, it may be two different men.'

'Thank you, Gilbert, that is some consolation, but the landlady only mentioned one tenant, Mr Facey, living there.'

'Unless she doesn't know.'

'True. Let us be sure it was our cad in disguise or see if anyone else is present. We'll visit Mr Joseph Facey again now. I bet he has departed and left a cheque for his landlady that will be worthless.' Harland rose and donned his jacket.

'Yes, Sir,' Gilbert said and then stepped back and gasped.

'What is wrong?' Harland asked, wheeling around, alarmed.

'How could I not have seen it? I have let you down, Sir.'

'I doubt that, Gilbert, as I haven't seen whatever it is, either,' Harland said, joining Gilbert at the board, looking for enlightenment.

'He loves puzzles. Mr Nash said Winnifred's fiancé, Isaac Wenton, loves puzzles!' Gilbert grinned. 'I believe Miss Astin was right, Sir. I think we will find Joseph Facey and his disguises gone.'

'Why? What has brought about this confirmation?' Harland asked impatiently.

Gilbert pointed at the four fiancés' names. 'Joseph Facey might be his real name, but the names he used when courting the ladies are all anagrams.'

'Anagrams,' Harland repeated, looking at Gilbert's list of names.

Oliver Newton, Isaac Wenton, Edwin Ownnet and Walter Tewnon.

'They are all the same surname – Newton, Wenton, Ownnet, Tewnon, just the letters jumbled,' Gilbert said with a shake of his head. 'One name, four uses.'

'Excellent work, Gilbert; we've linked the crimes now,' Harland said with a satisfied smile. 'Let's see if Joseph Facey has departed. To think I had him within my reach last night!' He wrung his hands before grabbing his hat, and Harland hurriedly departed. Gilbert scrambled for his hat and caught up with him in the hallway.

As expected, they soon discovered that the man had quit his room. The landlady would not hear a bad word spoken about him.

'Mr Facey left this morning, early, detectives. He explained that a family member was ill and was most apologetic and distressed. He has left me a month's rent to cover his absence and plenty of time to find a new tenant.'

'And he was the only tenant?' Harland clarified.

'Yes. I have my rules and charge more if two are sharing a room.'

'Was that rent paid in the form of a cheque, Ma'am?' Gilbert asked.

'Yes, I shall bank it today.'

'We fear it will be valueless,' Harland warned her.

'The job has made you mistrusting of human nature, Detective,' she said curtly, and they bid her good day.

'I hope we are wrong, for her sake,' Gilbert said.

They were not. The ever cordial and charming Mr Facey had duped his landlady, and one of the police department's finest.

Chapter 21

In Julius's absence, Ambrose was to manage this afternoon's funeral, and he didn't like it, not one bit. It was never his ambition to be the boss, and he would rather focus on his date tonight, walking Miss Billie Prout home. He had lain awake at night since seeing her in the cemetery, imagining walking beside her, kissing, loving, and caring for Miss Prout. Billie.

Who was he fooling? If Ambrose was honest with himself, he looked forward to sparring with the beauty. She always got a rise out of him, and he hoped to give as good as he got. She captivated him, and most pleasing, she seemed to like him foremost, not his brother. Intriguingly, unlike his former belle, Kate, Billie Prout did not appear to gush for him. In truth, she disturbed him in all the right ways.

'Slow down,' Will whispered, 'you are losing the followers.'

Ambrose's eyes widened in alarm, and he glanced back. 'Good Lord, sorry, I was thinking of... something else.'

'Tonight's date with Miss Prout?' Will asked drily. In his mid-twenties, the senior stable hand to Claude and Charlie, who had been in the employ of *The Economic Undertaker* for several years and recently promoted, would likely be better in the management role, but it was a family business.

'Of course I would rather think of the lovely Miss Prout. I have wasted hours, days, weeks not knowing her, and now she might be my future,' Ambrose said and smiled.

Will squeezed his shoulder. 'Then I hope as much for you.'

Ambrose thanked him. 'There are the gates; we are almost there. Do you know what is wrong with Julius?'

'Julius has not started confiding in me,' Will said, making Ambrose chuckle, then quickly sober. 'He might confide in his wife.'

'Of course, Violet,' Ambrose said, slowing the horses as they arrived at the site of the grave where more mourners and the reverend waited.

'I thought he seemed his usual self,' Will added.

'Perhaps with you, but he is avoiding me. Unbelievable, I know, when I am such good company,' Ambrose joked as he stopped the hearse and the men alighted to remove the body.

Ambrose went through the motions of the funeral, twice nudged by Will to step up, or assist a grieving person to a chair. He was impatient to get back and would corner Julius this afternoon and demand an answer. Was it not bad enough he was nervous about this evening's walk without worrying about Julius?

He enjoyed Will's company, but today marked their second day as partners, and he missed the comfortable banter with his brother. Besides, he wanted Julius's advice on what to do tonight.

'You are definitely not here today,' Will said as they drove the empty hearse through the gates, having paid the grave diggers and bid the reverend good day.

'I am sorry, Will. Tell me how you met your wife?'

'Elly and I have always known each other. We went to the same church, the same school; our families were friends. When we were old enough, she became my sweetheart, and it has always been Will and Elly.'

'Now you've got your little son as well,' Ambrose sighed. 'I've never known that certainty of love.' He navigated a corner, doffing his hat to two elderly women who watched the hearse go by. 'I thought about marrying Kate and I was mad about Lilly, but...' he gave a shrug.

'My mother always says love finds you when you are not looking,' Will said. 'Well, that's what she tells my sister, who is keen to marry but has no prospects in sight. And no, I'm not saying that to push her your way. We don't need to be brothers.'

Ambrose chuckled but repeated the saying; 'Love finds you when you are not looking. Then I shall pretend to look away and see what happens.'

Mrs Ingliss was too weary to be wary or nervous about the meeting at the carpentry store. Mr Julius Astin had extended a great kindness to her, burying her husband free of charge, and the gift of the mourning dresses several days later showed great compassion. She believed that only a person who had been through some suffering would be as astute.

Now she wondered if he was seeking some kind of recompense. But asking her to bring Jack along to the appointment challenged that idea.

'We shall see what this is about, Jack, and then get on our way,' she said to her 15-year-old-son. 'Put your head up and don't shuffle your feet.' With a final tweak of his hair and a roll of the eyes from Jack, they entered the premises, noting the large back area where much activity was being undertaken.

'You must be Mrs Ingliss and this is Jack?' Lucian's secretary greeted them with a smile and showed them through to Lucian's office, where Mrs Ingliss saw the two men looking over paperwork. Both men rose as she entered. 'I believe you have met Mr Julius Astin, and this is Mr Lucian Astin.'

Declining a cup of tea, Mrs Ingliss thanked the secretary and, feeling most uncomfortable, said, 'I can see you are busy but I am pleased to have the opportunity to thank you again, Mr Astin for—'

Julius raised his hand. 'You have done so already, Mrs Ingliss, and I was pleased to be of service. I beg, do not think of it again.' He offered Mrs Ingliss a chair, and Jack took the seat beside her. 'My cousin has a proposal, which I hope will be of interest to you both.'

'Mrs Ingliss, Jack, I am pleased to say carpentry services are in great demand,' Lucian began, 'and I recently apprenticed Julius's brother-in-law, but am now in need of another apprentice. Julius mentioned to me he had met a hard-working young man who was good with his hands, and I wondered...'

The pair said nothing for a moment and then Jack exclaimed, 'Me?' He looked at his mother and back at Lucian. 'You would apprentice me?'

Mrs Ingliss sat forward, a look of surprise and delight on her face. 'You are seeking a carpentry apprentice and you would consider my son, Jack?'

'If it is something that would interest Jack, yes. We could take a tour and show you what we create,' Lucian suggested.

Jack looked at his mother and beamed. 'An apprenticeship.'

'Have you built anything of your own before, Jack?' Lucian asked, and the young boy shook his head.

'We don't have the money for tools, Mr Astin,' Jack said. 'But Mr Connors next door lends me his tools to do repairs and basic stuff. I've fixed the fence and kitchen cupboards, and I'm good at fixing things, aren't I, Mum?'

'He is very capable and always sees a job through. I am sure you would find him a most diligent employee, Mr Astin.'

'What are your school marks like, Jack?' Julius asked.

The young man's face fell. 'They are average, Sir,' he said honestly. 'I am good at arithmetic and drawing, but not good at writing and grammar.'

'You will do fine then,' Julius said and smiled at Jack's surprised expression. 'Well, if you will excuse me, I need to get back to the office and shall leave you with Lucian to discuss the finer details.' Julius rose and thanked his cousin.

Mrs Ingliss jumped to her feet. 'Mr Astin, you must know your kindness has changed our lives for the better.'

'That's kind of you to say, Mrs Ingliss, but I only opened a few doors, as others helped my family when we were in the same situation in my youth. Good luck, Jack.'

The young man shook Julius's hand enthusiastically, and Julius headed to the corner to catch the omnibus back to the office. As he arrived, he saw the hearse slightly ahead, going too fast, and he sighed. *Ambrose!*

Chapter 22

REPORTER LILLY LEWIS WAS in a hurry to get to the police station to meet the detectives for a briefing. Looking up, she smiled triumphantly at her writing partner, Fergus, and held out her copy. 'I believe we have met the deadline.'

'And just,' he said, taking her copy to add to his own and file with the editor. 'You have time, hurry off then.'

'Tomorrow then, thank you dear Fergus,' she said, and bidding the reporters around her good day, Lilly took to the steps and rushed out of the offices of *The Courier*. She lifted the skirt of her sky-blue dress, and with a hand on her hat, paced along the street to hail a ride. Then she heard a familiar voice calling.

'Miss Lilly Lewis, halt immediately!'

Turning her head without breaking stride, it took Lilly a moment to stop when she saw who was hailing her. She grinned at seeing the handsome Bennet Martin learning from a hansom, hand extended for her to climb in. Lilly rushed to him, accepted his hand, and once settled inside, her eyes took in his most dashing appearance.

That a man of Bennet's standing found her interesting.... To hear Lilly's father speak of her dreadful job and her reckless nature, she had come to believe she would be on the shelf unless a man was desperate.

'As always, your timing is perfect,' she thanked him as she settled beside him.

'I received an invitation to the same briefing, and I knew you would rush to get there after your late deadline.'

'You are the best man I know,' she said, sighing and leaning against him, as the hansom continued on.

'Seriously? Better than your father?'

'Well, definitely as good as my dad, and better looking.'

'And your brothers? Am I a better man than they?' he teased her, and she hit his arm.

'Remind me to compliment you in the vaguest of terms next time. I will say you are a good person and reasonably handsome and be done with it.'

He chuckled. 'You are the best woman I know, and the loveliest. Not to mention the most talented.'

She laughed. 'I bet you say that to all the reporters you know. Do you have an update or a clue?'

'Yes, the former. Do you?'

'Yes. I bet mine is better than yours,' Lilly teased.

'Oh, I doubt that. I'll have you know I am a very skilled private investigator. My name has appeared in *The Courier* quite a few times.'

'How impressive!' Lilly laughed, being the one who wrote the articles featuring the private investigator's name.

'Indeed. I am surprised that you can keep your lips off me.'

Lilly smiled and shook her head at his brazenness. Looking up at him and leaning in, she granted him a kiss or two until the driver announced they had arrived at Roma Street Police Headquarters. Bennet, mumbling that of course today there were no obstructions to their journey, helped Lilly—who needed no help—alight.

When Julius arrived back in the office, not long after the hearse had arrived in the backyard, he walked in to find Ambrose standing in the foyer and his grandfather completing the diary appointments for the next day.

'Ah, you are back,' Ambrose stated the obvious.

'Yes. Here I am. Did all go well?' Julius asked, greeting his grandfather, hanging up his hat and giving Rufus—who was most pleased to see him—the required several minutes of attention before the large dog would settle.

'As well as can be expected,' Ambrose said. 'We buried the deceased; the mourners mourned, and the reverend imparted blessings.'

They heard Phoebe climbing the stairs from her room, and on arrival, she greeted her family. 'I have finished the illustration, Grandpa,' she said, drawing in hand. 'I am expecting Harland in an hour to walk me home. Perhaps he could take this with him and give it to Detective Ashdown tomorrow.'

'Ah, thank you, dear. May I?' Randolph asked.

'Of course,' Phoebe said.

Taking the illustration and unrolling it, Randolph said, 'A remarkable likeness, Phoebe; you are a deft hand. I shall ask Claude to take it now, and he can head straight home afterwards. Detective Ashdown will appreciate getting it sooner.'

'I shall head off early too, if no objections. I'm walking Miss Prout home this evening,' Ambrose announced smugly, as if this were news they hadn't heard a dozen times since the date was confirmed. He leant over to check the first appointment for tomorrow and slammed his hand down on the desk.

Phoebe jumped.

'Ambrose!' Randolph berated him, and the room stilled. Ambrose angry was a rare sight.

'I'm not partnered with you again tomorrow!" He glared at Julius. 'Two funerals and you are missing both?'

'I have meetings to attend,' Julius said with indifference.

'Then I am not attending either,' Ambrose declared. 'Grandpa, Claude and Will can do the funerals; I will do other work.'

'Other work?' Julius stared at his brother, trying to read him, before turning to his grandfather. 'I shall do the funerals with Claude.'

'And now you are free? No! No, Julius, this ends now,' Ambrose said.

'Why don't you both go into the meeting room, close the door and discuss this?' Randolph said with a nod to the nearest empty room. 'You are distressing the ladies.'

Julius noted how uncomfortable Phoebe appeared, and Mrs Dobbs quickened her departure, her shift done, and a wave in their direction. Julius headed to the nearest room, where Randolph met with his clients. Ambrose followed and closed the door behind him.

The pair stared at each other. 'What did you wish to say?' Julius asked.

'What is going on? You have abandoned your post without explanation, and I assume I have done something—unbeknown to me—to annoy you.'

'Not at all,' Julius said, surprised. 'I am not angry at you, nor have any reason to be so. Are you angry with me?'

'Yes. Why are you not working with me? Tell me now and be upfront about this,' Ambrose demanded, leaning over a chair, his hands on the meeting table.

Julius took his position, lounging in the window seat. 'I listened to your request, and I am giving you more freedom to work without me.'

'What request?' Ambrose spluttered, surprised. 'I didn't request that. I enjoy working together. Don't you?'

'I did. But you have made it clear my appearance has ruined your chance at love and that you would rather I were seen less in your company.'

'No, I did not say that! Well, I did not mean that. I just meant that if Miss Lewis had not seen you, perhaps she might have considered me.'

'And if I recall, you requested I keep well clear of Miss Prout. As I do not know when we might encounter her on a job, nor wish to be a burden to you, Ambrose, I am sparing you of my company.'

'That is not what I intended when I—'

Julius cut him off and continued. 'You may not know that Grandpa and Uncle Reggie were estranged because they both loved Grandma. It was enough to separate them for life. I couldn't conceive of that, but I could not rule out that you might as easily wish me out of your life.'

'No, Julius. That is ridiculous.'

'So, I am giving you freedom. You are a man now, and you and Phoebe do not need my protection.' Julius stopped and exhaled. Baring his soul and saying so much of an emotional nature had taken it out of him, and he watched and waited, as Ambrose stared at him, incredulous.

'No. That was never my intention,' Ambrose said in a conciliatory tone. 'It was a throwaway line I meant in jest. I would never permit a woman to come between us, nor would I ever separate from you or the family. We are closer because of what happened to Mum and Dad, and nothing will change that. Nothing.'

'Thank you, Brother, but nonetheless, it is good for us both to make our own way in the world. As I cover for Grandpa two days a week and you work with Will on those days, what does it matter if it extends over the week? You could partner with Claude occasionally if you prefer. You are the manager; work it out with Grandpa.'

'I do not prefer,' Ambrose said angrily, before softening. 'Do not do this, Julius. Forgive me for being so glib and ungrateful.'

Julius shook his head. 'There is nothing to forgive, and I am the one grateful to you for the work you do. But I have thought a great deal about your comments, and I believe you are right. You and Phoebe will soon have your own families, as I have now with Violet and Tom. Inevitably, we will go our own ways.'

'Why do we have to change just because we have our own families? Would it not strengthen us, as we all spend more time together as an extended family?'

'Time will tell,' Julius said. 'But for now, I am stepping back from what both of my siblings most likely consider interfering. Of course, I am always here if you need me.' He delivered the words with a coolness from having rehearsed them in his head. He had been expecting this confrontation, and he did not want it known that his siblings' indifference injured him.

'I need you now,' Ambrose said, surprising Julius with his vulnerability. 'I enjoy my job because I do it with you. Because of the comfortable companionship we share, and the history we have together on the job. The tragic, the funny, the odd, it is all more enjoyable because we do it together,' he said, pacing, agitated. 'When I do the funerals with Will or Claude, it is just a job and not one I want. Work with me, Julius, or I do not want to work here at all.'

Julius's eyes widened in surprise, and he rose, coming over to the table. 'Did you want to try your hand at another company, something completely different?' he asked curiously.

'No!' Ambrose exclaimed and rolled his eyes. 'I am loyal to the family business, and as such, I want to work with the family. With you.'

'And what if I see Miss Prout when we are out and about? Am I to hide in the hearse or behind a headstone?'

Normally, Ambrose would have accepted this suggestion with a laugh, but instead, drove his point home. 'You met her first and have already seen her several times. Yet, she still likes me,' he said with a small smile. 'A lady of good taste.'

Julius gave a small huff of laughter and shook his head at his brother's always present confidence, even if it was often bravado.

'I need your advice,' Ambrose added, and Julius gave a small groan.

'I don't think so. Go walk your lady friend home; the hour is approaching.'

'I do want your advice,' Ambrose insisted. 'I have enjoyed little success in matters of the heart, and I don't want to ruin this.'

'And you think I have been successful in love?' Julius scoffed. 'I nearly lost Violet several times, and before that, I met women who fell for my looks, as you would say, but did not like this business. Who am I to offer advice?'

'My brother,' Ambrose said. 'If not advice, tell me what you would do tonight on this first date. It may be a long walk. How should I approach it?'

Julius thought for a moment.

'Please,' Ambrose added.

Julius sighed. 'We are very different people, so my suggestion is to be yourself. It is tiresome trying to be something else for someone else. You are fun and charming, and Miss Prout has already expressed an interest in you.'

'I was that way with Lilly and Kate too, to no avail.'

'Do you really want me to be honest with you? To tell you my observations?' Julius asked and pondered the risk.

'Desperately.'

He hesitated before saying, 'Then you were not yourself with Miss Lewis or Miss Kirby. You set your cap at Miss Lewis when she was clearly not interested and set yourself up for failure. Once I was with Violet and out of the picture, you might have tried again. Miss Kirby was infatuated with you; it took little effort on your behalf to please her, but you were not truly engaged. You were in love with the way she loved you, and that is a very easy trap to fall into when you are recovering from feelings for another.'

Ambrose thought for a moment. 'I accept all that is true. So why will it be different now? I am delighted Miss Prout notices me, but how do I keep her interest?'

Julius looked uncomfortable. 'This is my opinion only, and if you repeat it, I shall deny it.'

'Agreed. Go on,' Ambrose said keenly.

'I believe there is a reason a beauty like Miss Prout remains single,' Julius said. 'Men are enamoured of her, flatter her, and bend to her will. I doubt they listen to her. That is insulting and boring to intelligent ladies like Miss Prout, Phoebe, and Violet.'

'Yes, it is an easy trap to fall into when she is so charming and attractive,' Ambrose conceded. 'What should I do?'

'Be yourself and allow Miss Prout to do the same. Invite her opinions and listen, but do not change yours to fit, Ambrose. Be the man. If you decide on something, then do it. Unless her persuasion makes more sense, then you can bow to her wisdom and let her know you agree. But you need to show her you are strong enough and a man of principle. Miss Prout is a very strong woman, bold enough to approach me on matters of business and to succeed in a very manly business. She needs a man to be the same, or she will walk all over you and lose interest.'

'Yes. I see,' Ambrose said, eyes narrowing as he thought about his brother's words. 'Yes, thank you, Brother.'

Julius moved toward the door. 'And good luck.'

Ambrose grinned, and hurrying after his brother, added, 'I will tell Grandpa we are working together tomorrow as usual, yes?'

'If you wish,' Julius said. Exiting, he could not help but smile as he collected Rufus before heading next door to meet his wife.

Chapter 23

HARLAND APPEARED PARTICULARLY FRUSTRATED and contrite when reporter Lilly Lewis and private investigator Bennet Martin hurried into the shared office of the detectives. He was pacing, hands fisted, with a look of concern upon his countenance.

'Whatever is the matter, Detective Stone?' Lilly asked.

'You look most glum, Harland,' Bennet offered and closed the door behind him as requested.

'Glum indeed and frustrated, Bennet, Miss Lewis. We have had some developments,' Harland said, 'and we believe Phoebe was right. The four suitors appear to be one man, a very convincing actor whom I have allowed to elude me.'

'Well, you did say not to ignore Phoebe's warning, and that there was likely something in it,' Lilly reminded him.

'Did I?' Harland said, brightening. 'I am pleased about that, but I have let the man slip from my grasp. Gilbert, however, has discovered why he is likely the one man. Shall we begin? Will you update Miss Lewis and Bennet, Gilbert?'

'Yes, Sir,' Gilbert said, rising and going to the board as Lilly and Bennet took their seats at the meeting room table and Harland continued to pace. Gilbert explained what they had uncovered.

'Oh my, an anagram. I didn't see that. You are brilliant, Detective Payne,' Lilly said admiringly.

'Thank you, Miss Lewis, but I should have seen that much earlier, especially as Miss Winnifred Nash's fiancé, Isaac Wenton, was said to love puzzles. I am annoyed with myself,' he confessed.

'A fine pair you are,' Bennet said. 'It is part of the role of an investigator to unearth some truths, miss a few clues and wrap them all up at the end, when you hopefully catch the criminal. Do not be so hard on yourselves.'

'Thank you, Bennet,' Harland said, 'but I have put the case back now by letting Joseph Facey slip away.'

'So we are looking for one man, a very clever disguise artist and clearly a master forger,' Bennet said. 'My news? Well, I spoke with the bank teller, Mr Bailey Sutton, who released Mr Gardner and Mr Edmonstone's advances by accepting the forged wills.'

'Excellent,' Harland said, now sitting at the table as Gilbert remained at the board.

'As Mr Gardner is a very large customer of the bank, Mr Sutton admitted they did not do their customary checks. They assumed that if Mr Gardner believed the papers were legitimate, then they had no reason to question him as the money was coming out of the sizeable Gardner account and not an advance from the bank.'

'And it was the same when Mr Edmonstone presented similar paperwork?' Harland said.

'Exactly so. However, Mr Sutton said he had tried to warn Mr Edmonstone of the strange case a year ago and the forged papers. But Mr Edmonstone insisted that his future son-in-law, Edwin, could be present for any conversation, and the pair dismissed the warning. They seemed very close, according to Mr Sutton.'

'Which makes the betrayal even worse,' Lilly said.

Bennet agreed. 'I believe the teller was in earnest and had no reason to consider anything nefarious was underway. I took the liberty of speaking with his manager, and he assured me, after a discrete enquiry, that there were no large sums of money that had appeared in the young bank teller's account, and he vouched for his honesty.'

'Thank you, Bennet; that's excellent. Assuming Joseph Facey might be our rogue's real name, I will enquire to see if he has a bank account and funds under that name,' Harland said, and his lips thinned in anger at being fooled.

'On that, the teller told me that Edwin Ownnet took the funds with him, saying he had his own business account with another institution,' Bennet finished.

'I bet he did. It was very clever to get the money out of the bank and tucked away elsewhere,' Harland mused. 'So it is unlikely he would have gone back to bank the money in an account for Joseph Facey, unless in disguise.'

They all looked around on hearing a rap on the door; it opened to reveal the desk sergeant.

'Apologies for the interruption, but a cranky lady just left this for you. I told her you were in a meeting, but she insisted it was important and I give it to you urgently.'

'Thank you, John,' Harland said. 'Has she departed?'

'Yes, she chose not to speak with you directly; you've been spared,' John said with a grin before departing.

Harland placed the heavy item wrapped in brown paper and string on the table and read the note, saying, 'Gilbert, this will not surprise you. It is from the landlady of Joseph Facey. The cheque was fake, and he left this behind. She offers an apology for mistrusting us.'

Harland unwrapped the item to find an iron leg brace. 'So much for his childhood illness that made one leg shorter than the other,' he said with annoyance, placing it back on the table. 'Miss Lewis, what have you then?'

'What a master of disguise,' Miss Lewis said, looking at the leg frame before beginning. 'While we are on the subject of the fiancé Edwin Ownnet and Mr Edmonstone, the latter granted Fergus an interview, given they had formed an acquaintance during Fergus's shipping news days. He spoke with him for a good hour, and I summarised the salient points. But there is one in particular that will greatly interest you all.'

'Do tell, Miss Lewis, what is that?' Harland asked, his interest piqued.

'The very next morning after the wedding cancellation, the Edmonstone family received a card and gift. I have the card.' Lilly pulled it from her notepad and gave it to the detective.

'And Mr Edmonstone kept this?' Harland asked.

'Yes, it accompanied a piece of wedding cake.'

'Oh, that is heartless,' Gilbert said.

'Yes, detective,' Lilly agreed. 'Mr. Edmonstone, as you can imagine, was incensed, but he kept it from his daughter Grace and his wife.'

'And he kept it from us,' Harland said drily.

'Yes, but he allowed Fergus to give it to me for your information,' Lilly said.

Harland read the card and huffed in disbelief. 'It reads: *"Dear Grace was plain but kind, and I am not sorry to leave her behind. Signed, The Vanishing Groom."'*

'I am very pleased Mr Edmonstone did not tell his daughter or wife of such cruel correspondence,' Gilbert said.

'But now we have another clue,' Harland said. 'Where is he purchasing a slice of wedding cake from, and did all the jilted brides get one?'

'I shall add bakers to our list to visit along with theatres, Sir,' Gilbert said.

'Was there more, Miss Lewis?' Harland asked, keen to hear anything that might advance his cause to arrest Joseph Facey.

'Yes,' Lilly lightly cleared her throat. 'The sum he advanced to Mr Edwin Ownnet was five hundred pounds.'

'Good Lord,' Gilbert exclaimed from the board. It would take the young detective years in the job to make that amount.

'An outrageous amount,' Harland said.

Even Bennet, who came from money, agreed and reminded them, 'But if Edwin had that much coming to him in wills, then Mr Edmonstone could be sure of getting it back.'

Lilly continued. 'The fiancé also claimed he had very good connections in the shipping industry in the mother country. He told Mr Edmonstone that he had written to introduce his future father-in-law and advance his business interests in Great Britain.'

Bennet huffed. 'He had the old man wrapped around his little finger.'

'That is all I have to report,' Lilly said.

'Very insightful and much appreciated, Miss Lewis,' Harland thanked her.

'May I add some concerning information?' Gilbert asked and continued. 'Emily is worried that one of her young ladies might be at risk.' Gilbert briefed the group on Miss Martha Hampstead and her beau, Benson. 'The Hampstead surname was on the list of the country's wealthiest a few years ago – she is to inherit shortly, on her 21st birthday. I do not know his surname yet, but he is keen to marry, according to the young lady. Emily is going to try to discover more, as discreetly as she can.'

'Benson. I wonder if his surname will also be one of the anagrams,' Lilly mused, reading the names on the board.

'Yes, that will be telling,' Harland agreed. 'Why does he continue when surely he has enough money by now?'

'Compulsion maybe, Sir,' Gilbert said. 'I read in one of my science magazines that an English defence counsel used it to defend a petty thief, excusing him because he apparently couldn't control his actions.'

Harland huffed. 'If this man tries that line of defence, I shall see to his punishment myself.'

'I know a very good grave digger,' Bennet suggested, and the group laughed.

'Thank you all for your contributions. We are advancing,' Harland said, sobering. 'This is a man who has meticulously chosen his victims and spent a good year wooing each one and their families. He knows how to con and present documents that are as good as the originals. He is cruel, clever and cunning. But he will have slipped up.'

'May I write of its possibly being one man? That is a wonderful story with the surname anagrams,' Lilly said. 'And, as Fergus was given the card sent to the jilted bride, we would like to run with that story, too.'

'As you discovered that clue, I will not stop you, Miss Lewis. But please do not list all the surnames. That will send him fleeing if he is currently wooing his fifth bride, and I want him to pay. I know it is newsworthy and I assure you that you will have the story, I just ask for your cooperation a little longer,' Harland requested, and as the small party said their farewells and departed for the night, he knew it was time to face Phoebe and admit his failures.

Chapter 24

Ambrose felt ridiculously nervous for a man who was usually so well put together around the ladies, or so he and cousin Lucian told each other on their nights out at the club. But perhaps there was no lady before who had caused his heart to flutter like Miss Billie Prout, and now that all was well in the world with himself and Julius again, he felt relieved and present.

He had worn his best suit and shirt, his newest hat, and had spruced up before arriving. As Ambrose approached the door of Prout Monumental Masons, it opened, and the beautiful Billie Prout stepped out in a light blue dressed fitted to her curves with a fetching straw hat and matching ribbon.

'You are timely, Mr Astin.'

'I would never keep a lady waiting, Miss Prout, unless, of course, I am delayed by the dead in the process of burial.'

'As it should be,' she agreed. 'I only see their plots, so they are rarely waiting for me.'

'I will pay my respects to your father before we depart. Is he in?' Ambrose asked.

'Yes, but there is no need to do so. He knows I do not stand on ceremony and you are only walking me home this evening,' she said, and moved from the door to take his arm.

'Ah, but I will stand on ceremony. Will you introduce us?' Ambrose said, standing firm. Before his talk with Julius this afternoon, he would have given in to Billie's wishes, but he wanted to begin right. It was a courtesy to meet her father, and he would do so.

'Of course,' she said, surprised, and he held the door for her as they entered the business. Billie led the way to a small office at the back, and Ambrose acknowledged the business employees as he passed, greeting several he recognised from crossing paths in the cemeteries. He stood back as Billie knocked on her father's door and entered.

'Pa, may I introduce Mr Ambrose Astin?'

Her father stood as Ambrose entered the office. 'Mr Prout, how are you, Sir?'

'Very well, Mr Astin, very well. It is a pleasure to meet you. I'm sorry I couldn't attend when my daughter presented to your company; my attendance wasn't permitted,' he said, giving his daughter an affectionate look as she laughed.

'The ladies know their minds,' Ambrose said. 'My sister is our mortician, and my sister-in-law runs our merchandise business most capably. We don't readily admit it, but Grandma manages us all.'

Mr Prout grinned. 'We wouldn't have it any other way, would we? Will you sit down?'

'No, Pa, we will get going,' Billie said.

'I wish to have your daughter home before dark,' Ambrose agreed. 'The winter days are short.'

'Then let us catch up another time. Perhaps Billie might bring you to dinner,' the kindly man, who shared Billie's finer, fair features, said.

'Thank you, Mr Prout, I would be happy to accept should she invite me,' Ambrose said in jest.

Departing, Billie put her arm through his offered arm, as Ambrose walked on the roadside to protect her.

'Well, aren't you charming?' she teased.

'Yes, I am,' Ambrose joked, making her laugh. 'Have you been thinking of me since I saw you in the most romantic of locations, the cemetery?'

'Oh, non-stop,' Billie assured him. 'I've even plotted the longest way to walk home. Have my designs been selling well?'

'As the Operations Manager, I can report that there has been considerable interest in them. Long term, I imagine your headstone with the roses will be one of our best sellers.'

'I am pleased. Did you check those figures before you met me tonight?' she asked teasingly.

'Of course. I knew you would ask me,' he nudged her. 'I update the figures weekly to report to Julius. We don't influence our customers' choice of headstones, though. We simply present them by price bracket.'

'As you must, being *The Economic Undertaker.*'

'Indeed. So,' Ambrose continued, 'if they are selling well, then there is much to recommend them in the design.'

Billie beamed. 'Thank you for the compliment.'

'And what have you done this week since last I saw you?' Ambrose asked, having prepared several topics in his head should silence prevail.

'Well, on Sunday I attended a violin recital with my mother.'

'Ghastly,' Ambrose said, taking Julius's recommendations to the extreme. He decided he would let her see the real him. There was no point in pretending he would enjoy a recital when he would rather attend a funeral.

Miss Prout turned to look at him, shocked, and for a moment, Ambrose suspected he had lampooned one of her favourite passions.

'I am so glad you said that. I would rather eat fish, and I don't like fish at all.'

He laughed, relieved. 'Nor do I. It's the smell, and the soft texture.' He shuddered.

'Good,' she declared. 'Then we will not endure a recital nor eat fish together. What do you like to do then?'

'Be with friends, have adventures. I would like to take the moonlight ferry to the Queensport Aquarium to hear the band and dance. Julius and Violet had a wonderful night there.'

'Oh, I would love that!' Billie agreed. 'So you like to dance?'

'Do I like to dance? You won't get me off the dance floor,' he teased. 'Shall we venture there this Saturday night? I will secure tickets.'

'Yes, thank you, Ambrose. I would enjoy that very much. Did you wish to invite your brother and Mrs Astin along, or your sister and the detective?'

'I shall mention it if you are happy for me to do so, and to my cousin Lucian; we are very close. He will bring his lady, Miss Elizabeth Jensen.'

'That will be great fun,' she agreed.

And a lot less pressure in a group, Ambrose thought, relieved. Just being himself, the walk went remarkably well, and afterward, on his way home, Ambrose swung by Julius's house to tell him.

'You are just in time for dinner,' Julius invited him in.

'Do you have a new cook yet?' Ambrose asked.

'I heard that Ambrose Astin,' Violet called out, and Julius grinned.

Ambrose sighed. 'Well, you said to be myself.'

'Sometimes discretion is the better part of valour,' Julius warned. 'Tom and I suffered for weeks. You could suffer one night.'

Violet called, 'I can still hear you,' and her brother Tom could be heard laughing.

'Hello Violet, hello Tom,' Ambrose said, entering the kitchen.

'Hello, brother-in-law. As the cook does not start until tomorrow, you will be pleased to know Grandma has prepared tonight's meal,' Violet told him with a smile, 'and there is plenty for one more.'

'Excellent,' Ambrose said. 'Fancy a trip to the Queensport Aquarium this Saturday?'

Half way through their walk, Phoebe sensed Harland's reservation.

'Is something bothering you, other than the case, of course?' she asked, looking up from underneath her hat to study him as they strolled, arm in arm.

'Yes,' he said bluntly. 'Forgive my distraction.'

'It is perfectly understandable,' she said kindly. 'You do not need to meet me on afternoons when you are busy. I am quite adept at seeing myself home.' She nudged him playfully, and he smiled at her momentarily before frowning again.

'But I want to be the one to see you home, Phoebe. I do not take the honour lightly. In fact, I often marvel at my good fortune that you should turn your eyes on me. I can't imagine what I have done to deserve it. Shall we sit?' he asked as they approached the bench under a grand tree, halfway along their journey where they normally rested.

Once seated, Harland turned to face Phoebe. 'I am distracted, but it is not what you think. Well, yes, I am thinking about work, but I have let you down.'

'How so?' she asked, surprised.

'Joseph Facey slipped through my fingers.'

Phoebe gasped. 'Had he left the premises before you arrived? I am sorry to make you go out of your way.'

'No,' Harland said and winced. 'I interviewed him, and he was nothing like you and the ladies described. He had blue eyes and dark hair, not blond hair. He wore an iron frame on his leg from a childhood illness that stunted his growth and had a prominent facial scar.'

'I see,' Phoebe said softly.

Harland hurried on. 'The man I spoke with was awkward, humble, and a far cry from a charming rogue physically and by nature,' Harland sighed. 'He got the better of me, Phoebe, and I did not believe that was him. However, I know your information has always been sage, so I left a constable watching the premises.'

'Did he depart during the night then?' she asked, disappointed by his lack of faith in her, but doing her best to hide it.

'Yes, and no. He departed as a blond man with no walking frame. The constable noted the comings and goings from the boarding house in his pocketbook, and the man he was looking for—the man I described—did not exit.'

'Because he was in disguise.'

'Yes. He left with all his worldly possessions except the iron frame from his leg, as if he were mocking me. The landlady has advised his rent cheque was forged and now she is out of pocket.' Harland looked away with a shake of his head. 'I am sorry, Phoebe.'

She smiled. 'You need not be, Harland. You have a job to do, and you can only go on your instincts. Shall we continue?' she asked, rising, and he hurried to his feet.

'You are justified in your disappointment in me. I am sorry,' he said again, offering his arm and feeling her hand slip through it.

She did her best to hide her feelings, but felt something shift between them. *Had she ever given him inaccurate information? Did he not trust her?*

'Don't be silly,' she said. 'He is very good at what he does. Good enough to fool the ladies, their astute parents, and you. He must be masterful.'

'Or I am an idiot,' Harland muttered and looked down to see Phoebe smiling. He asked, 'Will you let me know when the ladies have an update for you?'

She nodded but did not commit her promise to words. *Was there any point in doing so?* Now she would have to tell Alma and Winnifred that the heartbreaker had got away again.

Chapter 25

AT THE THEATRE THE next morning, Detective Gilbert Payne felt right at home amongst the thespians, musicians, poets, writers, and artists. He valued the skill and discipline of the creative arts, and aspired to be considered a respectable poet himself one day. His superior, Detective Harland Stone, did not feel comfortable. His brief stint performing in his school plays was only because it was compulsory to earn his grade; he preferred to work in reality, not that which required some suspension of disbelief.

'I will let you lead in this interview, Gilbert,' he said as they entered the New Theatre Royal, where several of the performers had also arrived for rehearsals.

'Thank you, Sir,' Gilbert said enthusiastically, and he sought and found the theatre manager and renowned actor, Mr Sherman Bird.

'Of course, detectives, how might I assist?' the middle-aged man with the flamboyant waistcoat asked.

'I believe I saw you in "*The Forty Thieves*" earlier this year, Sir. You were marvellous, as was the production,' Gilbert gushed.

'Well, thank you, Detective. Sometimes I feel as if that role was written just for me. It is great fun to play.'

'I can't imagine anyone else playing it,' Gilbert agreed, and then, seeing his superior's impatience, added, 'but work prevails, Mr Bird. We are seeking a gentleman who is a master of disguise, changing character regularly. We understand that he is also a theatre lover. He might have used a variety of Christian names and the surnames Facey, Ownnet, Wenton, Newton, or Tewnon. Might he have performed with your company?'

'His connection may go back three or four years or be quite recent,' Harland added.

'We have auditions twice yearly, and several artists have come and gone during that time. What gall to be on the run using fakery,' Mr Bird said, as if he had the measure of the man. 'Let us hear those names again.'

Behind him, a minor disagreement had broken out on the stage, and a louder voice took charge, most likely the stage director. That did not stop one man from calling out, 'Sherman, shall we use your stand-in or are you intending to be part of this?'

'I am busy speaking with two detectives about you. Use my stand in.'

'About me! What do you mean?' the actor spluttered, ready to defend himself if required.

'I am joking. Use my stand-in and do get back to your rehearsal; I will be there shortly.' Sherman Bird rolled his eyes and Harland did his best not to smile at the surrounding melodrama, while Gilbert watched with much excitement.

'They are like children, these temperamental artists,' Sherman sighed. 'Forgive me, detectives, those names again?'

Gilbert read the list of names. 'Oliver Newton, a salesman with fair hair and a limp.'

Sherman Bird thought for a moment, then shook his head in the negative, and continued to do so as Gilbert read each name.

'No,' he said, until hearing the last name read. 'Wenton? I am sure we had a Wenton in our cast, but his name was not Issac. Molly,' he yelled, 'what was Wenton's first name? The fellow who left before Christmas?'

'Oliver,' she called back.

Gilbert gasped and, showing Harland his notes, pointed at the names. 'He is mixing his aliases, Sir. It was Isaac Wenton, Irish and blonde, and Oliver Newton, a local with a limp. He has created an Oliver Wenton.'

'Fair-haired, with a local accent and no impediment if memory serves,' Sherman added.

'How many actors have joined your company this year, Mr Bird?' Harland asked.

'That is an easy question to answer. Oliver left at Christmas, and after auditions, we accepted three new members. They are all onstage presently.'

'May we come closer to study the cast and could you point them out please?' Harland asked and Sherman Bird agreed, taking them closer to the performers and gesturing toward the three new players, one of which was female and the other two were not in the same age bracket or height as Joseph Facey even if disguised.

'Thank you, Mr Bird,' Gilbert said. 'Neither is the man we are looking for today.'

'So we had a real live criminal on stage, playing an actor, and a very good one he was too,' Sherman said. 'Rather exciting.'

'We would be more excited if he were on your stage right now, Sir,' Harland said. 'Would you have an address for him even though he has departed the company?'

'Of course. Come this way and Molly will find that for you?'

Harland nodded for Gilbert to follow while he stood to watch the thespians in action. He wanted to be sure Joseph Facey, the master of disguise, wasn't on that stage and about to slip through his fingers again.

Phoebe had not slept well and was pleased to have a quiet day ahead. She scolded herself for overreacting, but felt the need to speak with Julius. He knew her better than anyone, and they were the closest of siblings. He would understand her feelings or put them in some context for her.

'Will you send him downstairs if he has time before the first funeral, Grandpa?' she asked on arrival at the office, after greeting the senior Astin and Mrs Dobbs.

'He will have time if he arrives at his usual hour,' Randolph assured her.

She did not wait for long—just long enough to prepare her brushes and powders for the day—when she heard Julius's footsteps. Heavier than her grandfather's, lighter and slower than Ambrose's scuffles, and the next minute he was coming down the stairs.

'Phoebe, good morning. Grandpa said you wish to speak with me?' he asked, looking ready for the day in his dark suit and presentable appearance.

But his manner took her by surprise. Julius was always so big-brotherly, so concerned for her, but now his tone was more businesslike.

'It is a personal matter. Have you got time now?'

He hesitated.

'Oh, you are too busy this morning. Later then, perhaps.'

'No, please go ahead,' he said, moving into the room now, but Phoebe felt the situation was odd. Awkward. Was Julius expecting to be accused of some wrongdoing? He had mended his relationship with Ambrose, but why was he being so standoffish?

'It is about Harland,' she said and cleared her throat lightly, emotion and exhaustion bearing down upon her. 'After we informed him of the location of Joseph Facey, he visited him and let the man slip away.'

'Really?' Julius asked, surprised, then appeared to temper his reaction. 'How peculiar.'

'He was very contrite and said that, like the ladies and their fathers, he had fallen victim to a deception. But it is more than that. Harland did not believe me.'

'Ah,' Julius said, understanding the situation now. 'I am sorry for that.'

She moved to her desk and leant against the chair for support. 'I thought we had got past that. I thought he had faith in me.' Her voice hitched, and still Julius remained impassive. Phoebe continued, 'If it were the reverse, Julius, I would trust him without question.' She reined in her emotions and took a deep breath.

Julius's jaw locked, and he swallowed. But he did not move to take her hand or sympathise as he normally would. Phoebe stared at him as if he were a stranger.

No opinion? No anger at Harland? No defence of the gamble I took or the truth I told? Will you not tell me I am right to feel betrayed?

Julius exhaled. 'I am sure he regrets it, Phoebe, and will know not to second guess you next time. Was there anything else?'

She was sure her mouth had dropped open, and she shook her head and muttered, 'No.' She wanted his soothing words, his support.

'I had best get to work then; it is a busy day.'

'Yes. I shall see you later,' Phoebe said to his back as he raced up the stairs.

'Where are you, Julius?' she whispered.

Julius exhaled as he made his way out the back of *The Economic Undertaker* office to check on the hearse and horses. It was unnecessary, of course. His staff knew what they were doing, but he needed to get out of the office for a moment to gather himself. He had been aloof with Phoebe, and it had pained him as much as it seemed to have distressed her. But she wanted her space from his over protectiveness, from being overbearing. How was he supposed to know when to give it and when to withdraw?

It went against all his instincts not to support her; she looked so broken and vulnerable, and he was angry at Harland for dismissing her warnings. Of course she knew where Joseph Facey was; the spirit ladies had told her. Now she felt hurt and alone.

But he could no longer be the brother she confided in and could expect to defend her. Last time, she had told him in no uncertain terms that she would keep her secrets if he were to be overprotective, and that he should tend to his own family.

And so, he took those barbs on board, wearing them close to the heart; Julius gave her the new brother she wanted. Even if it felt like a betrayal.

Chapter 26

A BREAKING NEWS STORY by reporters Lilly Lewis and Fergus Griffiths ran on the front page of *The Courier* again.

'So exciting,' Lilly whispered to Fergus, not meaning to gloat amongst the other writers.

'Well done, young ones,' Ted called from his desk, and the pair thanked him. Not everyone was as supportive as Ted, but most enjoyed stirring Lilly for a bite.

'If you marry that good-looking boy from the mother country, Lilly, what will become of your front-page spreads?' the down-to-earth, horse betting, chain-smoking Frank asked.

'I won't be going anywhere, Frank. Because my beau accepts and supports me working; Fergus won't be rid of me too soon.'

'But if your man gets you in the family way, then there'll be no ink under your dainty fingernails,' Lawrence, the persistent flirt, said with a wink. 'The little Lillies will have to come first.'

'I thought I would bring the babies in, Lawrence, while I work. You have such charm about you, I am sure you could lull them to sleep.'

The office men laughed and ribbed Lawrence, who, as always, took it in good humour. When all had settled, Lilly and Fergus read their copy, taking pride of place on the front page.

The Courier – Morning Edition
THE VANISHING GROOM – FOUR BRIDES JILTED CRUEL NOTE AND WEDDING CAKE TAUNT
An exclusive report by Lilly Lewis and Fergus Griffiths

He is a master of disguises, a man who breaks women's hearts, abandoning them in the worst way at the altar, and now your reporters can tell you it is likely the work of one man who taunted his brides and is this city's greatest rogue.

We recently reported that over a four-year period, four men professed to love four worthy ladies, while, meantime, presenting forged wills to receive advances from their dowries. Two of the ladies died from emotional distress after being abandoned at the altar.

Your reporters can now reveal that Roma Street Station detectives Harland Stone and Gilbert Payne recognised the surnames were anagrams, and one man was likely responsible for this crime. He is still at large, and the names are withheld while the investigation continues.

The detectives recently discovered that the groom had sent a note and a slice of wedding cake to Miss Grace Edmonstone after abandoning her at the altar. But it was not an apology. Her father, Patrick Edmonstone, withheld the note, believing it was too distressing to give to his daughter. The rhyme signed *"The Vanishing Groom"* mocked the jilted bride.

Yesterday, "The Vanishing Groom" sent a slice of wedding cake to the detectives to taunt them, apologising for slipping their notice. Despite Detective Stone's penchant for the treat, he assured us the rogue would not have his cake and eat it too.

So rest easy, ladies; soon it will be safe to love again.

It was Miss Emily Yalden of the *Miss Emily Yalden School of Deportment*'s usual practice to allow her students to enjoy a social cup of tea of a morning before classes started. This served several purposes – it allowed Emily to watch their progress at the art of serving tea and to determine if their socialising skills were improving.

Today, however, she had another motive. Having heard all about the vanishing groom case from her beau, Detective Gilbert Payne, Emily was worried that her student, Martha's beau—Benson—might be the vanishing groom.

But how to bring about the conversation without being a busybody or offending the young lady? Emily had an idea – she displayed the newspaper for all to see with Lilly and Fergus's story on the front page. It didn't take long for the girls to notice it.

'Oh, it's the *"Jilted Bride and Vanishing Groom"* story!' Amy, a student with abundant wealth, figure and hair, exclaimed. 'I truly admire the reporter, Lilly Lewis. How amazing she is to work in that field.'

'I know, but my father says her male partner probably writes most of the story,' Tess said, and Emily refrained from groaning, given she was pretending not to listen in.

'Rot,' Martha said. 'Of course Lilly Lewis writes the stories. If a man can do it, a woman surely can.'

No one contested Martha, as she was the strongest of the students. Catherine, a meek young lady, returned to the headline. 'It is so terrible. I would die if left at the altar.'

'And two ladies did just that,' Martha retorted in her matter-of-fact manner. She had obviously read the newspaper.

Emily spoke up. 'Tess, do not gulp your tea, sip, and Martha, slow down your process of pouring tea. It is not a race; it is an art, a seduction.'

'Miss!' Amy exclaimed, shocked.

'Well, it is, ladies. You are saying without words that you have time for the recipient, that how they like their tea is your concern, that they are important to you, be it your beau or your great aunt. You feel privileged to entertain them.'

Martha grinned. 'I shall never pour a cup of tea in the same way. I will go very slowly when I pour for Benson tonight.'

The ladies tittered at the naughtiness of Martha's inference, except for Catherine, who did not really understand what was being said.

'How did you meet your beau?' Amy asked Martha, and Emily could have hugged her and graduated the girl with honours. As the subject was now raised, Emily was free to speak of it.

'I bumped into him outside a hat store, or rather, he ran into me and apologised profusely.' Martha smiled at the memory. She was not the blushing type. 'He introduced himself, and then Benson insisted he must see me home in case he somehow injured me. He was so handsome and charming, naturally I accepted.'

Hmm, Emily thought, *that sounds in character for the cad in question.* She spoke up. 'Your beau surely did not introduce himself by his Christian name, Martha? Sacré bleu!'

'No, Miss. He was a perfect gentleman. He bowed and said, Mr Entown at your service.'

'So, if you marry him, you will be Mrs Benson Entown,' one girl teased.

'How is that spelt?' Emily pushed on.

'E-n-t-o-w-n,' Martha said. 'It is a difficult surname. But no trickier than Hampstead, which I always have to spell,' Martha said with a sigh. 'Do you know him, Miss?' the thought just occurred to Martha.

'I don't believe so,' Emily said, feeling a thrill of excitement as she noted the name to tell Detective Payne. 'Forgive me for saying this, Martha, but are you sure of his origins?'

'Do you think he might be the vanishing groom, Miss?' Amy asked, and all the girls began talking at once, until Emily rang the little bell on her desk.

'I could not say, but I will ask him and watch for his reaction,' Martha said assuredly. 'Although he corrected me when I said his name recently. He said, "Benjamin" and then he laughed and told me he thought I had called him Benjamin, and that was his brother's name. It was odd, and we had a laugh, but I never gave it a second thought.'

Emily stored that fact away, too.

'What if he is the vanishing groom using one of his disguises on you, Martha?' Tess asked dramatically, and all eyes turned to Martha.

'Then I shall drag him to the police station myself!' she stated, satisfying them all.

'As much as I would like him to be captured, do be careful, Martha, won't you?' Emily said.

'You don't really believe I am dating the vanishing groom, do you, miss?' Martha laughed. 'I have told him I am in no hurry to marry, so he would not waste his time with me if wealth was his pursuit.'

Emily smiled. 'Of course not, but I am protective of my girls.'

Martha thanked her, and for a moment her face softened; the pair had turned a corner. Emily imagined Martha had experienced very few people on her side and, most likely, very little maternal care.

Meanwhile, across town in a new boarding house, Joseph Facey slammed the paper down on the breakfast table before him.

They are on to us! I need to hurry along with my romance and desertion. This will be my final job, and then we'll live comfortably ever after. Next time I fall in love, it will be true love for an eternity, not for money.

Chapter 27

RETURNING TO THE THORNTON mansion on a chilly winter's morning, the atmosphere was notably different. There was no long queue of citizens staring at the jilted bride's house, and no line of ladies snaking their way in for a viewing of the deceased lady herself.

'It feels so desolate and truly abandoned now, Sir,' Gilbert said, 'like Miss Alma Thornton herself.'

'It does, even for the non-poetic,' Harland said with a glance and a smile at his protégé as they entered through the main gate, with the permission of Alma's aunt, Mrs Frances Neale.

Gilbert chuckled before adding, 'I can understand why Mrs Neale wants to hold off before selling it. Some people are superstitious and might believe that buying the house will bring them bad luck.'

'I am not one of them,' Harland said. 'This home does not run to my salary, but for the right price, I can get past its history.'

'As can I, Sir. Besides, my mother would likely get a priest in to bless the house.'

'That is one solution to ward off the evil past,' Harland agreed, and he fetched the key from the location advised by Mrs Neale.

Entering the house, it felt gloomy and silent, like a tomb. The air had a faint scent of stale flowers, no doubt from the many displayed at the viewing of Miss Thornton. Like all closed-up houses, it had a stuffiness to it, as if the house itself had breathed in all the fresh air.

'I can't imagine living here alone,' Gilbert said quietly. 'I wonder if Miss Thornton sometimes felt frightened.'

'Perhaps after her abandonment, it was a sanctuary. I shall take the upstairs if you start down here,' Harland said. 'Many people keep paperwork in their kitchen, and the study is on this level. Call out if you find anything of relevance.'

'I will, Sir,' Gilbert said and watched as his superior headed up the stairs. He felt like he was being watched, an odd feeling, and, reeling around, there was no one there.

Gilbert chided himself for being silly and got to work.

Julius held the reins as the horses pulled the hearse along a familiar route to the South Brisbane cemetery where the priest and mourners would be waiting. The two Astin men looked impressive in their dark suits and hats, acting as escorts on the last journey for the body on board.

'Isn't this nice?' Ambrose said, grinning at his brother as the cemetery came into sight.

'Do not look so happy. We are supposed to be sombre,' Julius chided him.

'Ah, just like old times,' Ambrose said and sighed. 'How I have missed it.'

Julius rolled his eyes. 'We were not paired for two funerals; one would think we haven't seen each other for weeks. How did you cope when I was on my honeymoon?'

'Not well,' Ambrose said in jest. 'But I knew you were coming back, and I imagined you were missing me, too.'

This time, Julius could not help but chuckle. 'Stop it and do try to look like we are respectful funeral directors taking our roles most seriously.'

'So, did you and Violet decide you will come to Queensport for the band and dance on Saturday night?'

Julius hesitated. Although things might be better between him and his brother now, the recent slight had made him cautious. Was socialising together a good idea, especially if Miss Prout was going to be there?

'No, we won't attend, but thank you for the invitation,' he decided.

'Why not? Are you worried that the fish that followed you at the aquarium last time will be there again?'

Julius smiled and then berated himself. 'Good Lord, you are a bad influence on me. Let's be serious.'

'But why?' Ambrose persisted.

'If Lucian and Miss Jensen go along, that will make up the party. You do not need us to be there, and you and Miss Prout definitely don't need chaperoning.'

'You are right; we need no chaperoning. I feel confident I can hold my own, as I might have mentioned—'

'In considerable detail,' Julius butted in.

'Well, I knew you would be keen to know that I followed your advice and was my own man. But it will be fun with a large group, and you and Violet enjoyed it last time. Come with us, Brother. I have asked Phoebe as well. She can invite Harland, and if you and Violet come along, then we better invite Bennet too, so that will mean Lilly comes along. Did you want to ask Tavish?'

'His twin brother might be here by then. If it is a large party, it sounds like a good night.'

Ambrose agreed, pleased, and then quickly sobered as the mourning party came into sight. 'Right then, let's get this one below ground and I shall go make a booking for our large group.'

'I hope the fish is there,' Julius said quietly, forcing Ambrose to hide his amusement in the guise of a cough.

Several mourners stood by the gate, as if forming a guard of honour, and then followed the hearse to where the gravesite waited for its new inhabitant.

Julius gasped, and Ambrose glanced left and right to see what had alarmed him. 'What is it? All seems as it should be?' he whispered.

'That young woman, she is wearing Violet's wedding dress, in black. I know it well from the design in the window.'

'It looks beautiful, does it not? Or does it disturb you?' Ambrose asked.

'It is a bad omen,' Julius said, slowing the hearse as they arrived, and glancing around. He muttered something to his right, but Ambrose could not hear the words.

'What are you seeing, brother? Who are you speaking with?' Ambrose asked, concerned, and Julius winced.

'Nothing, no one.'

'We have worked in the funeral industry for years, and you have never spoken of omens. I know you have Phoebe's skills. You can deny it all you like. But you can trust me, Julius. What do you see? What worries you?'

But before Julius could tell him, the priest and family approached, and Julius stepped down to greet them and begin the tradition of burial.

On returning to the Roma Street Police Headquarters after having had a small victory at the late Miss Alma Thornton's manor, Harland and Gilbert stopped inside the doorway of their office and looked around in surprise. Small gifts, boxes, and baskets, each featuring wedding fruit cake, covered the meeting table and several benches. Before they could call for the sergeant, he arrived behind them with two more small boxed cakes in hand.

'Ah, apparently the reporter, Miss Lewis, mentioned in her article this morning, that you received a wedding cake from the criminal at large and you have a penchant for fruit cake, Detective Stone,' Sergeant John said. 'These are gifts from concerned citizens and a selection of bakeries who wish it to be known you have their support.'

'Good Lord,' Harland said. 'Sergeant, we'll put all of these and any further arrivals in the kitchen, and anyone who wishes may help themselves. I will have Miss Lewis thank the gift givers; replying personally is beyond us.'

'No problem, Detective. However, the one on your desk is from Mrs Dobbs. I believe she works for *The Economic Undertaker* and said you liked her fruitcake.'

Harland looked over with interest. 'I shall definitely keep that slice, thank you, Sergeant. There is none better.'

'Sir! This slice is from the Whitehouse Bakery! And this one is from the Fernberg Bakery at Rosalie. Both are excellent.'

'Then I suggest you and the Sergeant secure yourselves a piece now, and please find me one for the inspector, Gilbert, and I shall take it to him with my report.'

'Bribery now, Detective?' Sergeant John said, grinning and happily accepting the Fernberg Bakery cake.

'Whatever is required, Sergeant,' Harland said with a smile.

As the cakes were being removed by two juniors, reporter Lilly Lewis arrived. 'Goodness, what on earth is this?' she asked, and Sergeant John explained.

'How thoughtful and what a show of support. Ooh, is that cake from Mailer's Bakery?'

'It is, Miss Lewis,' Gilbert said. 'Do store that away for yourself, and one for Mr Griffiths as well,' Gilbert said, and Lilly took him up on the offer, taking a slice for Fergus and happily agreeing to write a small thank you piece on their behalf.

After the removal of the cakes and Gilbert's return to his desk, Lilly asked, 'Do you have news, detectives?'

'Yes, and you may report this, Miss Lewis. We went to Miss Alma Thornton's home and found a similar card to that sent to Miss Grace Edmonstone,' Harland said and nodded to Gilbert, who produced it.

'We're assuming she got a slice of wedding cake, too,' Gilbert said. 'The note reads: "*Alma, your affection is not all I took; with your money I am fleet of foot. Signed the Vanishing Groom*". Disgraceful, and he is no poet,' Gilbert declared.

'As if his abandonment is not insult enough, but to send these mocking cards afterward,' Lilly shook her head with disgust.

'It is unthinkably cruel,' Harland agreed.

'And yet Miss Thornton hoped he would return,' Gilbert mused. 'Perhaps she ignored this or convinced herself Mr Oliver Newton did not send it.'

'She was in a heightened state of grief,' Harland agreed. 'Any updates from you, Miss Lewis, aside from your cake drive on our behalf?'

Lilly grinned. 'Sorry, Detective, I didn't know the people of Brisbane held you in such high regard they would bake for you. As for my news, I have a message from Emily.'

At the sound of his beloved's name, Gilbert snapped to look at Lilly, who further explained, 'I sent Emily a note this morning to see if her suspicions about the heiress in her school might have come to fruition. She sent back this reply and asked I pass it on to you as I was en route to see you today.'

'Let's have it then,' Harland said, frustrated by the cake delay.

'Emily said Miss Martha Hampstead's beau's name is Mr Benson Entown.'

Gilbert wrote the name on the board and gasped. 'Sir, it must be him. His name is an anagram, like all the other names – Entown, Newton, Ownnet, Tewnon, and Wenton. Good gracious!'

Harland's thinning of lips and look of determination were a sight many a boxer had experienced when entering the ring with him. But now, the "Vanishing Groom" was in the senior detective's sights.

'I believe you are right, Gilbert. Only this time, he will not get away. We need to know when Miss Hampstead is next seeing her beau. He knows we are on to him, so he may flee soon. And what I am about to say is not for reporting, Miss Lewis, yet.'

She nodded solemnly. 'Agreed.'

'We believe we know where he is. In residence, hiding, in the deceased Miss Alma Thornton's empty manor.'

<h1 style="text-align:center">Chapter 28</h1>

JULIUS DID NOT YIELD to Ambrose's interrogation on the return trip to *The Economic Undertaker* ninety minutes later. He couldn't take his eyes off the woman in the black wedding—now mourning—dress; plus, the constant begging of the woman he was burying, who stood beside him in spirit, asking him to tell her daughter where to find her will, exhausted him.

How did she know he could see spirits? Was there some marker on him that others did not possess? He would ask Uncle Reggie. But he could not reply to her despite her persistence.

'It is in the attic, in my bible. Her inability to find it will prevent her from inheriting my house. There's a cousin, you see, who believes he has the right... tell her, please tell her. It was her father's wish too, but we are both gone now. Please help.'

He gave her a brief, inconspicuous nod so she could rest in peace.

'Thank you; you are so very kind. My daughter will believe you. She is open to messages from the other side.' The woman reappeared once more before his departure, to remind him of his promise.

Julius's brow furrowed while he thought, *How can I tell the daughter about the will?* Did the recently deceased think he could just walk up to her daughter and say, 'Your mother, before we buried her, wanted you to know her will is in the bible in the attic? Good luck, then.'

But she left his side, leaving her problem with him. Julius was already uneasy about the daughter wearing Violet's dress in black. The whole funeral had unsettled him; he needed to see his wife to right all in his world.

On arrival back at their office, he thanked Ambrose, assuring him all was well, as he handed the reins to Claude. Hurrying inside, Julius went through his washing routine, leaving Ambrose to update his grandfather.

'All went well, except Julius was shocked to see a woman wearing...'

Julius did not hear the end of the sentence as he exited *The Economic Undertaker* for *Beyond the Veil.* But there were several customers in the store, so he turned and returned to his business.

'Are you all right, lad?' Randolph asked.

'I am fine, Grandpa, thank you. We had a lovely time together,' he added, finding his sense of humour, and Ambrose laughed.

'Just two brothers burying the dead,' Ambrose agreed. 'Such good times.'

Randolph laughed at his grandsons' antics.

'Is Phoebe in?' Julius asked, and his grandfather confirmed she was, as Violet came by the front windows and gently opened the door.

'Come in, dear, all is clear,' Randolph said.

'Thank you, Grandpa,' she smiled, still getting used to calling him as such. 'Hello Ambrose, Julius. Were you looking for me, husband?' Violet teased.

'It's about your wedding dress,' Ambrose said. 'It spooked us.' He made an eery sound, and Violet looked at Julius, confused.

'Yes. A word, if you have time?' He didn't wait for her to respond, but was pleased to see Ambrose lose interest and head for the kitchen to see what Mrs Dobbs might have on hand.

Julius led Violet to the stairs, and they hurried down to Phoebe's workroom.

'Can we come in?'

'Of course. Hello, Violet. Is all well?' Phoebe stopped attending to an elderly lady and draped her with the shroud, before moving towards the small sitting area where her plant, Florence, a gift from Detective Stone, was flourishing.

'I cannot say. I too am in the dark,' Violet said, and both ladies looked at Julius to explain now they were all seated.

'I need both of your help. Violet, today a lady was at the funeral wearing the black version of your wedding dress.'

'Oh, yes. She requested it, and we were able to do so. Did it look good on her?'

'No. It looked like a terrible omen, and I confess it startled me.'

Violet reached for his hand. 'Of course, I can imagine so, especially when the dress is so familiar from the window display.'

'I do not care about profit over my family. Please, for me, do not allow it to be made for mourning wear again. I don't wish to invite misfortune to visit.'

Violet gave a little shudder. 'Now you have frightened me.'

'I did not mean to do so,' Julius said, stroking her hand, 'but I can't look at that dress daily and remember such a happy day and then see it in the throes of death.'

'Of course,' she soothed him. 'I do not want to see that either. I shall tell the ladies it is to be done in wedding fabric or ball gown fabric only. Never black or half-mourning grey.'

He exhaled as if the weight of an impending death had fallen off his shoulders; a feeling that he could not shake until he spoke with his wife.

'Thank you. And Phoebe, I need your advice.' He spoke of the mother's wishes. 'But how do I tell the daughter without revealing what we know?'

'A note,' Phoebe said, most decidedly. 'I confess I have done it by note form before. I shall scribe it for you and have it delivered by a postal boy this very afternoon. We have the address, or Grandpa will, and we will sign it, a concerned friend of your mother.'

Julius smiled. 'That will work very well. I promised her mother, but did not know how I might deliver on it. Thank you both.'

'I shall get back to work,' Violet said, rising, and Julius rose to see her off.

Phoebe bid Violet farewell and said, 'Julius, may I ask a favour of you now?'

He returned as Violet took to the stairs and sat opposite Phoebe again. 'What do you need?'

'For you to be my big brother again,' she said, and Julius, not expecting this, huffed.

'I will always be that.'

'No,' Phoebe looked ashamed. 'Please accept my humble apology. I was hurtful to you and ungrateful. I offended you and pushed you away. But I need you, Julius. I need you to be outraged on my behalf, to defend me, to hear me, to continue to respect me and my work, as you always have, and I took for granted. Please forgive me,' she whispered, tears welling in her eyes.

Julius gently squeezed his sister's hand. 'There is no need—'

'There is every need,' she insisted. 'Please forgive me.'

Julius nodded. 'Let us not speak of it again. Now, write that letter for me, and then you can tell me if I should challenge Harland to a fight at the club or not.'

Phoebe gave a small laugh of relief, and as he rose, she jumped to her feet and wrapped her arms around him. Pulling away, she smiled.

'It is good to have you back, Julius.'

'I never left. It is good to have *you* back.'

Detective Gilbert Payne approached the door of Miss Emily Yalden's deportment school with excitement and trepidation. The thought of seeing his beloved in an official capacity gave him the opportunity to impress her, but knowing he would most likely be studied by several young ladies was daunting. He knew he was not a handsome man like Julius Astin or Bennet Martin, but he was presentable and courteous with good prospects. For some, that was enough to encourage affection, and to his good fortune and amazement, Emily took the time to get to know him.

He knocked, and one of Emily's staff—a young maid who assisted Emily's administration manager with tea and lunch making, and general business duties as required for the deportment school—opened the door.

'Good morning, Miss. Detective Gilbert Payne to speak with Miss Emily Yalden, if she is available, please?'

'Come in, Sir. The ladies are about to break for lunch. If you will wait here, I shall let Miss Yalden know of your arrival,' she said, showing Gilbert into the parlour room, of which he was most familiar.

He could hear voices drifting from down the hallway, where Emily conducted her classes in a separate part of her townhouse. Now and then, he heard her dulcet tones and strained to hear the conversation. And then, a door opened and the sound of girls escaping a classroom filled the air – laughter, hurried steps and Emily calling, 'Girls, young ladies do not stomp to lunch.'

Gilbert was grinning when Emily entered the room, her eyes relaying her delight to see him despite her formal welcome in case young ears were listening.

'Detective Payne, this is a pleasant surprise.'

'Miss Yalden, the pleasure is all mine,' he said, holding her gaze and would have kissed her hand if it were not a work-related visit. 'Detective Stone and I very much appreciated your message via Miss Lewis, and I hoped to speak further with you on the subject.'

'Of course,' she said. 'May I offer you a drink, or would you like to sit?'

'Thank you, no. I best get to business, and it might be best if Miss Martha Hampstead were present, if possible? Is there a guardian who must be on hand when I speak with her?'

'No, I can fulfil that role,' Emily assured him. 'I'll fetch her, but be warned,' she whispered, 'she's quite opinionated.'

'That might work in our favour in this instance,' Gilbert said with a conspiratorial smile and Emily, agreeing, departed to fetch Miss Hampstead.

While doing so, Gilbert bore the glances and giggles of several young ladies passing by to take some fresh air with the express purpose of viewing the gentleman in the front room, rumoured to be Miss Yalden's beau.

Entering the room with Miss Hampstead, Emily sent two girls back to lunch. 'Girls, I encourage you every day to take some fresh air and rarely have any takers. But today, you are all keen. I shall remember that tomorrow.' She closed the door. 'Detective Payne, may I introduce Miss Martha Hampstead?'

The pair exchanged appropriate greetings and took the offered seats on the couch setting.

Adopting his most empathetic tone and expression, Gilbert said, 'Miss Hampstead, I imagine this will be distressing news, but I must inform you we believe your beau, Mr Benson Entown, to be the man named the "vanishing groom".'

'Truly!' she said, eyes wide and a smile on her face.

To his surprise, Martha was not at all distressed; she was excited.

'Miss Yalden, you were right; I knew you suspected him,' she said, looking at Emily as if the deportment teacher had gone up considerably in her estimation.

'Detective Payne discovered early in the case that that the vanishing groom used surnames that were anagrams of each other,' Emily said proudly.

'And Entown is one of them?' Martha asked with delighted. 'So, how will we trap him?'

'Ah, well, it could be dangerous, Miss Hampstead, so Detective Stone and I will manage that, but I am requesting your discretion and calling on your acting skills.'

'Marvellous,' she said. 'What do you wish me to do?'

'First, do you know where Mr Entown is currently residing?'

'Yes. He said he was minding his cousin's house in Highgate Hill as she was abroad. He described it as a large mansion on a small block that constantly needed his attention.'

Gilbert, most happily, received this information believing it to be Alma Thornton's property.

He exchanged a look with Emily. *Cousin indeed! More likely the deceased fiancé.* He was sure the man, Joseph, now calling himself Benson Entown, was there earlier this morning when he and Detective Stone were on site; he felt his presence. Then, Detective Stone had found evidence of a male inhabitant – a man's comb, shoe polish, and a current newspaper in the bin.

'And when might you be seeing Mr Entown next?' Gilbert asked.

'He is collecting me after class today, and we are going for a walk. Should I ask him to show me his home?' she suggested excitedly.

Gilbert thought about this. 'That might work, Miss Hampstead, but I would prefer you were as far away from that man as soon as possible, not just for your safety, but for your heart's sake.'

'As would I,' Emily agreed, and looked admiringly at Gilbert for his sensitivity.

'Do not worry, Detective, Miss Yalden, I am not in love, nor will I be heartbroken,' Martha announced. 'Benson was always a pleasant distraction, but he was keener than I to marry and settle down. I have a large inheritance coming my way in a matter of weeks when I come of age, and there are many things I want to do. Marrying is not one of them.'

'Perhaps if you were in love, you might feel differently,' Emily suggested.

'I imagine so, Miss Yalden,' Martha agreed, 'and maybe if I had met Benson in a few years' time, I might find him more appealing. But I have spent years at boarding school and now Uncle insists I do this deportment course,' she said and then added, 'although I have surprisingly enjoyed it. But I want my freedom, for a time anyway. So let me help trap him, please, Detective. For all the other ladies he has slighted. I am confident I can do anything you ask.' She looked at Emily to support her.

'Detective, I believe Martha is sensible and confident enough to assist, and as long as there is no danger, in fact, you are saving her from danger, then there's a rogue to be caught.'

Martha beamed. Emily looked at her detective with great affection, and in that moment, Gilbert had admired no two women more, except for his mother, of course.

Chapter 29

Bennet Martin knew he needed to do some work to earn his private investigative fee and not rely too greatly on the detectives' investigation. His client, Mr Patrick Edmonstone, whose daughter Grace was a victim of fraud and desertion one year ago, wanted an update, and Bennet had little more than that which his belle, Miss Lilly Lewis, covered in the newspaper.

He sat back and studied his clerk, Daniel Dutton, until the young man noticed he was being observed.

'What is the matter? Is my tie crooked or is your desk not in order?' Daniel asked, looking up from his current workload.

'On the contrary, they are both straight and neat. I have been thinking, and that grimace is not warranted,' Bennet said in good humour.

'I look forward to this, do tell,' Daniel encouraged him with a grin.

'As you wish. My last report earned a positive reception from Mr Edmonstone, but now I need a sting of my own, and I know just the thing, Daniel!'

'You do?' Daniel asked, surprised. 'Ah, your father had a similar case, and you are using his intelligence.'

'Yes, but it is my intelligence now,' Bennet said, tapping his fingers on his desk. 'My father would tell me about his cases in excruciating boring detail in the hope I found them exciting and wished to join the police force.'

'Instead, you left the country. Rather drastic,' Daniel said with a huff of laughter. 'So what is your sting, dare I ask?'

'It is to do with the list you are compiling for me of stationery stores where this rogue might buy his papers and stamps for forging documents. I am going to pass myself off as Joseph Facey – the blond version.'

Daniel's face brightened. 'Are you? How exciting! Can I come along to witness this performance?'

'Of course you must. You are my clerk, who will collect the orders. I have the blue eyes and a British accent, as Grace's fiancé did. But there are risks. Did Joseph Facey adopt the accent when purchasing his stock, and was he fair or dark-haired when in-store?'

'If you keep your hat on, and the original encounter with the sales clerk was brief, then perhaps you could pass for, or be mistaken for Joseph Facey.'

'My thoughts exactly, assuming we can find the supply store,' Bennet said with an expectant look in Daniel's direction. His clerk waved a piece of paper before him.

'Three. I've found three that deal in the quality of stationery and stamps you, or rather our rogue, needed. They are all in the city, so we could go from one to the next.'

'Excellent. Let us go then, my good man,' Bennet said, rising and calling to his housekeeper, Mrs Clarke, that they were both departing and should return within a few hours.

'I shall have a late lunch ready,' she assured them.

'What if Joseph Facey has collected but not yet paid for his goods and they demand payment from you?' Daniel asked as he rose, donning his hat and jacket.

'Then I will reveal my true identity to them, inform them they were misled, and instruct them to contact Detective Harland Stone immediately.'

Satisfied with this response, Daniel closed the door behind his employer and, with his other hand, hailed an approaching hansom. Bennet consulted the note Daniel had just given him and, climbing in, gave the driver the first address.

The ride from his South Brisbane office across the bridge to the city took little time, and Bennet thanked the driver, paying him with a generous tip.

'Play along, Daniel,' Bennet said, putting his chin up and adopting his most arrogant expression as Daniel opened the door to the business for him and they strolled him.

It was not long before a gushing sales person approached to assist him in preference to other customers in the store who did not look as wealthy, nor arrived with their own clerk.

'Good afternoon to you. I am after a quality paper, similar to that which I purchased last time,' Bennet said happily, using his British accent to best effect. 'I have a new clerk, and the last one did not record the purchase. Hence, the new clerk,' he said, waving a hand in Daniel's direction, who gave a small bow to the salesperson.

'Understandable, Sir. Do you have an account with us? If so, I can tell you exactly what you purchased last time.'

'Excellent, how very efficient. I believe I do,' he said.

'Mr Facey, F-a-c-e-y, Joseph,' Daniel said, stepping up to play his part.

The sales person nodded and hurried behind the counter to look in the store's supply book. His frown told the men all they needed to know.

'I can't seem to find that order, Sir. Would your clerk have paid in cash?'

'Never,' Bennet said, as if that was for people of no importance. 'Forgive me, my man, we must have the wrong store.'

'Nevertheless, I am sure we could help you, Sir.'

'No need, but thank you. I am quite particular about my papers.' With that, Bennet swanned out of the stationery store, Daniel offering further apologies, and hurrying after his boss.

'Right then, next one,' Bennet said.

'Just around the corner,' Daniel said as they strolled along together, drawing admiring looks from ladies of marriageable age and their mothers. 'You do very well in that pompous role.'

'It comes naturally,' Bennet said, amused. 'Let's try again then, shall we?' He stood back as Daniel opened the door for him. This time, the salesperson studied him with greater attention.

'I cannot place you, Sir, forgive me. Perhaps you have an account with us?'

'No doubt,' Daniel said on behalf of Bennet and spelled the surname again.

'Ah, that is odd. Perhaps an error. We have an account for Mr Benjamin Facey, but not Mr Joseph Facey. It is an order due in tomorrow, Sir.'

'And it is quality papers?' Daniel asked.

'Yes, our best, and several rubber stamps and ink pads,' the salesman said.

Bennet sighed. 'I suspect my former clerk put the order in my brother's name. Truly, could a man be more inept? When did he place that particular order?'

'Three weeks ago, Sir. I apologise that it has not come in yet. I guarantee it will be here with the noon delivery. As mentioned at the time of ordering, the paper you requested had to come from across the border.'

Bennet nodded and waved his hand in dismissal; those details were not something he had time to record to memory.

'We shall collect it tomorrow then, thank you kindly,' Daniel confirmed.

'Will you fix up the account then, Sir?' The salesman addressed Bennet.

'Indeed. Once I inspect the goods,' Bennet said.

'Of course. If you could allow me some time to unpack it. I believe we had an appointed time for collection,' he said, referring again to the book. 'Yes. It was 4.30pm. Will that still be convenient?'

'That will be fine. We will return then, thank you,' Daniel agreed, and the two men left the store, looking pleased with themselves.

Once they were far enough away, Bennet said, 'Benjamin Facey. Could they be brothers?' He did not wait for an answer. 'I need to let Harland know and ensure we are watching this shop tomorrow late afternoon, if not all day, in case a Facey of any description arrives early,' Bennet said, delighted.

'I wonder if Benjamin is dark-haired,' Daniel said.

Bennet considered his clerk. 'You are onto something there, Daniel. And now I have something more to report to Mr Edmonstone this afternoon. I will tell him I have advised the police.'

'That was very clever of you, Bennet,' Daniel said.

'Thank you, Daniel. Once I knew he was a forger, I knew he had to have a certain type of paper and speciality stamps. Of course, he need not have bought those here in Brisbane, but if he has been in residence for some time, it is likely he would.'

'He's so close now,' Daniel said.

'Yes. But he is the master of disguise and escape, so I will not count my counterfeit notes until they are banked,' Bennet joked. 'To the police station, then.'

It was a chilly winter afternoon, more so in a bleak and windswept cemetery. Detective Harland Stone stood beside Winnifred Nash's grave, waiting for his protégé to collect him on Gilbert's return to the office. He had been present for an hour now, in no rush. There was no reason to be at the graveside, but as there was no crime scene, Harland needed the benefit of the outdoors and fresh air to clear his head. Here, it was cool and silent.

Three years ago, Isaac Wenton deserted this young woman. Her suspicious father discovered the ruse, ensuring no money was stolen, and the vanishing groom had vanished. Plain, quiet Winnifred, 25, had thought at last love had come for her. It had not. Thus, she neglected herself until illness took her.

The grave featured a large angel, in keeping with her family's wealth and a measure of their grief.

Our beloved Winnifred

What we keep in our memories

Is ours unchanged forever.

Until we meet again.

'Harland,' a voice called, and he looked around to see Bennet Martin approaching on foot, a hansom parked near to the gates. 'Your sergeant said you were here.' Bennet arrived beside him and looked around. 'Why?'

'Time away for thinking, until Gilbert collects me on his return to the office.'

'Oh, I am sorry to intrude on your solitude.' He looked at the headstone. 'Ah, this is one of the ladies.'

'The first to die, three years ago.'

They heard a whistle, and Harland looked up, smiled, and raised his hand. Of course, Gilbert kept his police whistle from his days on the beat. He had arrived and waited by the large black gates with a hired hansom.

'I shall send his hansom off, and you can both ride back with me, yes?' Bennet said.

'Thank you,' Harland agreed and watched Bennet hurry to the gate before returning his attention to the grave. 'Miss Nash, I know you spoke with Phoebe. I apologise for letting you down, but rest assured, I will catch this dishonourable man.' With that, he put his hat on his head and headed to Bennet's ride.

Once settled in the cab's warmth and on their way, Harland said, 'If only I brought the man in for questioning and searched the boarding house room for papers and stamps. If I could fight myself in the ring, I would knock myself out.'

Both men smiled at the odd thought.

'You must let it go, Harland. Is Phoebe upset with you?' Bennet asked.

'No. She is a kind soul, but I felt her disappointment. After consulting Gilbert about the best colour of roses for an apology, I have sent her a large white bouquet.'

'Most considerate,' Bennet said. 'Well, I have good news for our case, so cheer up. Daniel and I had a break-through this morning while I was playing the role of Joseph Facey, who I believe was Grace's fiancé, Edwin Ownnet.'

'Edwin Ownnet,' Gilbert said, scrambling for his notebook. 'Ah, yes, British and dashing. The description could well fit you, Mr Martin.'

'Thank you kindly, Detective,' Bennet said with a flourish of his hand, and told of finding three stationery shops that sold the quality of paper needed for official documents and how he played the role of Mr Facey. Daniel appeared as the trusty, nervous clerk. 'It was quite a challenge for Daniel,' Bennet joked. 'But this is the most important news. A Mr *Benjamin* Facey had arranged to collect that order tomorrow afternoon at 4.30pm, if he remembers.'

'Benjamin!' Harland exclaimed. 'Could they be brothers? Might he have dark hair?'

'I said the same to Daniel,' Bennet said.

'My, that is excellent work,' Gilbert said.

'I have my moments of brilliance,' Bennet agreed with a grin.

'Did you enquire when the order was placed?' Harland asked.

'Of course, Harland,' Bennet said, looking wounded, and Harland chuckled.

'Forgive me. I forgot you were a private investigator first and an artist second.'

'I wish it were the other way around,' Bennet said. 'Mr Facey placed the order three weeks ago. So it appears he still has a need for fresh papers and is likely wooing a young lady.'

'Excellent work,' Harland repeated Gilbert's earlier sentiment. 'I will have the paper store watched all day tomorrow, and we will be there ready to make an arrest.'

'Unless we get him earlier,' Gilbert said, and both men turned to him. He said for Bennet's benefit, 'Detective Stone and I visited Miss Alma Thornton's house yesterday looking for a card sent after the fact. We found it, but while there, I had the sense we were being watched.'

'How disconcerting,' Bennet shuddered.

Harland agreed and told of finding evidence of a man in residence. 'How did you fare this morning, Gilbert?'

'Very good, Sir. I spoke with Miss Martha Hampstead, who confirmed her current beau, Mr Benson Entown, is minding a large house in Highgate Hill for a cousin, or so he would have her believe. He is collecting her after school today for a walk.'

'Well done, Gilbert,' Harland said.

'Thank you, Sir. Miss Hampstead wishes to be involved for the sake of the other victims and is quite practical. She is not mooning over Mr Facey or Mr Entown in this case, and suggested asking him to show her his house, and for us to follow and arrest him on site if we have the right house. Emily feels Martha is capable of assisting us.'

'It could work, but we cannot let her out of our sight, especially if there are two men present in that house – Benjamin and Joseph Facey,' Harland said.

Gilbert agreed. 'I warned her about the dangers. At least now we have the potential to arrest him this evening; failing that, tomorrow late afternoon.'

Harland looked pleased and added, 'I also visited the registry where the four marriage licenses would have been issued under the four different aliases. They did not exist.'

There was silence while everyone thought about the implications of this. Bennet concluded, 'He never applied for a licence as the groom. He simply created the forged, faked papers and presented them to the priest, or the girl's father, or the bank, or whoever required them. No one thought to check. Why would they?'

'The man is thorough,' Harland said.

'And devious,' Gilbert added.

They all braced as the hansom lurched slightly, and the driver called down an apology, as the cab shook with the wind whipping up George Street en route to Roma Street.

'It is the same story for the addresses given by our fake grooms,' Harland told Bennet. 'We discovered the three addresses did not exist. The fourth address was a theatre company.'

'Ah,' Bennet said, nodding. 'He has us running in circles. He may well have slept in the theatre or props room with no one being the wiser.'

'He appears to be quite comfortable in Miss Thornton's mansion now,' Gilbert agreed.

'She must be rolling over in her grave knowing the man who slighted her at the altar is now living in her house without her,' Bennet said, disgusted. 'We are almost at the station. I have one more piece of news.'

Both men looked surprised.

'I have to do some work to earn my investigator's fee,' he told them with a small grin. 'I have been doing further research on Mr Bailey Sutton, the bank teller, who released Mr Gardner and Mr Edmonstone's advances by accepting the forged wills. He seemed most sincere in our previous interview and has his manager's support. But I found out he had only been in the role for a few years. His timing is interesting.'

'I don't think we should rule out his involvement then,' Harland said.

'Agreed,'Bennet said. 'If he is involved, then he would have recognised Mr Facey or the two Facey men when they appeared as the fiancés.'

'If there are two or more involved, it might explain the desire to do a few more jobs to share in the rewards,' Gilbert said.

'Yes,' Harland agreed, as the hansom came to a stop outside the Roma Street Police Headquarters.

'I shall change hansom here too and let him rest the horses,' Bennet said. 'Allow me to pay, or rather, my client.'

'The inspector and I thank you,' Harland said with a chuckle. 'Let us go in and work on a plan. Knowing what a slippery character Joseph Facey is, we will give ourselves as many opportunities as we can to catch him. This afternoon, we will follow Miss Martha Hampstead and stand ready.'

Chapter 30

As promised, after delivering his second funeral for the day in the company of Ambrose, Julius returned to speak with Phoebe. He came down the stairs, paperwork in hand to sign, and found his sister and Charlie preparing a young girl for viewing.

'Hello, Mr Astin,' Charlie said, addressing Julius formally as he always did, despite all invitations to do otherwise.

'Hello, Charlie, Phoebe, Rufus!' he acknowledged the large black dog that bounded off the couch to greet him before promptly returning to his comfortable spot. Joining them to see their work, Julius gave a heartfelt sigh. 'The saddest of all funerals is when the young die.'

'Heartbreaking,' Phoebe agreed. 'I have not permitted Charlie to assist before with younger clients, but I thought it was time.'

'I can handle it,' he said assuredly, in his usual quiet manner. The young man, who had wielded a knife at his uncles, stabbing Julius by mistake, had landed on his feet with a job and apprenticeship with Phoebe. Though no relation, he was like them both in nature, and the work interested him.

'You have done very well, but I will not expose you to too many young clients,' Phoebe promised.

'I am quite comfortable with death,' Charlie assured her. 'My mother lost a child before I was born and believed I was the blessing that followed. She always said that life was full of heartbreak and happiness, and it was only fair you had your share of both.'

'I believe both are necessary to appreciate the good times,' Julius said. 'I have some paperwork to sign for Grandpa; I'll do so over here while you finish your work.'

'I can depart if you need to speak with Miss Astin,' Charlie offered.

'No need,' Julius assured him. 'I am in the office for the rest of the afternoon.' He stopped, looked above, and rolled his eyes at the sound of Ambrose stomping around at a hurried pace.

'Are there no clients in the house?' Phoebe asked, hiding a smile.

'Hopefully not,' Julius said.

Phoebe continued her lesson with Charlie, as Julius nudged beside Rufus and raced through the papers, signing where indicated. He was an astute businessman, but trusted his grandfather implicitly. If the papers were ready for signing, then they were correct, be it bills, wages, or accounts.

Fifteen minutes later, Phoebe declared, 'We are done. Thank you, Charlie. Young Meg looks beautiful.' The pair stood back. 'Her viewing is late today and burial tomorrow,' she added for Julius' benefit.

'She looks as if she is resting and might wake any moment,' Charlie agreed.

'Then you have done an excellent job,' Julius said, rising, and Charlie departed with thanks, his lessons over for the day.

Rufus gave a sharp bark announcing Uncle Reggie, who appeared beside the young deceased lady.

'Stand down, Rufus, I am a friend, not a foe,' Reggie said, and the dog settled again. 'A dear little soul.' Reggie glanced at the girl on the table.

'Have you met her already, Uncle?' Julius asked. He no longer pretended not to see his uncle, to Reggie's relief and Phoebe's delight.

'Yes. It is a shame she was taken so soon. I can think of several ne'er-do-wells that the living would not miss.'

'If only it worked like that, Uncle. Is this a social call or have you news?' Phoebe asked as she cleaned her brushes and packed away the powders.

'Social, my dear niece, although I can report both Miss Alma Thornton and Miss Winnifred Nash have been singing your praises. You might be sainted by the time you come over to my side,' he teased her, and Phoebe laughed.

'Hopefully, you will be a little old lady by then and have some sins to account for,' Julius said, and Reggie agreed.

'Thank you both,' she said, smiling at the thought. 'I am glad you are here, Uncle. I was going to seek Julius's opinion on whether my feelings are irrational, and now I have two gentlemen to consult.'

'I imagine your brother will be much more helpful,' Reggie said, pacing around the room, his hands behind his back as he studied all that was on display. 'Remember, my opinions are rather dated now. I have been dead for some 25 years, and these are modern times you are living in.'

'Stay, Uncle Reggie,' Julius encouraged him. 'Manners never date.'

He gave a firm nod, and Phoebe began her story, finishing, 'I know Harland has no reason to believe me; I am only delivering messages from the dead, but somehow I feel slighted, as if I am untrustworthy. Am I being silly or overwrought?'

'I have never known you to be overwrought, Phoebe,' Julius said, 'and I think your hurt is understandable. What do you think, Uncle?'

'Hmm,' the ghostly uncle said as he considered the pair. He was very much like his nephew, Ambrose, and bound to see things differently from Julius and Phoebe. 'I don't wish to be blunt, but I doubt that in the heat of the interview, he gave the source of the information a second thought. He was there because of your tip off, and then his instincts went into action; he made a decision based on what he saw before him.'

'Of course,' she said, feeling foolish. 'But he knew the man was adept at deception,' Phoebe said, unable to let it go.

'True, and your information has always been accurate,' Julius said. 'But from what you say, he did not dismiss it out of hand. He left a constable on watch all night.'

'Yes,' Phoebe considered this. 'But if he had even looked through the man's possessions, what might he have found? It is upsetting to let Alma and Winnifred down.'

'That cad must be a very impressive conman,' Reggie said. 'I think you will have to make allowances for your detective, Phoebe dear. He is governed by the factual. Do not take it to heart.'

'Thank you, Uncle Reggie. I appreciate your insight. Thank you, Julius,' she said, turning to her eldest brother.

Julius grimaced. 'I think you and I put too much value in our relationships to our own detriment.' He did not need to say it, but the recent shift in the relationship between Ambrose and Phoebe was one such example of how loved ones pained each other.

'Yes, perhaps that is true. What hurts me most is that I would have believed him above all others and all evidence.'

'Romantic love,' Reggie said with a shake of his head. 'It has the power to undo us.'

'Yes.' She blinked away her tears, raised her chin and took a breath. 'I have learnt my lesson. I was never after excitement or riches, just a man who considered my thoughts and actions worthy of consideration. But I guess the best we can hope for in life is comfort, and he provides me with that.'

'No, Phoebe!' Julius said firmly. 'Surely you aspire to more than just a comfortable life? You have succeeded in a difficult position, so apply that determination to secure a love that is worthy. I am not biased when I say you are beautiful, clever and self-sufficient – a fortunate position that means you do not need a man to provide for your comfort. So hold your partner to your standards, to what you need. If that is not Harland, so be it.'

And as if on cue, Ambrose came down the stairs with a delivery for Phoebe – a dozen white roses.

293

Chapter 31

FOR FEAR OF WORRYING her neighbours and damaging her business reputation, Miss Emily Yalden requested no large police presence outside her townhouse, the location of the *Miss Emily Yalden School of Deportment*. Detective Harland Stone readily agreed as he sought to study the culprit and his actions before arrest, thus strategically placing two officers nearby, briefed on the necessity of remaining unseen. Harland also requested Constable Rogers—who had executed his duties so capably last time—be present at the manor, and the young man was excited to be called up.

Gilbert was inside the building, on the pretence of visiting Miss Yalden, and would remain hidden, but watching – a protector for the ladies, which showed him in his best light. And so, they were ready; the assignment required all participants to do nothing but follow Miss Martha Hampstead and Mr Benson Entown. Harland hoped to arrest him at the house of the deceased fiancée.

Mid-afternoon, right on time, classes were over and the girls drifted out of the building, several linking hands and laughing, another hurrying behind them, waving and dashing off in another direction. Then Miss Martha Hampstead came to the gate.

Harland's breath stilled; he loved the moment of reckoning. A quick glance around told him his officers were playing their part, remaining out of sight. Now, Miss Hampstead, the detectives and two constables waited while, at the late Miss Alma Thornton's stately home, reporter Lilly Lewis, private investigator Bennet Martin and Constable Rogers, hoped all would go to plan and the expected couple would arrive soon. Naturally, Harland would prefer Miss Lewis was not present, but given her contribution, he allowed it as Bennet was on hand to protect her.

And then, unexpectantly, a hansom pulled up, and a hand extended to Miss Martha Hampstead.

Joseph Facey, acting as Benson Entown, was very wary since the visit from the detective at his boarding house, the raid on Miss Thornton's home and that strange message from the ethereal blonde girl at the omnibus stop. He sensed pursuit, felt the net closing in on him, but it was his one last job to secure his future – an easy one with no parents involved.

Unfortunately, Martha was proving to be a challenge. She wasn't madly in love with him like Alma and Winnifred had been, and she was quite headstrong. He had mentioned marriage a few times, but she had changed the subject. Martha, or rather her fortune, was a prize worth pursuing, and time was running out.

Facey had listened to her ambitions and desires, and today, he would propose, ensuring he liberally sprinkled his declaration with the right promises to snare her. He would offer her adventure, sell the dream of having the longest honeymoon exploring the world together on their two fortunes. They will make memories that will last a lifetime, falling in love at every port from Paris to the Mediterranean. He impressed himself with the vision; what girl who wanted to be free and see the world could resist that opportunity in the company of a handsome, rich companion?

Of course, he was presenting forged wills to her uncle, and while he and his brother had amassed a considerable sum from duping the other ladies, he had no intention of sharing that with Martha, or living up to any of his promises once he secured her funds. It would be *adieu* to *you*, Miss Martha Hampstead. He smiled at his own cheek.

Now wary, Facey glanced out as the hansom approached Martha's school and breathed a sigh of relief to see her waiting at the gate. He became Benson Entown in mannerisms and charm, and as the cab pulled up, he opened the door and extended his hand to her.

'Miss Hampstead, I believe?' he teased. 'Let me take you away from all this.'

Her eyes widened with surprise, and she glanced momentarily to her left and back at him again. 'I thought we were walking! Should I tell someone where I am going?' she asked saucily. 'Are you alone in there?'

'I am indeed alone in here, and I thought a drive around the park might be in order.'

Martha pouted. 'We have done that before, and it will be crowded at this hour. I have an idea...'

'Oh? Let's hear it then,' Benson encouraged her, keen to get Martha onboard and spirited away.

'Show me your cousin's manor, the one you are minding for her. That would be fun.'

His eyes lit up. 'Miss Hampstead! How forward you are,' he played at being shocked, and then gave her a wink.

Martha grinned, biting her bottom lip, before saying, 'You are correct, Benson; I didn't learn that in my ladylike classes,' she said with a cheeky smile.

'Let us go then,' he said, keen to move on as quickly as possible. With that, he gave the driver the address, offered his hand again to Martha, who stepped inside, and Benson Entown tapped the roof for the driver to depart.

The game was afoot.

Martha was delighted they were going to the abode as planned, but the plan was to walk there. Could the detectives catch up in time?

She had played coy before entering the hansom, stalling for as long as she could so the detectives could hail a ride. Martha was also conscious of the fact that she had glanced away as if looking for someone. She tried to hide that faux pas by asking if she should inform someone that she was entering his hansom. He seemed none the wiser. Now, to keep him on the hook.

'How was your class today? Any deportment tips you care to share?' he teased, and Martha laughed.

'Not one. The idea is that you don't notice how naturally charming I am. If I tell you how I practiced pouring tea with your needs at the forefront of my mind, the impact would be lost, would it not?'

He chuckled. 'I have never thought of the act of pouring tea to be so enticing.'

'Oh, but it is. I shall show you if your dear cousin has the elements on hand. Just wait until I put sugar in your cup!'

Again he laughed at her playfulness, and while she was dying to glance behind and see if they were being followed, Benson had insisted she sit beside him, and far too close for her liking.

'I have a confession to make,' he said.

'Oh?' Martha turned side on, wary of what was coming now that she knew of his character.

'My cousin wishes to sell, and I am thinking I might buy her manor... for us.'

Martha's eyes widened in surprise. 'For us?'

Benson hurried on, knowing his future rested on getting Miss Martha Hampstead's fortune. 'There is more. Even if I decide to buy the house for our future, I am intending to travel within the next month. To Paris.'

'To Paris. But I want to go there; you know that. And to London, and to all the dreamy places.'

'Yes, we share that desire. I want to treat the world as if it were my playground, and I am in the enviable position to do so as the benefactor of my father's will,' he bluffed, continuing to hold her hand and her attention. 'But I don't want to travel alone. I want to share it with someone who will laugh with me, dine and dance with me and create memories for a lifetime.'

He was saying everything Martha wanted to hear, and she could easily allow herself to be swept up in his words and promises. For a girl who had grown up alone, to have someone's companionship, their love, while sharing their dreams... *No!* She scolded herself. *Play along.*

'—that someone is you, Miss Martha Hampstead, the woman I want to discover the world and spend my life with. Will you do me the great honour of marrying and escaping with me? We will honeymoon around the world.'

She drew a sharp breath, as expected, and looked at him with surprise and delight. 'Benson, I thought I wasn't ready to marry, but we could do that. We could have the longest honeymoon, a grand tour, yes?' she gushed.

'Yes indeed. Is that a yes you will marry me?'

'Will you hold to your promise? The world will be ours to discover?'

'Absolutely. You will tire of travelling before I shall,' he threw down the gauntlet.

'Never,' she declared. 'What memories we will make!'

'So, your answer, Miss Hampstead? Do not keep a man in love in suspense.'

She laughed. 'Yes. I will, Benson. I will become Mrs Benson Entown.' She looked at him lovingly, feeling slightly disappointed no one was on hand to see her performance.

Martha had an audience, however. Broken-hearted Miss Alma Thornton and Miss Winnifred Nash sat on the seat opposite, holding hands, watching as their fiancé spoke of his love for Martha. Now, like Martha, they waited.

Chapter 32

THE MOMENT GILBERT SAW the hansom pull away with Miss Martha Hampstead inside, he hurried out of the building to follow. What good fortune that a hansom pulled up just in time.

'The top cop said for you to get in and we'll follow the cab in front without being obvious,' the driver said, enjoying the espionage underway. Gilbert jumped in and sat as close as he could to the corner in order to keep an eye on the ride carrying Miss Hampstead and her cad of a suitor.

Meanwhile, Detective Harland Stone had identified himself to another hansom driver and requested that he take the quickest route to the Highgate Hill address, as a young lady's life was in danger.

'I know a shortcut. Sit back, Detective,' the driver said, and they were off at a good pace that would well and truly arrive before Benson Entown and his victim.

The brief journey gave Harland another chance to berate himself for letting Joseph Facey slip through his fingers. The thought that the couple might not go to the Thornton manor, leaving him waiting while Gilbert followed them, added to his worries. Still, his protégé knew by now not to put himself in danger. Or so he hoped.

Arriving, Harland told the driver to let him out in the back street, where he paid handsomely with a tip from his own pocket, thanked the man, and accepted his encouragement to 'Get the job done, Detective!' He saw one police officer he had briefed earlier, in position and indicated for him to remain so. The officer nodded his understanding.

Coming around the corner, Harland spotted Bennet Martin and Miss Lewis waiting on a park bench, and briefly acknowledged them. They would pretend to be a young couple arriving home at a nearby residence when Facey came into sight, but be close enough to assist Miss Hampstead to escape if need be, and for Lilly to get her story, although that was the least of Harland's concerns.

He stealthily made his way down the side of the large home, hoping on this occasion that the neighbours did not do their civic duty and question him about who he was and what he wanted.

In the clear, he entered the house, stood silent and listened. Not a sound. His voice echoed loudly when he called out, 'Constable Rogers, it is Detective Stone. Show yourself.'

A few moments later, a face peered over the banister at the top of the stairs. 'Here, Sir. No one has arrived yet.'

'They will be here any moment, hopefully. Mr Entown collected Miss Hampstead in a hansom; we were expecting him on foot. Remain unseen and do not play the hero, Constable. I will call for you if needed, but overhear the conversations as best you can so you may serve as a witness.'

The young constable answered, 'Yes, Sir. Constable Ferris is also here on patrol in the street if you need him. He knows to stay out of sight and to come if he hears the whistle.'

'Excellent.'

The two men heard the clip-clop of the horses' hooves drawing closer.

'They are here,' Harland said with relief, seeing the carriage coming up the drive. He turned to ensure the constable was out of sight and was pleased to find he had slipped away and returned to his position. Gilbert would arrive momentarily too; it was all hands on deck.

Harland hurried out of sight, dashing into the living area so he could follow or listen in. As soon as Facey made his demands for Miss Hampstead to sign over her fortune, he would show himself and arrest the rogue.

Maintaining his character, Benson Entown congratulated himself on his plan. Removing Miss Hampstead from the deportment school quickly and without revealing himself safeguarded his ruse. And now Martha had accepted his offer of marriage. The future looked brighter than it ever had. He was so relieved to succeed at his plan, and ecstatic at the thought of all that was to come that he did not need to perform; she would believe he was genuinely happy to take her as his wife.

'Oh, it is grand,' Martha said, looking out of the hansom at Miss Alma Thornton's palatial home on a small manicured block of land. The large gates were imposing, and the house matched its neighbours; the street spoke of wealth.

After paying the driver, Benson handed her down from the hansom, turning his focus on his fiancée. He took her hand and placed it in the crook of his arm.

'Now imagine this,' he said, continuing up the steps to the front door. 'In the social column of the newspaper, an announcement reads: "Mr and Mrs Benson Entown have finally returned home from their years abroad to their Highgate Hill manor. How long they will stay is anyone's guess, but no doubt dinner parties and great tales are to follow,"' he said dramatically.

She gave a small laugh of delight. 'I can imagine that. Can you?'

'Of course. I have dreamt about it, and now that you have accepted my hand in marriage, there is nothing stopping us. I shall give you a tour of the house and if you give it your imprimatur, we shall secure it!'

He opened the front door with the confidence of a rightful inhabitant using a key previously found in a drawer in the kitchen.

'Look at that staircase,' she said, delighted.

He had no inclination that her eyes were scanning the room, not for its beauty, but for the detectives. Nor could he read her mind, which was racing with thoughts, none of them romantic. Rather, *how long would it take the detectives to catch up with her? Were they here now?*

Benson Entown was delighted with her response to the manor and stopped in front of the large window in the living room, where the sun was lighting the trees with a dusky glow and the scene was peaceful and romantic.

'What do you say, Miss Hampstead? Shall we make this our home?'

'Yes, let's do so, Mr Entown,' she teased, and leaned in to kiss him on the cheek. 'But how do we secure it now so your cousin does not change her mind?'

'We can do so immediately if we are clever. Since we're getting married, we'll combine our incomes. We will use my fortune to travel with... my legal man is expecting the payment from the wills any day now, and we can use your income to purchase this house now. Then we are set.'

'That will work,' Martha agreed.

'So let us get married now, today, tomorrow, immediately,' he said, picking her up and swirling her around as she laughed. 'Let us see your man to organise the documents, and then visit a priest, and plan where we will travel to first.'

She held up her hand to slow him down. 'It is only a matter of weeks until I am of age, and then we need no one's permission. My uncle will no longer be my guardian, and the funds will be mine to do as I please.'

'Then, my dear fiancée, we have much to plan in secret before then.'

Detective Harland Stone stepped into the room. 'I think your days of planning are over, Mr Facey.'

Hearing the detective stepping forward to make the arrest, Constable Rogers appeared on the stairs and, opening a nearby window, blew his whistle loudly, bringing Detective Payne—who arrived only moments after Martha—running in, followed by Bennet Martin, Lilly Lewis and an excited Constable Ferris.

But to Harland's shock, this man was not Mr Facey, who had eluded him earlier, and no amount of disguises could hide that fact.

Chapter 33

Phoebe knew the day would come when Detective Harland Stone would not arrive. When, because of duty, he would miss their walk home. But for it to happen on the day when she already felt slighted by him pained her more than she cared to admit. Of course, if they should wed, she would wait at home for him. Her eyes always looking at the front door, her ears straining for the sound of footsteps. Perhaps that would not be so bad if there were children to care for and mortician work to fill her days.

'I shall head home with you then, Grandpa, if that suits?' she asked, patting Rufus on the head, as he sat alert in the reception area, aware of the hour and awaiting Julius's return.

'Of course, my dear,' Randolph said as the door to *The Economic Undertaker* opened and both looked up to see what client required services at the end of a business day. To Phoebe's delight, Emily entered.

'Hello Phoebe, Mr Astin, and this must be Rufus,' she said, greeting them all. 'Forgive the intrusion when I imagine you are about to close shop, but I was eager for news.'

'It is always lovely to see you, Miss Yalden,' Randolph greeted her.

'What has happened?' Phoebe asked.

Emily smiled. 'I shall assume, then, that you have no news. The game is afoot. Martha left after class with her beau, and our detectives were in pursuit, hopefully following them to Miss Thornton's house.'

'Goodness me,' Randolph said, 'It sounds as if an arrest may be imminent.'

'I very much hope so, Mr Astin,' Emily said. 'I do hate the waiting, though, and hoped that if Phoebe were free, we might have tea or an ice cream?'

'Yes, please, I am at a loss,' Phoebe said. 'It was Harland's afternoon to walk me home. So now I know where he is and he won't be coming, I welcome the distraction, and your company, of course.'

'Then on your way, Phoebe, and enjoy yourselves. I shall lock up. It is lovely to see you again, Miss Yalden,' Randolph said.

'And you, Mr Astin.'

'You won't stay back late, Grandpa,' Phoebe warned. 'Grandma has her charity concert tonight, and I believe you are to go along.'

'Yes,' he said drily, making her laugh. 'I am just waiting for the boys.' The back door burst open. 'And here they are now.'

'All buried and done with, Grandpa,' Ambrose said. 'They won't be coming back.' He stopped dead on seeing Emily, as Phoebe and Randolph hid their smiles. 'Ah, Miss Yalden, trade talk, forgive me.'

'Not at all, Mr Astin,' Emily said with a grin. 'I hope when I die, I can be sure of being all done with and not unexpectantly coming back.'

Phoebe could not help but laugh, and Randolph shook his head and sighed. He said, 'It is not from lack of coaching, Miss Yalden. You have students, you know what it is like. But still, Ambrose insists on talking before checking the premises.'

'I could offer him a discount deportment course if you think that might help,' she suggested, making Ambrose smirk and his family laugh. Julius entered, having left the horses in Will and Claude's care, and heard Emily's suggestion.

'Miss Yalden, that has merit. Could we discuss it?' Julius asked.

'Very amusing, brother,' Ambrose said. 'Where is your detective, Sister?'

'Not here. On a case with Detective Payne. We believe they are arresting the vanishing groom,' Phoebe said.

'Excellent,' Julius said, stroking Rufus, who sat beside him, pressing his weight against Julius' leg.

'So, given Phoebe and I may find ourselves abandoned in the line of duty quite often in the future, we must stick together,' Emily declared. 'We are going for ice cream.'

'What a grand idea! Can I come?' Ambrose asked.

'Of course, you are all welcome to join us, although Mr Astin Senior has a recital and Phoebe may wish to be free of her brothers,' Emily said.

She smiled. 'Occasionally, but not today. Come along, Ambrose. Will you and Violet join us, Julius?'

'Thank you both, but it is winter,' he said, stating the fact as if it appeared to be overlooked. 'I am not envisaging ice cream, but our new cook's roast, hopefully. She has only been with us for a matter of days, and Tom has put on a few pounds, and Violet is happy not to have to feed us,' Julius joked. 'Would you both like to come to dinner, oh, and you too, Ambrose?'

'Forgive me, Miss Yalden, but that is a better offer,' Ambrose said, and Randolph chuckled.

'We would hate to impose on your cook and Violet,' Emily said, always mindful of her manners.

'On the contrary, Miss Yalden,' Julius assured her. 'A full house would delight us both. Besides, the wonderful new cook prepares large servings, allowing for leftovers. She believes Tom is a growing boy who must eat, and I must keep up my strength. Consequently, Rufus has done very well for himself.' The large black dog appeared to nod, as if the arrangement suited him very well.

'That's decided then,' Ambrose declared, taking charge. 'I shall see the stable lads off and get the trap to take us all home. Grandpa, you lock up. Julius, you collect Violet from next door, and we shall be off. Come, Rufus.'

Phoebe linked her arm through Emily's and smiled. 'Let us always be each other's company if our lives continue on this path.'

'If there is an offer of a roast dinner, you can be sure of that,' Emily agreed, laughing.

Chapter 34

THE LIVING ROOM OF the late Miss Alma Thornton suddenly filled with people. Detective Gilbert Payne and Constable Ferris rushed in on hearing the whistle; Constable Rogers hurried down the stairs to be of service; Bennet Martin came to usher Miss Hampstead away to safety, and Lilly Lewis followed, agreeing to stay close by.

'What is going on?' Benson Entown asked, his head snapping from Martha to Detective Stone and the gallery of people.

'We know what you are up to, Benson, or should I say Mr Joseph Facey?' Martha said, standing back and crossing her arms across her chest.

'He is neither Benson nor Joseph,' Harland said, and all eyes turned to him, including a smirking villain. It was a dark-haired Mr Facey that Harland had met in the boarding house, not this man.

'Am I not? Then who am I?' he asked smugly. 'Martha, do you truly doubt your fiancé?'

'I know you as Mr Bailey Sutton,' Bennet said, looking at Harland, who nodded his confirmation. 'The bank teller whom Detective Stone and I both spoke with, but now you are pretending to be Benson Entown.'

'Ah,' Lilly said. 'Working at the bank, you ensured the inheritances of the Misses Grace and Caroline went to Joseph Facey. Where is he then?'

'Or are you Joseph Facey too?' Bennet asked, eyes wide, as the thought just occurred to him given the man before them was blond and blue-eyed.

'How could I be the groom and the bank teller at the same time when the father of the bride is present?' he scoffed.

'Bailey Sutton, then, is it? It doesn't matter who you are,' Martha said angrily, her temper apparent. 'You were going to get me to sign my inheritance to you, and we were never going to travel together, were we?'

'Please, everyone, Detective Payne and I will handle this,' Harland said, trying not to show his exasperation. 'Identify yourself then, and I refer to your birth name, or we shall assume you are an accomplice of Joseph and Benjamin Facey, a relation perhaps, who we also seek for fraud.'

Sneering, his charming persona gone, he looked at Martha, and then the detective, but did not speak.

Harland issued orders. 'Detective Payne, Constable Rogers, will you see if there are any personal items on the property please that might assist us with identification?'

Constable Rogers raced back up the stairs as Gilbert proceeded to the desk in the corner of the living room. Bailey Sutton hurried forward, and Martha yelped in surprise as he grabbed her, his arm restraining Martha around her neck.

'I am leaving now, and she is coming with me,' the cad said as Martha fought him, resulting in the tightening of his stance.

In one swift movement, Detective Harland Stone hit out at the man, the punch landing on the bridge of Bailey Sutton's nose. He wailed in pain and surprise, releasing Martha, who Bennet grabbed and pulled away as a flailing Sutton fell to the ground, blood gushing from his nose.

Harland called on the well-sized Constable Ferris to assist, and manhandling a dazed and bloodied Sutton, Harland ordered, 'Cuff him.'

'How exciting,' Lilly whispered to Martha.

'Who are you?' Martha snapped, rubbing her sore throat and taking offence at Lilly's comment.

'She is Miss Lilly Lewis, reporter extraordinaire,' Bennet said with a wink at Lilly.

'Oh my word, I love your work. You are amazing,' Martha gushed. 'How exciting!'

Harland gave a small shake of his head, exasperated with the surrounding drama.

'Sir, I have found this,' Gilbert said, holding up a tan leather satchel that, when opened, revealed quality papers and stamps.

'Ah, the materials for your forgeries,' Harland said to Sutton, and as Gilbert emptied the bag, they found identification papers for two men. 'It appears you are a Facey—Joseph Facey—but have papers to support your alias of Bailey Sutton. Who is Benjamin Facey to you?'

'You broke my nose,' he spluttered to the chief detective.

'And you threatened a lady,' Harland reminded him. 'One that you intended to fleece of her fortune. The dark-haired man I met pretending to be Joseph Facey, is that your brother, Benjamin Facey?'

'I know no such man,' the now identified Joseph Facey said, spitting blood and saliva on the floor.

'Very noble of you,' Harland said. 'I am to assume that it was all your doing then. That you are proficient with a British and Irish accent, can walk convincingly with a limp, play the role of a bank teller, and happily play the role of a suitor at the same time. An amazing feat.'

'He was definitely playing that role with me,' Martha agreed. 'I will be a witness to it.'

Harland nodded. 'We require that to make our case, thank you, Miss Hampstead.' He returned his attention to Joseph Facey. 'I imagine Benjamin Facey will take his leave now when Miss Lewis reports of your capture and will enjoy the spoils gathered to date, while you do time for both of you.'

'He wouldn't do that to me.'

'Ah, so you do recall him now,' Harland said. 'Your brother, is he?'

A yell from Constable Rogers upstairs interrupted the interrogation.

'Someone is up there,' Bennet exclaimed.

'Bennet, Constable, stay with the prisoner!' Harland ordered as he and Gilbert took to the stairs two at a time in pursuit of locating the cries for help. Constable Rogers had been searching for incriminating objects, and he found a most significant one.

'Good Lord,' Harland said, racing into a large bedroom where the constable was holding the legs of a man trying to escape out the window. Reporter Lilly Lewis, who had boldly raced up the stairs behind the detectives, gasped and hurried back downstairs to inform Bennet, and to avoid being accused of getting underfoot.

'Not so quick,' Harland said as the three men bundled the man back into the room and restrained him, as the man's fists flew and he kicked in all directions.

'Your handcuffs, Constable, use them,' Harland said, and they held the man down until Constable Rogers secured him.

Stepping back and exhaling, Harland looked at the man's face and smiled. 'Ah, we meet again. Mr Benjamin Facey, I assume? We have your brother downstairs; join us for a reunion.'

Gilbert and Constable Rogers lifted the man to his feet and brought him along.

'Are you managing well without your leg brace, Mr Facey?' Harland asked as they took to the stairs and he heard only a grunt in reply.

Bundling the brother downstairs, the Facey men quickly turned on each other.

'You idiot, I told you we had enough, and it was time to stop,' Joseph hissed at his brother.

'If you had hurried up, we would have been long gone,' Benjamin shot back. 'You took too long each time. How hard is it to get these plain girls over the line?'

'Plain!' Martha exclaimed, most indignant.

'We had enough!' Joseph yelled at him.

'Don't give me that. You loved every minute. Having the girls adore you, making up our names with your silly puzzles.'

'The anagrams,' Gilbert said, looking at the fair-haired Joseph Facey. 'Clever, but risky.'

'See! They worked it out. I told you not to play around.' Benjamin glared at his brother.

'You sent the poems and the wedding cake! And we would have got more from Grace if you had married her and then deserted instead of just taking her dowry.'

'And if you hadn't blown it with Winnifred, we would have had enough money already. All that work and not a cent from her.'

'I didn't know her parents were going to get their solicitor to look at the wills—'

'Why did you not take a year apiece?' Gilbert interrupted, curious.

All eyes turned to him, and he continued. 'According to my notes, three years ago the fair-haired brother, Joseph, wooed Winnifred. Then there were two dark-haired fiancés in a row. Now, it appears in the two most recent cases, the fair-haired brother wooed Miss Thornton and Miss Hampstead. Would it not be safer to undertake a romance every second year and stay out of sight?'

'Don't answer him,' Joseph said.

His brother scoffed. 'Why, so we don't incriminate ourselves? You put an end to that when I came down the stairs and you bandied about that we did one too many jobs.' He turned to Detective Payne. 'Joseph got the job at the bank under the alias Bailey Sutton. It was best he stayed there.'

'It was too good of an opportunity, given it was the bank of choice for several of the fathers of the women we were wooing,' Joseph said. 'But sometimes we let the girls pick,' he smirked.

'We both met them, and let them select the brother that most appealed to them,' Benjamin said, looking at Martha with disdain.

Martha gasped. 'Did I meet you both?'

Joseph smiled as if he had won the prize. 'You did, but you only had eyes for me.'

'Shut up, you idiot,' Benjamin snapped at his brother. 'You think I care about winning the hand of a plain miss?'

As Miss Hampstead arced up, Harland put an end to the discussion. 'Constables, remove the men.'

'I will call for transport, Sir,' Gilbert said loudly over the men's continuing argument, and hurriedly departed.

'Bennet, could you please deliver Miss Hampstead home?' Harland asked.

'I will, and see Miss Lewis back to *The Courier*. Then I shall inform my client,' Bennet said.

'Thank you, yes, I am sure I can make the late deadline for the morning's paper,' Lilly said, all a fluster.

Harland thanked him and then departed to assist the constables with restraining and bringing the Facey brothers down the driveway. Lilly Lewis's departing words reached his ears: 'Two vanishing grooms, who would have thought?'

'Who indeed?' he muttered.

Chapter 35

SHORT OF BREATH, REPORTER Lilly Lewis rushed into the office of *The Courier* late that afternoon and despite her desire to celebrate the case with her beau, Private Investigator Bennet Martin, it would have to wait – there was an amazing story to write, and her editor and writing partner to brief.

'Sensational, stop the presses! We've got a new front-page story for the morning edition,' Mr Cowan bellowed, sending several staff members outside his office scurrying to obey. 'Write it up now, Lewis and Griffiths! Get me the illustrator,' he yelled, startling his secretary. 'We'll illustrate the constable holding the man's legs as he tried to escape out the window!' He chuckled at the thought, and seeing his two reporters were still in his office, bellowed, 'Go, write, hurry!'

Lilly and Fergus rushed out of his office, Fergus saying as they hurried to their desks, 'I will write the introduction appraising the case, if you write the conclusion as it played out today. Agreed?'

'Agreed,' Lilly said, and the pair got to work. Fergus wrote the headline and provided the context:

SENSATIONAL ARREST
TWO VANISHING GROOMS CAUGHT
THE CULPRITS – THE FACEY BROTHERS

An exclusive report by Lilly Lewis and Fergus Griffiths.

A theatre production could not be as exciting or heartbreaking as the story of two brothers who proved to be the masters of disguise.

While Fergus summarised the unfolding drama, Lilly assembled her copy for the story's conclusion:

Detectives Harland Stone and Gilbert Payne caught the two brothers, who had broken the hearts of four ladies, and were wooing a fifth.

At the time of their capture, the men revealed they shared the role of wooing a lady—or allowed her to choose the brother of her liking—while the other brother worked behind the scenes as a bank teller, managing the forged documents for their scheme.

The brothers, Benjamin Facey, 29, and Joseph Facey, 28, affected accents, limps and scars to be unrecognisable to any former abandoned ladies.

It was thanks to the intrepid work of the detectives that a case going back four years has now been solved. But it may never have been so, if Benjamin Facey had not insisted they needed one more inheritance, given their first victim, Miss Winnifred Nash's parents hired a solicitor who found no such wills existed under the supplied names, and the men decamped before receiving any funds.

Lilly told of the bravery of Miss Martha Hampstead and the bold capture of one brother upstairs by Constable Rogers, and the other downstairs, felled by a well-placed punch. She concluded:

Ladies, the rogues are now behind bars, and while one must always be wary, our city's worst will not have the opportunity to destroy any young lady's life anytime soon.

Across town, Bennet Martin called on his client, Mr Patrick Edmonstone, to advise that he was on-hand, along with the detectives, in a successful plan to catch the culprits red-handed.

Whether the detectives could recover any of Mr Edmonstone's daughter's stolen fortune remained to be seen, but Grace, her father, the other jilted brides, and their parents would receive justice.

A delighted client immediately wrote a cheque, paying Bennet for his services, despite Bennet's insistence on sending an account and a full report within the week.

Bennet was then required to recount the story to Mrs Edmonstone, and one hour later, he departed to his club with the cheque in his pocket and a hand buzzing from a vigorous handshake.

The night was young, he mused. Who might he find to share a drink or two with?

Nearby at the Roma Street Police Headquarters, Detective Harland Stone advised his protégé they would interrogate the prisoners in the morning. There was no need tonight; the scoundrels were in separate cells and could not collaborate on their stories.

Thus, Gilbert left for the evening with Harland's commendation on another successful conclusion to a case, and as the inspector had also departed, Harland left a note on his desk advising him of the outcome and that a report would follow in the morning.

Preparing to depart, Detective Harland Stone placed his hat on his head and took a deep breath. He didn't want to be alone; there was often an emptiness that followed a case being concluded. Now that he had caught the rogues, he could face Phoebe again. For the evening ahead, he was a man, not a detective; a visit to her home was in order. Noticing a half dozen recently delivered boxed and wrapped wedding fruit cakes addressed to him, Harland scooped the cakes from reputable bakeries into the largest of the bags so he would not arrive at the senior Astin household empty handed.

Out in the dark, cool night, standing on the street outside the station, he hailed a hansom and made his way to *The Economic Undertaker.* Perhaps Phoebe had worked back late, but a glance from the hansom on arrival told him the business was in darkness and locked up.

He gave the driver the Astin family's home address and sat back. Harland needed to see her, and the sensation intensified as he arrived to find the Astin house empty. A flicker of panic unsettled him. *Where was she? Where was everyone?*

'Driver, one more address if the horses are not too weary?'

'Not on this cool night, Sir. Where to now then?'

'Nearby,' Harland said and gave the driver Julius' address. Perhaps Phoebe's brother—his friend—might know the whereabouts of Phoebe this evening. Perhaps she went out with her grandparents.

On arrival, he paid the driver handsomely, and released him. Even if Phoebe was not present, he would stop and have a drink with Julius, if Violet did not object. The lights were on, and he imagined what it would be like to return to his own home at night, with the welcoming warm glow and Phoebe waiting.

He rapped on the door. Moments later, it swung open, and Julius grinned at the sight of him.

'You are just in time for dinner, but it will be rations, so hopefully you are not too hungry.'

'I would be happy with a drink and a friendly face, but I am looking for Phoebe,' Harland said, shaking the offered hand and stepping inside. The door hurriedly closed behind him to keep the warmth in. He gave his hat and coat to Julius, as requested.

'She is here; come through.'

'Dessert then,' Harland said, handing Julius the bag of iced cakes.

'You've been baking, you shouldn't have,' Julius stirred him and chuckled when Harland explained, 'I didn't risk bringing the cakes from home bakers; not everyone is a fan of the police.'

'Harland! We were worried,' a voice that could soothe his soul said, and he turned to see Phoebe, resplendent in her innocence and beauty.

Emily appeared behind her. 'Detective! Is Gilbert all right?'

'He is fine, and all went well. We have arrested the culprits. Thank you, Miss Yalden, for your tolerance, and thank you both for your assistance.'

'Culprits? More than one?' Phoebe gasped. 'But the girls assured me...' she did not finish her sentence, remembering Tom did not know of her visions.

'The ladies were correct, Phoebe. In their case, their suitor was the same, but a brother was also involved and wooed more ladies by interchanging names, aliases, and disguises.'

'Detective!' Violet exclaimed, joining the group in the hallway. 'Do come in. We have plenty to eat. I have warmed up last night's leftovers as well. It is safe; I didn't cook.'

Harland laughed. 'You are too hard on yourself, Mrs Astin. I don't wish to impose; I was just wishing to apologise to Phoebe for missing our walk.'

'You must call me Violet, and—'

'Come in, you lot,' Ambrose called from the dining room, cutting off his sister-in-law. 'Or Tom and I will eat it all.'

Harland followed the family into Julius's spacious dining room, where a large timber table for eight took pride of place, as if Julius was always expecting family to drop in. The detective shook Ambrose and Tom's hands and was directed to sit next to Phoebe.

Harland had never known the joy of siblings or of being welcomed into a family home for dinner. Growing up in boarding schools, this was only something he read about in books, and he could not believe how fulfilling it felt.

'We will ask you a thousand questions later, but first, relax and eat,' Julius said.

'You are both safe, and made an arrest; bravo,' Phoebe said, smiling up at him.

'Does Lilly have her story?' Emily asked.

'Indeed, she was there for the whole adventure,' Harland said drolly with a roll of the eyes, which earned a laugh. The intrepid reporter's presence in the thick of the action surprised no one.

Harland returned his attention to the young lady beside him, gazing into Phoebe's eyes until a nudge and a teasing smile from Violet pressed the bowl of potatoes into his hand.

Julius drank in the moment. At his table in his house sat his brother and sister; just last week, he'd felt abandoned by them and irrelevant to their lives. He caught Violet's eye, and she, too, looked happily at the gathered family before them.

Tom and Ambrose kept everyone amused with their antics, while Emily assured Julius she would design a deportment course just for Ambrose and suggested some lessons that might be of value.

'I refuse to walk with a book on my head; my posture is excellent,' Ambrose said, straightening up.

This was what the future would look like, Julius mused. He did not want to think of a time without his grandparents, but if the family continued to expand, life would continue on, as it should. Tom would one day partner and always be by their side as Violet's only brother. Harland and Phoebe may marry and have a brood of their own. He imagined Ambrose and Miss Prout providing plenty of amusement over the dinner table and then, hopefully, his own family filling the chairs around the table. Tonight was just the beginning.

Phoebe glowed in the breast of her family and breathed easy knowing that Harland and Detective Payne were safe. Before Harland told of the night's adventures, she sat in quiet contemplation, a little nervous beside him with the family watching them, but happy for the noisy banter to disguise it.

And then, when dessert was served and with everyone's encouragement, Harland told the tale of the arrest, reminding them that Miss Lewis would feature a more colourful version in *The Courier* in the morning.

'And just when I thought I had caught the man I released the other evening, I was wrong. It turned out that Miss Martha Hampstead's fair-haired beau was not only the bank teller, Mr Bailey Sutton, but also Joseph Facey.'

There were gasps around the table, and Phoebe stared at him wide-eyed, trying to make sense of it.

Harland continued. 'Meanwhile, upstairs, further drama was unfolding. Constable Rogers secured Benjamin Facey as he tried to escape through the bedroom window. Dark-haired Benjamin Facey is Joseph's brother and appeared to me the other evening in his brother's stead.'

'That is why the man you released was so different from the man I witnessed,' Phoebe said sheepishly.

'Exactly,' Harland said to her, 'but we weren't to know,' he added kindly.

She felt a wave of relief. He was different because he wasn't the same man. Phoebe could not blame Harland for releasing him or for not trusting her.

'So they not only wooed the ladies, but had an entry to the bank where they could continue to fool the ladies' parents,' Emily said, shocked.

'That is correct, Miss Yalden,' Harland said. 'The brothers were very talented forgers, but went too far with their game. Now they are both in a cell, and we cannot save the ladies from their humiliation, but hopefully, we can return some of their fortunes.'

'But two ladies died from the heartbreak,' Violet said. 'I hope they are held accountable for that.'

'They most likely won't be, Violet,' Harland said, accepting her earlier invitation to address her as such. 'That is the injustice of it.'

'You have caught them, and they won't have the chance to take advantage of any innocent hearts again,' Emily said.

'These fruit cakes are delicious,' Tom proclaimed, accepting a second slice from Violet, who, as the hostess, served the dessert.

'Perhaps you should use these cakes as a trial for your own wedding,' Ambrose said to Harland. 'I am sure these bakeries could all produce a superb wedding cake.'

Harland looked immediately at Phoebe and smiled, and she felt herself flush, embarrassed. She turned to glare at her brother, making Ambrose laugh.

'There has been so much talk of brides and weddings since your case began, Detective,' Emily said. 'I could not imagine the pain of being left at the altar.'

'It has been our preoccupation for weeks,' he agreed and added confidently, 'Your detective is an honourable man, Miss Yalden. You can rest assured that would never happen to you,' and Emily agreed.

Phoebe glanced at Harland, which suggested a declaration of his own actions might be in order. Harland continued. 'As for me, I would never leave my bride at the altar. I would be there very early, in anticipation, and so I could take up chase should she run away at the last moment.'

Laughter and assurances filled the air that he wouldn't meet that end, as the group smiled and gazed at Phoebe, who once more experienced a delightful mix of joy and embarrassment at being the centre of attention. Harland's openness also surprised her; he was not the most romantic of men, and perhaps Detective Payne was influencing him.

'You could station some constables around the church just in case she is fleet of foot,' Ambrose suggested, earning another round of laughs.

Violet rescued the pair. 'Mrs Dobbs did a wonderful job with our wedding cake; we were very spoilt.'

'Oh, have you put away the top layer to be eaten at the christening of your first child?' Emily asked, referring to the usual tradition for brides and grooms.

Violet scoffed and looked at her brother and husband. 'I intended to do so, Emily, but the two men I have been starving ate it.'

Everyone around the table burst out laughing, and Julius explained as all present ribbed him, 'It was desperate times.'

Phoebe noted how regularly Julius smiled these days, how much happier he was, and how it changed his already handsome countenance. She risked a glance at Harland, who returned her smile.

A movement in the corner near the door caught Phoebe's eye; two young ladies stood, one waving a white handkerchief to get her attention. Though no one else could see them, Miss Alma Thornton and Miss Winnifred Nash were present, and smiling.

Both ladies blew Phoebe a kiss before curtsying and disappearing. Julius saw it too and gave her a smile, as did Harland, believing her reaction was to his success and the happy gathering. And in a way, that was true. After all, being dead was no excuse for letting crime go unpunished, and no one knew that better than the Astin family.

THE END

From the author

Thank you for visiting the Astin family with me for another adventure. The crimes committed in this novel were based on two actual crimes from Australian history.

If you thought I borrowed a story line from the great Mr Charles Dickens's novel, *Great Expectations*, printed in 1861, you may be surprised to know that the story might have originated in Australia. A lady by the name of Miss Eliza Emily Donnithorne was a bride jilted on the morning of her wedding in 1856. Guests were turned away from an elaborate banquet that stayed on the tables, untouched, and it is said she remained in her wedding dress for the rest of her days. Sound familiar? It is also the story of Dickens's fictional Miss Havisham.

Australia's Eliza came to our shores with her father, James Donnithorne, an East India Company Judge and Master of the

Mint in Calcutta. He was successful and wealthy, and believed to have come to Australia to retire in 1836. Eliza was one of five children; she had two older sisters, Penelope and Maria, but the girls, along with Eliza's mother, died in the Calcutta cholera outbreak of 1832.[1] Her two older brothers—William and Edward—remained in England.

As her father's only remaining daughter, Eliza was cherished and spoiled. Settling in Sydney, her father, James, became renowned for his hospitality and attempted to arrange a society marriage for his daughter. She rejected this and instead fell in love with a modest shipping clerk, George Cuthbertson – not too different in surname from Dickens' villain 'Compeyson' who jilted Miss Havisham.

But Eliza's father died before Eliza was to marry, and despite being survived by his two sons who remained in England, Eliza inherited most of his estate. She was now a very wealthy young woman.

In 1856, Eliza was preparing to wed George. Her betrothal at the age of thirty was quite late for a woman of that era, although there was some contention about that date and a claim that it was eight years earlier. But, back to the pending nuptials... because of her wealth and social standing, the wedding was to be a grand affair.

Unlike Miss Havisham, Eliza did not get a letter that morning to save her from the horror of facing her guests. Poor

Eliza and her maid were already dressed for the ceremony; the wedding-breakfast was laid, the wedding guests were assembled, but the groom did not appear.

Devastated, betrayed and humiliated, Eliza never left the house again. It is said that the wedding breakfast remained where it was placed, disintegrating and moulding until it was dust[2] – a macabre proposition. Heartbreakingly, for the rest of her life, Eliza left her front door slightly ajar, just in case her groom returned. This was never going to happen: allegedly, Cuthbertson died in India not long after jilting Eliza.[3]

Eliza remained in the house another thirty-five years, dying on 20 May 1886 at approximately sixty-five years of age (if her birth date was 1821). Although, according to *The Telegraph*, cemetery records disclose that Miss Donnithorne was buried on 22 May 1886, and that she was 58 years of age at the time of her death. Eliza's estate was considerable, and included property in the U.K., Sydney and Melbourne – quite a bounty. Beneficiaries included her housekeeper, her nieces, the diocese of Sydney, and her pets.[4]

There are as many naysayers of the validity of this story as there are devotees, but it bore some remarkable similarities and, at the time of the novel's success, Eliza was widely regarded to be the model for Miss Havisham.

But how did Charles Dickens hear of it? Well, Dickens is believed to have had many English friends who settled in Australia, which was quite common at the time, and to whom he corresponded. His correspondents could have easily conveyed Eliza Donnithorne's story to him. He is no stranger to Australia as it features in *Great Expectations* – Pip's benefactor, Abel Magwitch, who gave Pip his 'expectations' hailed from New South Wales.

There was also some conjecture that Dicken's sons, Albert and Edward, who resided in New South Wales for some time, conveyed the story to their author father.

An interesting aside: when Eliza's grave was vandalised in 2004, a grant from the Dickens Society contributed to its repair. Eliza shares her father's grave in the beautiful Camperdown Cemetery in Sydney.

The news clipping that appears in Chapter 2, fictitiously written by reporter Lilly Lewis, is based on a real clipping from an Australia newspaper, telling Miss Donnithorne's story.[5]

The second crime that influenced this story was that of one of Australia's greatest fraudsters, Walter Thomas Porriott, also known as Doctor Darling, Andrew Gibson, Sir Harry Cooper, Surgeon Major Swinton Holmes, Dr Boyd, Dr Scott and you get the picture. One of his descendants also believed him to be Jack the Ripper, given he lived near Whitechapel at the time of the murders and departed England for Australia after the last of the five canonical murders.

He deserted many a wife, presented fake wills with fortunes that were coming, defrauded them, took their money and abandoned them. Porriott spent time in jail, and died aged 85 while performing his last sting, leaving the mature-aged woman who loved him widowed and broke. Scandalous.

As always, I have tried to stay as accurate to the era as possible – 1891 Australia. For any phrases that I am concerned about, I check on our wonderful resource, Trove – the National Library, to see if they appear in 1891 or earlier editions of the newspaper. Where possible, I try to use actual locations and events. For example, the New Royal Theatre existed in Brisbane in 1891, and Gilbert may well have gone along to see the performance of "*Forty Thieves*" in January that year.

I hope to see you next time.

Cheers and thank you, dear reader.

Helen x

About the author

Helen is a hybrid-published, Amazon best-selling author. After studying English literature, media, and communications at universities in Queensland, Australia, and obtaining a counselling diploma, Helen has worked as a journalist, producer and marketer in print, TV, radio and public relations. Born in Toowoomba, she has made her home in Brisbane, Australia, with her journalist husband, Chris, and Boxer dog, Baxter. She is published by Next Chapter, Podium Entertainment, and her own imprint, Atlas Productions.

Connect with Helen:

Website: www.helengoltz.com

BookBub:www.bookbub.com/authors/helen-goltz

Facebook: www.facebook.com/HelenGoltz.Author

Instagram: https://www.instagram.com/helengoltz1/

Also by Helen Goltz

If you like the Astin family, you might enjoy:

Miss Hayward & the Detective Series (historical mystery/romance):
Murder at the Carnival

The Artist's Missing Muse

Mystery at the Asylum

The Mortician's Clue (introducing Phoebe and staff from The Economic Undertaker)

Murder in Bridal Lane

The Clairvoyant's Glasses (supernatural/romance)
Volume 1 – A vision unexpected

Volume 2 – Time has a shadow

Volume 3 – Love knows no bounds

Volume 4 – Fate comes to call

And coming soon, Volume 5 and Volume 6, The Raven's Son.

The Jesse Clarke series (cosy mystery):

Death by Sugar

Death by Disguise

Death by Reunion

The Mitchell Parker series published by Next Chapter (crime thrillers):

Mastermind

Graveyard of the Atlantic

The Fourth Reich

Writing as Jack Adams (psychological mystery/suspense):

Poster Girl

Delaney and Murphy childhood friends series:

Asylum

Stalker

Cult

Hitched

Carnival.

Coming soon… Forgotten.

With journalist Chris Adams, The Grave Tales series (non-fiction) x 9 titles:
Grave Tales: Brisbane Vol.1
Grave Tales: Great Ocean Road – Geelong to Port Fairy
Grave Tales: Sydney Vol.1
Grave Tales: Bruce Highway
Grave Tales: True Crime Vol.1
Grave Tales: Queensland's Great South West
Grave Tales: Melbourne Vol.1
Grave Tales: Queensland's Scenic Rim & Surrounds
Grave Tales: Tasmania.
Grave Tales: Cold Cases (an amalgamation of stories from existing titles)

The Lady Mortician's Visions (historical mystery/romance/paranormal twist)
The Missing Brides
The Fake Child
The Dastardly Debutante
The Deathly Dolls
The Potent Perfume
The Watery Grave
The Vanishing Groom

The Fallen Angel

And the last volume in the series to come....

Writing as Ally Adams:

The Saints team (contemporary romance):

Team Lucas

Team Tomas

Team Niklas

Team Alex

Stand-alone titles:

The House on Findlater Lane (mystery/romance paranormal)

The Forgotten House (historical romance)

Three Parts Truth (mystery suspense)

Morphers (middle grade fiction).

1. Edward Harris Donnithorne, Soldier and Magistrate, 1810 – 1885, The Twickenham Museum. Retrieved 10 November 2017 from URL: http://www.twickenham-museum.org.uk/detail.php?aid=302&cid=15&ctid=1

2. J.S.Ryan, *Australian Dictionary of Biography*. Op.Cit.

3. Janilye, 'Eliza Emily Donnithorne 1821 – 1886', *Family Tree Circles*. Retrieved 10 November 2017 from URL: http://www.familytreecircles.com/eliza-emily-donnithorne-1821-1886-44927.html

4. J.S.Ryan, *Australian Dictionary of Biography*. Op.Cit.

5. Two Houses. (1902, March 22). The World's News (Sydney, NSW: 1901 - 1955), p. 15. Retrieved March 30, 2025, from http://nla.gov.au/nla.news-article128448315